ASK DR. ASIMOV

How would life on Earth change if there were no Moon?

Would we be better off changing the month system to a World Season Calendar with ninety-one days to a season?

Why does the complexity and versatility of life hinge on carbon? Could another element do the job, or is carbon the one and only key to organic life on Earth?

Will computerization lead to the obliteration of individual privacy or to a world free from injustice and war?

These are but a few of the questions Isaac Asimov asks and answers in his own inimitable famous style. Doctor A. ranges from microbiology and sociology to astronomy and a special eyewitness view of the spectacular nighttime Apollo launching, possibly man's last Moon mission for many decades to come.

Dedicated to:

Some of the places that have inspired some of the articles herein included:
    The Bread Loaf Writers' Conference (chapter 13)
    The Institute of Man and Science (chapter 14)
    The S.S. *Statendam* (chapters 2 and 16)
        and alas,
    The University Hospital (chapter 12)

The Tragedy of the Moon

ISAAC ASIMOV

A Dell Book

Published by
DELL PUBLISHING CO., INC.
1 Dag Hammarskjold Plaza
New York, N.Y. 10017

All essays in this volume are reprinted from *The Magazine of Fantasy and Science Fiction*.
Individual essays appeared in the following issues:

Dell ® TM 681510, Dell Publishing Co., Inc.

ISBN: 0-440-18999-3

Reprinted by arrangement with
Doubleday & Company, Inc.

Printed in the United States of America
First Dell printing—March 1978

CONTENTS

CONTENTS

INTRODUCTION

Douglas W. Jerrold, a nineteenth-century English author, was once told that he was going to have a book dedicated to him by a friend of his who was, alas, a pronouncedly mediocre writer. A look of melancholy crossed Jerrold's face. He shook his head and said, "Ah, that's a fearsome weapon the man has in his hands."

With dedications clearly inscribed in over a hundred of my books, Jerrold's sad remark occurs to me at times and unnerves me. I never ask permission before stigmatizing someone or something on the dedication page, and I sometimes think in hangdog fashion that some good friend of mine would not wish to be so conspicuously pilloried. (As a matter of fact, I was once blessed with a strenuous letter demanding the removal of a dedication, which was accordingly removed—but that is another story.)

Then, too, dedications tend to be so cursory and mysterious. You dedicate a book "To So-and-So, for helping," and at once everyone wants to know when and how he helped and what was the difficulty you got into. Did he give you money, an alibi, a kind word, what? Chances are, you never find out.

In this one case, then, let me take some space to explain the dedication:

I

In 1971 I was persuaded, much against my better judgment, to attend the Bread Loaf Writers' Conference, in Bread Loaf, Vermont, and lecture to the assembled students on how to write non-fiction. My protestations to the effect that I didn't know how to write non-fiction, but just did it instinctively, were brushed aside with contempt.

As it happened, I did manage to make up a few lectures and enjoyed myself thoroughly. The only thing that caught me by surprise was the fact that every member of the faculty was expected to give one evening lecture, and, as I attended these, I discovered that each read from his works.

I had not brought any works to read, but during the first ten days, I had written an article on Ruth (the heroine of the biblical book of that name) for Reader's Digest Books, and thought I might as well repeat the gist of that. As it happened, though, I got off the subject (I frequently do, since my talks are not prepared in advance) and began to preach a sermon—unintentionally, I assure you.

Well, I never look at my audience. I gaze at the space above their heads. But I *listen*, and by the sounds I hear, I guide my talk. And what I always listen for most eagerly, and virtually never get, is dead silence. This time I got it, and it drove me on to give the best talk (well, the most effective) of my career. When I finished, I got a standing ovation.

I can't let something like that go. A cardinal rule for me (and surely for anyone who writes as much as I do) is that nothing must be wasted. So I wrote up a version of the talk as "Lost in Non-Translation" (chapter 13), and then I wrote a full-length treatment which has appeared as a book for young pepole, *The Story of Ruth* (Doubleday, 1972).

But I can't dedicate the book to the place alone. The poet John Ciardi, who directed the conference for many years, is a long-time friend of mine and the cause of my being there. Tall and large, with a proud nose of aristocratic dimensions and a rolling bass voice that could make the telephone directory sound like great literature, he presided over the nightly soirees with wit and good humor.

"Farewell, O minor poet," I declaimed magniloquently at the close of the conference.

"Farewell, O major pain-in-the-ass," he neatly riposted without missing a beat, and buried me under an avalanche of laughter.

It was all pleasurable enough to persuade me to go back for a reprise in 1972, and that occasion is mentioned in the opening paragraphs of "Through the Microglass" (chapter 9).

II

The Institute of Man and Science, at Rensselaerville, New York, is the "seminar in upstate New York" that I refer to in the opening paragraphs of "The Ancient and the Ultimate" (chapter 14). I was there in the first week of July 1972.

I cautiously refrained from identifying it more closely, because it occurred to me that the organization might not want their name bandied about in the kind of informal essays I write. I was mistaken. Just a week ago (as I write this) the Institute wrote to *The Magazine of Fantasy and Science Fiction* identifying themselves as the place mentioned and asking for permission to prepare sixty copies of "The Ancient and the Ultimate" for their own use.

What's more, in a personal letter to me, the director was kind enough to say that I had, if anything, understated the excellence of my talk on the occasion. (Thank heaven I'm not modest. If I were, you would be deprived of interesting tidbits of information like that.)

Again, I had an unexpectedly good time on this occasion. It was Miss Duncan MacDonald (a beautiful lady, despite the first name) who invited me to attend, ran that week's sessions, and asked me to give my talk on very short notice. And it was Beardsley Graham who gave the talk on TV cassettes that inspired mine.

To both of them I am grateful.

III

The S.S. *Statendam* is the ship on which I took the cruise that is described with perfect accuracy (barring a few flights of rhetoric) in "The Cruise and I" (chapter 16). The ship itself was luxurious and the officers and crew could not have been more co-operative and pleasant.

The reporters on board seem not to have enjoyed themselves, but that was *their* problem. I had a wonderful time, and so, as nearly as I could tell, did everyone else involved in the seminars, whether speaking or listening. Certainly the whole thing was poorly organized, but we all enjoyed ourselves, and for that I am grateful to Richard C. Hoagland, who (as described in the chapter) persuaded me to go.

IV

My stay at the University Hospital, as described in the opening paragraphs of "Doctor, Doctor, Cut My Throat" (chapter 12), was completely involuntary. I was there for one week to the hour, and, needless to say, the pleasure of my stay was limited.

However, it had to be; and I came out of it well. My gratitude goes to Dr. Paul R. Esserman, the internist who detected the condition; to Dr. Manfred Blum, the endocrinologist who analyzed it; and to Dr. Carl A. Smith, the surgeon who corrected it.

—And, of course, to all the nurses and other personnel of the hospital who did their best to see to it that all went well; and especially to Renée Vales, a beautiful Haitian nurse, who held my hand all that long first postoperative night when I could neither sleep nor (worse yet) type.

A

ABOUT THE MOON

one

THE TRAGEDY OF THE MOON

There was a full Moon in the sky this morning. I was awake when the dawn had lightened the sky to a slate blue (as is my wont, for I am an early riser) and, looking out the westward window, I saw it. It was a fat yellow disk in an even, slate-blue background, hanging motionless over a city that was still dreaming in the dawn.

Ordinarily I am not easily moved by visual stimuli, as I am relatively insensitive to what goes on outside the interior of my skull. This scene penetrated, though.

I found myself marveling at Earth's good fortune in having a Moon so large and so beautiful. Suppose, I thought, the Moon circled Earth's twin sister, Venus; suppose that it was Earth, rather than Venus, that lacked a satellite. How much beauty we would have missed! And how useless it would be to have it wasted on Venus, whose cloud cover would forever hide the Moon even if there were intelligent beings on the planet who could appreciate it if it could be seen.

But then, over breakfast, I continued to think . . .

Beauty, after all, isn't everything. Suppose Earth lacked the Moon. What would happen?

To begin with, Earth would have only solar tides, considerably smaller than the present ones. It would have a shorter day, because tidal friction would not have slowed it so much. It might have formed, during the birth pangs of the solar system, in a somewhat different fashion, in the absence of a secondary nucleus forming at the same time (if that was what happened). Or else, life must have evolved differently without the capture of a large Moon six hundred thousand years ago (if that was what happened).

But let's ignore that. Let's suppose that Earth formed as it did, that life evolved as it did, that the day remains what it is, that the smaller tides are of no crucial importance.

And now let us suppose that early man (twenty-five thousand years ago?) raised his questioning eyes to the sky—

And found no Moon!

What would have happened?

I am going to advance the thesis now that, had he found no Moon, mankind's history would have been altered far, far for the better—especially if that Moon were circling Venus. It was because Earth *did* have a Moon, and Venus did not, that mankind may well be approaching the end of its days as a technological society.

I'm not kidding. Bear with me . . .

Suppose we leave the Moon where it is for now and try to imagine what primitive man decided the objects in the sky must be doing.

To begin with, he must have been aware of the Sun rising, moving across the sky, setting—then rising again the next morning, and repeating the process indefinitely. The only possible rational explanation of what he saw was to suppose the Sun revolved around the Earth once each day.

At night the stars came out, and observation made it clear that they, too, revolved about the Earth once each day, while maintaining their relative positions fixedly.

It might have been possible for men to argue that the sky stood still and that the Earth rotated on its axis, but why should they have done so? The hypothesis of the Earth's rotation would not, *in any way,* have explained the observations any better. Instead the hypothesis would merely have raised the question of why the Earth should seem to be motionless if it were, in fact, moving—a question no prehistoric man could possibly have answered.*

Careful observation would show that, in actual fact, the Sun does not move around the Earth in exact step with the stars. The Sun takes four minutes longer, each day, to complete the circle. That means that the Sun drifts west to east against the background of the stars from day to day and makes a complete circle around the sky in 365¼ days.

If you ignored the daily rotation of the sky and considered the stars as a kind of fixed background (which was

---

* It wasn't till 1851 that the rotation of the Earth was directly demonstrated. Till then, it had had to be accepted by indirect reasoning.

mathematically equivalent to supposing the Earth to be rotating), you could say that the Sun revolved around the Earth in 365¼ days.

Actually you could explain the motion of the Sun against the stars just as well by supposing the Earth revolved about the Sun in 365¼ days—just as well, that is, *but no better*. And again, you would have to explain why the Earth should seem motionless if it were, in fact, revolving about the Sun.

And where does the Moon come in? It is almost as obvious an object for observation as the Sun is. It, too, rises and sets daily; and it, too, lags behind the stars. In fact, it lags behind far more than the Sun does. It makes a complete circle against the starry background in a mere 27⅓ days.

Now forget about the implausibility of the Earth's moving without anyone being aware of it. Let us suppose it could happen (as, in fact, it can) and ask merely this: If we imagine the Earth revolving about the Sun to explain the Sun's movements, and revolving about the Moon to explain the Moon's movements—which is it really doing? It can't do both, can it?

But then suppose some primitive madman, with the imagination of a science-fiction writer, had suggested that the Moon revolved about the Earth in 27⅓ days, while Earth and Moon together, the latter still circling steadily, revolved about the Sun in 365¼ days. That would neatly explain the apparent motion and the phases of the Moon, and the apparent motion of the Sun too.

Do you suppose, though, that any of his listeners would accept so complicated a system on the basis of what was known in prehistoric times? Why should there be two centers in the Universe? Why should some objects circle the Earth and other objects circle the Sun?

It was possible to explain the motion and phases of the Moon, and the motion of the Sun as well, by supposing Moon and Sun to be moving independently, at different speeds, about a common center, the Earth. This could not easily be done if Earth and Moon were pictured as moving in independent orbits about the Sun, or if Earth and Sun were pictured as moving in independent orbits about the Moon.

Only the Earth could easily serve as a common center

for both other bodies, and that, combined with the obvious
motionlessness of the Earth, must have fixed the geocentric
("Earth-centered") notion in the mind of any primitive astronomer capable of reasoning out such things. To the ordinary observer, the obvious motionlessness of the Earth was
enough.

Long after the motions of the Sun and Moon, relative to
the stars, were carefully studied,* the motions of the planets Mercury, Venus, Mars, Jupiter, and Saturn were studied and analyzed. That may not have been done in detail
until the time of the first high civilization (one based on
writing)—the Sumerian.

The planets, it was found, moved against the stars in far
more complicated fashion than the Sun and Moon do.

Consider Mars, Jupiter, and Saturn: Each makes a complete circuit of the sky, but more slowly than the Sun does.
Mars takes a little less than two years to make the circuit,
Jupiter a little less than twelve years, and Saturn a little less
than thirty years.

But instead of drifting slowly across the starry sky in a
steady west-to-east manner, as the Sun and Moon do, each
of the three planets periodically changes direction and
moves east to west against the background of the stars for a
comparatively brief period. These "retrograde" movements
come at roughly yearly (Earth time) intervals for each
planet.

The Sumerians and their successors in Babylonia apparently were content to work out the motions without ex-
plaining them. The Greeks, however, when they grew interested in astronomy, in the fifth century B.C., could not let
the matter rest there. They knocked themselves out trying
to work out systems that would allow Mars, Jupiter, and
Saturn to revolve about the Earth, while allowing also for
the periodic change in direction. More and more elaborate
schemes were built up, climaxing with that of Ptolemy in
the second century A.D.

Here at last was a case in which the hypothesis that the
Earth and the other planets revolved about the Sun would

---

* The primitive stone structure at Stonehenge has been described as
intended to follow the movements of Sun and Moon in an elaborate and rather sophisticated way, indicating perhaps thousands of
years of previous development and elaboration.

have made a difference. A moving Earth would explain the retrograde motion of Mars, Jupiter, and Saturn far more simply and logically than a stationary Earth could possibly explain it. If Earth and Jupiter, for instance, were both revolving about the Sun, the Earth would have to make one circle in one year while Jupiter made one circle in twelve years. Earth would move more rapidly. Whenever Earth was on the same side of the Sun as Jupiter was, Earth would overtake Jupiter. Jupiter would then seem to be moving backward in the heavens.

Unfortunately, if you assume that the planets are each revolving about the Sun in independent orbits, *that does not take care of the Moon.* The Moon has to be revolving about the Earth, and that would require two centers to the universe. The planets could all, *except* for the Moon, circle the Earth in independent orbits. The planets could all, *including* the Moon, circle the Earth in independent orbits. If I were a Greek, then, I would have voted for a geocentric universe rather than a heliocentric ("Sun-centered") one. The geocentric one would have seemed simpler.

I don't know whether this line of argument involving the Moon actually swayed the Greeks. I have never seen such an argument described. Still, I'm convinced the argument about the Moon must have had its effect.*

If only there were some object in the sky that was clearly revolving about another object in the sky as the Moon revolved about the Earth. Then, perhaps, men would accept, perforce, the notion of two or more centers to the universe and see nothing wrong in accepting a heliocentric universe in which the Moon remains geocentric.

Actually, there is such an object; two, in fact. The planets Venus and Mercury never leave the vicinity of the Sun. In this, they are in sharp contrast to the other planets.

The Moon, Mars, Jupiter, and Saturn all move against the background of the stars in such a way that they can, at one time or another, be at any given distance from the Sun, even in a spot in the sky exactly opposite to the position of the Sun. (This is true of the Moon, for instance, at every full phase, as when I saw it this morning.)

---

* And, of course, it's no mystery why the Moon spoils the heliocentric view of the universe. The Moon really *does* revolve about the Earth.

Not so Venus and Mercury. Venus, for instance, moves farther and farther from the Sun till it is separated by 47° (half the distance from horizon to zenith), but that is all. Having reached that 47° separation, it begins to move closer to the Sun again. Eventually it merges with the blaze of the Sun and then, after a few weeks, can be seen on the other side of the Sun. Again it moves farther and farther to a maximum separation of 47° and begins moving back. It does this over and over.

When Venus is on one side of the Sun, it is the evening star. Because it is never more than 47° from the Sun, it never shines later than three hours after sunset. By then, or earlier, it has set. On the other side of the Sun it is the morning star, never rising earlier than three hours before sunrise.

As for Mercury, it stays even closer to the Sun, never moving more than half as far away as Venus does, never setting later than one and one half hours after the Sun when it is an evening star, never rising earlier than one and one half hours before the Sun when it is a morning star.

It would be quite logical to suppose that both Venus and Mercury are revolving about the Sun, since this would at once, and without difficulty, explain their motions in every detail.

Easier said than done! In the first place, it was not easy to identify Venus the evening star with Venus the morning star. It took a pretty advanced astronomer to see that one was present in the sky only when the other was absent and that the two objects were therefore the same planet. Again, Venus and the Sun were never visible at the same time, for when the Sun was in the sky, Venus could not be seen (or just barely seen, at times, if you knew exactly where to look). The connection between Venus and the Sun was therefore not an obvious, at-a-glance one. Again, it took a sophisticated level of astronomy to see it; and the condition with respect to Mercury was even worse.

Nevertheless about 350 B.C. the Greek astronomer Heracleides Ponticus did indeed suggest that Venus and Mercury revolved about the Sun. And if two of the planets revolved about the Sun, why not all the rest, including Earth as well? In fact, about 280 B.C., the Greek astronomer Aristarchus of Samos took this step, and suggested a heliocentric universe.

But, by this time, geocentricity had fossilized itself into Greek thought. What's more, Aristarchus could not deny that the Moon, at least, had to remain in orbit about the Earth. So the geocentric notion was not abandoned, and Greek astronomers worked out ingenious schemes for allowing Venus and Mercury to circle the Earth and yet never move far away from the Sun.

You might ask yourself if, after all, it matters to ordinary human beings, and to history, whether philosophers decide in favor of geocentrism or heliocentrism. Who cares whether Earth goes around the Sun or vice versa?

Unfortunately it makes all the difference in the world. To the average person in early history (and now too!) the sky and all it contains is of minor importance (except perhaps for the Sun). It is the Earth that counts and only the Earth. And on Earth, only mankind counts. And of men, only one's country, one's city, one's tribe, one's family, one's self counts. The average person is geocentric, anthropocentric, ethnocentric, and egocentric.

If the intellectual leadership of the world—those who think, speak, write, and teach—agree that the universe is indeed geocentric, then all the other centrisms tend to follow that much more naturally.

If all the universe revolves about the Earth, who is then to doubt that Earth is the most important part of creation and the object for which the rest of the universe was made? And if it is Earth that is of central importance, must that not be for the sake of man, who is visibly the ruler of Earth? And if mankind is the ruler of all creation, the object for which all creation was formed, then why should it accept any bars or qualifications to its actions? Mankind is king, its wish is law, and it can do no wrong.

Those religions which are Earth-centered and man-centered make more intellectual sense too, in that case.

Because pagan philosophy and Christianity were alike geocentric and therefore anthropocentric, it was easier for the Roman Empire to become Christian. There was mutual reinforcement in this particular all-important respect, and Christianity, which made geocentricity and anthropocentricity a central dogma, called Aristotle, Ptolemy, and similar Greek thinkers to its aid, to impress those intellectuals who would not be satisfied by the word of the Bible alone.

And because geocentricity is not, in fact, an accurate picture of the universe, all scientific inquiry became undesirable. Any investigation that would try to go beyond Aristotle and Ptolemy and find a non-geocentric picture of the universe that might explain it better, became dangerous to revealed religion.

Even though the Ptolemaic system had become so topheavy as to be embarrassing in its deficiencies, it was not till the sixteenth century that the Polish astronomer Nicholas Copernicus dared present a heliocentric theory once more, and even he preferred not to publish till 1543, when he was sure he was going to die soon anyway. Then it took another full century before the intellectual world of Western Europe accepted heliocentrism fully in the face of religious resistance. Bruno had to burn and Galileo had to recant before geocentricity vanished.

Even then victory was not really won. Old habits die with exceeding slowness, and whatever the science courses in school teach us, most of the population of the "advanced" nations of the world still believe that man is the measure of all things, the ruler of creation, and can do as he pleases.

As a result, here we are in the waning decades of the twentieth century still destroying the plant and animal kingdoms, still ravaging the inanimate environment—all at our careless whim and for the pleasure and comfort of the moment. The clear indication that this will kill mankind, who cannot live without a functioning ecology, seems to bounce off the blank wall of those minds who see a universe built only for the sake of mankind and for no other reason.

To my way of thinking, then, this all goes back to a geocentricity that was riveted on the minds of man by the glowing intellect of the Greek philosophers who were influenced by a number of things including the fact that the Moon *does* revolve about the Earth.

But suppose that the Moon does not revolve about the Earth, but revolves about Venus instead, and that it is Earth, not Venus, that is moonless.

Let us suppose that it is our Moon, the same size, the same characteristics, and the same distance from Venus' center that it is, in actual fact, from ours. And to avoid confusion, let us call the Moon, while it is Venus' faithful companion, Cupid.

Cupid's period about Venus would be a trifle longer than its period about Earth, since Venus is slightly less massive than Earth and has a slightly less intense gravitational field in consequence. Without laboring the point, let's say Cupid will revolve about Venus in thirty days.

Let's not worry—at least not here—on the effect this would have on Venus. Let's ask only how this would affect Earth's sky.

In the first place, Earth's sky would be perpetually moonless, so that viewing would be considerably better. There would never be a glaring Moon, washing out the dimmer stars in the neighborhood.

In the second place, Venus itself would be the brightest object in the sky, after the Sun itself, and certainly the brightest object, by a good bit, in the night sky. Beautiful and noticeable as Venus is in our present sky, it would be nonpareil in an eternally moonless one. It would be studied with an admiration no other object in the sky could possibly attract.

In the third place and most important, Cupid, as it circles Venus, *would be visible to us*. Its brightness would depend upon its position relative to the Sun and to the Earth, as does the brightness of Venus itself. Cupid would, at all times (assuming it has the size and characteristics of the Moon), be almost exactly 1/100 the brightness of Venus.

This means that at its brightest, Cupid would shine in our sky with a magnitude of +0.7. It would be a first-magnitude object, roughly as bright as the planet Saturn or the star Arcturus.

Would Cupid be so close to Venus as to be drowned in the latter's glare? It would depend on where Cupid was located in its orbit about Venus. When it is at its farthest from Venus, and when Venus is closest to us, Cupid would be separated from Venus by 0.6°, which is slightly more than the width of the Sun. We would have no trouble seeing Cupid when it was that far from Venus, and even when it was rather closer—especially if we knew it was there and looked for it.

This brings us to the crucial point. Without a Moon in

our sky, there would be no object whose motions could be explained *only* by supposing it to revolve about us.

Instead, we would see in Venus and Cupid something that would be easily and even inevitably interpreted as a double planet. Cupid would spend fifteen days on one side of Venus and fifteen days on the other, in alternation. During a single stretch of nights in which Venus remains an evening star, we would see Cupid go through eight complete cycles.

There could be no mistake. No one could reasonably doubt that Cupid was revolving about Venus.

The next step would be to note that the bright morning star present in the sky before dawn would also be accompanied by a companion that behaved like Cupid. With Cupid as attendant in both cases, the identity of evening star and morning star would be obvious from the start. There could not be two different objects so spectacularly alike in detail.

That means that from the very start of sky watching, primitive man would clearly see that Venus went from one side of the Sun to the other and back, precisely as Cupid went from one side of Venus to the other and back. With morning and evening stars recognized as one object, and with Venus and Cupid showing the way, it would be impossible to fail to see that Venus, *carrying Cupid with it,* revolved about the Sun.

Furthermore when observers noticed Mercury also serving as an evening star and morning star, with a shorter period than Venus', they would have to conclude that Mercury also revolved about the Sun, and in an orbit closer to the Sun than Venus'.

With Mercury and Venus both circling the Sun, it would be easy to speculate that the other planets were doing the same, Earth included. There would be no Moon to confuse matters, and even if there were, the case of Cupid would be convincing evidence that a Moon could circle Earth and yet move along with Earth around the Sun as well.

The Greek astronomers, and possibly the Sumerian astronomers before them, would have seen that the assumption that the Earth was revolving about the Sun would easily explain the otherwise irritating retrograde motions of Mars, Jupiter, and Saturn. That, combined with the visibly heliocentric motions of Mercury and of Venus-Cupid would surely have overcome the difficulty of the apparent motionlessness of Earth, as it eventually did with Copernicus.

It follows that the heliocentric theory would have been established possibly as early as 2000 B.C., and by no conceivable stretch of the imagination as late as 300 B.C.

What's more, the revolution of Cupid about Venus and of Venus about the Sun would make it relatively easy to catch the concept of *universal* gravitation. Objects did not merely fall to Earth: everything exerted an attraction. The Sun and Venus would be doing so visibly, and if so, why not everything else as well?

It seems to me that Aristotle would have been perfectly capable of doing Newton's work if he had invented calculus and had not been anticipated by a still earlier thinker.

The heliocentric nature of the universe as seen by the astronomers, and by any layman, in fact, who watched Venus, Cupid, and the Sun with any reasonable degree of intelligence, would make it plain that the Earth was only one world among many and that it could not be the center and crown of creation. Mankind's world, and therefore mankind himself, was only a small part of creation and in no way occupied a particularly important part.

While religious systems might still be formed that centered on man and Earth, they would not have had a chance of capturing the scholarly part of society, unless they were modified to allow the plurality of worlds and to accept man as but a small part of a much greater whole.

Since both science and religion would then be on the right track, there would instead be mutual reinforcement.

Religion would be progressive, eager to learn more of the universe as it is, certain that there could be no conflict between the material and the spiritual. Science, on the other hand, would more easily accept the moral necessities. It would recognize the need for understanding man's small niche, both in the astronomical universe and on the biological Earth.

Ecology would have been the queen of sciences, the one embracing all the rest from the start. The integration of human population and economic activity safely into the ecology would have been the prime aim of science.

Experimental science and technology would be perhaps two to four thousand years further advanced than they are now; and a healthy Earth might today be establishing the

beginnings of a galactic empire or, perhaps, pushing ten-
drils toward other intelligences elsewhere.

But instead, our own lifetime may be the last that will be
lived out in a technological society at all—thanks to the
tragedy of the Moon, to the chance that placed it in our
sky and not Cupid in Venus'.

So now I'll never again be able to look at the beautiful
full Moon hanging in the western sky at dawn, without a
pang—except that there's another side to the story too, and
that I take up in chapter 2.

THE TRIUMPH OF THE MOON

Last night (as I write this) I stood on the deck of the Holland-American liner S.S. *Statendam*, seven miles off Cape Kennedy, and watched Apollo 17 rise into the air like the biggest firefly in creation (see chapter 16). It lit the sky from horizon to horizon, turning the ocean an orange-gray and the sky into an inverted copper bowl from which the stars were blanked out.

Slowly it rose on its tail of fire, and it was well up in the sky before the first shaking rumble reached us some forty seconds after ignition and shook us savagely.

Mankind was making its attempt to reach the Moon a sixth time and place an eleventh and twelfth man upon it. It was the last launching of the Apollo series (and the only night launching, hence incredibly spectacular, and I was delighted to see it). It may be decades before mankind returns to the task—after establishing a space station that would make it possible to reach the Moon more easily, more economically, and more elaborately.

And as I stood on deck watching Apollo 17 become a star among stars in a freshly darkened sky, while the hot gantry glowed forlornly on the low shoreline, a spasm of guilt swept me.

It was not so long ago that I wrote "The Tragedy of the Moon" (see chapter 1), in which I described how and why man would have advanced so much farther if only the Moon had circled Venus rather than the Earth. Yet that was only one side of the story. The Moon has had its triumphs too, if we accept man as the measure of all things, for at three crises in the development of man it was the Moon that was, in one way or another, the motive force. In chapter 1 I lightly dismissed them, but now let's make up for that.

To begin with, man might conceivably not exist at all if Earth had had no Moon. The dry land might have remained untenanted.

Life began in the sea some three billion years ago or more, and for at least 80 per cent of its entire history on this planet, it remained in the sea. Life is adapted for the surface layers of the ocean primarily, and only by the power of versatile adjustment over many generations has it succeeded in colonizing the surface's borderlands: downward into the abyss, outward into the fresh-water rivers and lakes, and outward/upward into the land and air.

Of the borderlands, dry land must in its way have been most exotic; as impossible to sea life as the surface of the Moon is to us. If we imagine a primitive sea creature intelligent enough to have speculated about land life, we can be sure he would be appalled by the prospect. On land, an organism would be subjected to the full and eternal pull of gravity, to the existence of wild oscillations of temperature both daily and yearly, to the crushing need to get and retain water in an essentially water-free environment, to the need to get oxygen out of dry, and desiccating, air rather than out of mild water solution.

Such a sea creature might imagine itself emerging from the sea in a water-filled land suit with mechanical grapples to support him against gravity, insulation against temperature change, and so on.

The sea life of half a billion years ago had, however, no technology to help it defeat the land. It could only adapt itself over hundreds or thousands of generations to the point where it could live on land unprotected.

But what force drove it to do so, in the absence of a deliberate decision to do so?

The tides.

Life spread outward into the rims of the ocean, where the sea water rose up against the continental slopes and then fell back twice each day. And thousands of species of seaweed and worms and crustaceans and mollusks and fish rose and fell with those tides. Some were exposed on shore as the sea retreated, and of those a very few survived, because they happened, for some reason, to be the best able to withstand the nightmare of land existence until the healing, life-giving water returned.

Species adapted to the temporary endurance of dry land

developed, and the continuing pressure of competition saw to it that there was survival value to be gained in developing the capacity to withstand dry-land conditions for longer and ever-longer periods.

Eventually species developed that could remain on land indefinitely. About 425 million years ago, plant life began cautiously to green the edges of the continent. Snails, spiders, insects developed to take advantage of a new food supply. Some 400 million years ago, certain fish were crawling on new-made limbs over the soggy mud flats.

(Actually we are descended from fresh-water creatures who probably came to endure land as a result of the periodic drying of ponds, but they could have completed the colonization only because the tides had already populated the continents and produced an ecology to become part of.)

And of course the tides are the product of the Moon. The Sun, to be sure, also produces tides, nearly half the size of those produced by the Moon today, but that smaller to-and-fro wash of salt water would represent a smaller drive toward land and might have led to the colonization of the continents much later in time, if at all.

Indeed, hundreds of millions of years ago, when land life was evolving, the Moon was surely closer to Earth, and the tides were considerably more ample. It is even possible that the Moon was captured late in the existence of life and that it was the long period of giant tides that followed which produced the necessary push for the colonization of the land.*

The second crucial effect of the Moon came sometime in the Paleolithic period, when men were food-gathering primates, perhaps not noticeably more successful than others of the order. Man's primitive ancestors were already the brainiest land creatures that ever lived, but it is possible to argue that brains in themselves are not necessarily the best way of insuring survival. The chimpanzee is not as success-

---

* I wonder if, when we explore the galaxy, we will find life universally present on all Earthlike planets, but always *sea* life. I wonder if we'll find that land life requires that most unlikely event, the capture of a large moon, and that we are therefore alone in the galaxy after all.

ful in the evolutionary scheme of things as the rat, nor the elephant as the fly.

For man to become successful, for man to establish himself as the ruler of the planet, it was necessary for him to use his brain as something more than a device to make the daily routine of getting food and evading enemies a little more efficient. Man had to learn to control his environment; that is, to observe and generalize, and give birth to a technology. And to sharpen his mind to that point, he had to number and measure. Only by numbering and measuring could he begin to grasp the notion of a universe that could be understood and manipulated.

Something was needed for a push toward numbering, as once something had been needed for a push toward dry land.

Man would have to notice something orderly that he could grasp—something orderly enough to enable him to predict the future and give him an appreciation of the power of the intellect.

One simple way of seeing order is to note some steady, cyclic rhythm in nature. The simplest, most overbearing such cycle is clearly the alternation of day and night. The time must have come when some man (or manlike ancestor) began to have the *conscious* knowledge that the Sun would certainly rise in the east after having set in the west. This would mean the consciousness of time, rather than the mere passive endurance of it. It would surely mean the beginning of the *measurement* of time, perhaps the measurement of anything, when an event could be placed as so many sunrises ago or as so many to come.

Yet the day-night cycle lacks subtlety and is too overwhelming and black-and-white (literally) to call out the best in man. Of course if men observed *very* closely, they might notice that the day lengthened and shortened and that night shortened and lengthened in what we would today call a yearly cycle. They might associate this with the changing height of the midday Sun and with a cycle of seasons.

Unfortunately such changes would be hard to grasp, hard to follow, hard to measure. The length of the day and the position of the Sun would be hard to observe in primitive days; the seasons depend on many factors that tend to obscure their purely cyclic nature over the short run; and in the tropics, where man developed, all these changes are minimal.

But there is the Moon—the most dramatic sight in the heavens. The Sun is glorious but cannot be looked at. The stars are unchanging points of light. The Moon, however, is an object of soft and glowing light that *changes its shape steadily.*

The fascination of that changing shape, accompanied by a changing position in the sky relative to the Sun, had to attract attention. The slow death of the Moon's crescent as it merged with the rising Sun, and the birth of a *new* Moon from the solar fire of sunset may have given mankind the first push toward the notion of death and rebirth, which is central to so many religions.

The birth of each new Moon (still so called), as a symbol of hope, may have exercised the emotions of early man sufficiently to give him the overwhelming urge to calculate in advance when that new Moon would come so that he might greet it with glee and festival.

The new Moons come sufficiently far apart, however, for the matter to prove an exercise in counting; and the count is large enough to make it advisable to use notches in a piece of wood or bone. Furthermore, the number of days is not unvarying. Sometimes the interval is twenty-nine days between new Moons, sometimes thirty. With continued counting, however, a pattern will appear.

Once the pattern has been established, it will eventually be seen that every twelve new Moons will include a cycle of seasons (it is easier to count and understand twelve new Moons than 365 days). And yet the fit is not right, either. With twelve new Moons the seasons drift forward. Sometimes a thirteenth new Moon must be added.

Then, too, every once in a while the Moon goes into eclipse. (Since eclipses of the Moon can be seen all over the world at once, while eclipses of the Sun—roughly equal in number—can be seen only in some particular narrow region only, then from a given spot on Earth one sees many more eclipses of the Moon than of the Sun.)

The eclipse of the Moon: its comparatively rapid death at the moment of complete maturity (the eclipse *always* comes when the Moon is full), and the equally rapid rebirth, must have had enormous impact on primitive people. It would have been important for them to know when such a significant event would occur, and calculations must have had to reach a new level of subtlety.

It is not surprising, then, that early efforts to understand the universe concentrated on the Moon. Stonehenge may have been a primitive observatory serving as a large device to predict lunar eclipses accurately. Alexander Marshak has analyzed the markings on ancient bones and has suggested that they were primitive calendars marking off the new Moons.

There is thus good reason to believe that man was first jolted into calculation and generalization by the need to keep track of the Moon; that from the Moon came calendars; from them, mathematics and astronomy (and religion too); and from them, everything else.

As the Moon made man possible as a physical being through its tides, it made him an intellectual being through its phases.

And what else? I promised three crises; for the third, let us move still farther forward in time, to a point at which human civilization was in full career.

By the third millennium B.C. the first great civilization, that of the Sumerians, in the downstream reaches of the Tigris-Euphrates Valley, was at its peak. In that dry climate the night sky was uniformly and brilliantly visible, and there was a priestly caste that had the leisure to study the heavens and the religious motivation to do so.

It was they, in all likelihood, who first noticed that although most of the stars maintained their configurations for night after night indefinitely, five of the brighter ones shifted position steadily, night after night, relative to the rest. This represented the discovery of the planets, which they distinguished by the names of gods, a habit we have kept to this day. They noted that the Sun and the Moon also shifted position steadily with reference to the stars, so they were considered planets too.

The Sumerians were the first (possibly) to begin to follow the motions of all the planets rather than of the Moon only, and to attempt the far more complicated task of generalizing and systematizing planetary motion rather than lunar motion. This was continued by the later civilizations inheriting their traditions, until the Chaldeans, who ruled the Tigris-Euphrates Valley in the sixth century B.C., had a well-developed system of planetary astronomy.

The Greeks borrowed astronomy from the Chaldeans and elaborated it further into a system, which Claudius Ptolemy put into its final form in the second century A.D.

This Ptolemaic system placed the Earth at the center of the universe. Earth was supposed to be surrounded by a series of concentric spheres. The innermost held the Moon, the next Mercury, then Venus, the Sun, Mars, Jupiter, and Saturn, in that order. The outermost held the fixed stars. Many subtle modifications were added to this primary scheme.

Now let's consider the objects in the heavens, one by one, and see how they would impress the early observer. Suppose first that only the stars existed in the sky.

In that case there would be no reason whatever for any astronomer, whether Sumerian or Greek, to assume that they were anything other than what they appeared to be: luminous dots of light against a black background. The fact that they never changed their position relative to one another, even after long periods of observation, would make it reasonable to suppose that the sky was a black solid sphere enclosing the Earth and that the stars were imbedded in that solid sky like tiny, luminous thumbtacks.

It would be further reasonable to suppose the sky and its embedded stars to be a mere covering, and that the Earth, and the Earth *alone*, made up the essential universe. It had to be *the* world, the only existent thing man could inhabit.

When Mercury, Venus, Mars, Jupiter, and Saturn were discovered and studied, they added nothing startlingly new to this picture. They moved independently, so they could not be affixed to the sky. Each had to be embedded in a separate sphere, one inside the other, and each of these spheres had to be transparent, since we could see the stars through them all.

These planets, however, were merely so many more stars to the primitive observer. They were brighter than the others and moved differently, but they had to be only additional luminous points. Their existence did not interfere with the view of the Earth as the only world.

What about the Sun, though?

That, it would have to be admitted, is unique in the heavens. It is not a dot of light, but a disk of light, many

millions of times as bright as any star. When it was in the
sky, it painted the sky blue and washed out any mere dot
of light.

And yet, although the Sun was much *more,* it was not
much *different.* All the stars and planets, and the Sun too,
were composed of light, while the Earth was dark. The
heavenly bodies were changeless, while all on Earth cor-
rupted, decayed, and changed. The heavenly bodies moved
around and around, while objects on Earth either rose or
fell. Heaven and Earth seemed fundamentally different.

About 340 B.C., Aristotle set the distinction in a fashion
that held good for two thousand years. The Earth, he said,
was made of four basic constituent elements: earth, water,
air, and fire. The heavens, however, and everything in
them, were made of a fifth element, peculiar to itself and
completely different from the four of Earth. This fifth element is "ether," from a Greek word meaning "glowing."

This glowingness, or luminosity, which seemed so fundamental to heavenly bodies as opposed to earthly ones, extended to temporary denizens of the heavens too. Meteors
existed only momentarily, but they were flashes of light.
Comets might come and go and have strange shapes, but
those shapes were luminous.

Everything, it seemed, conspired to show the heavens to
be separate and the Earth to be the only world.

. . . Except the Moon.

The Moon does not fit. Like the Sun, it is more than a
mere dot of light. It can even be a full disk of light, though
it is then hundreds of thousands of times less bright than
the Sun. Unlike the Sun or anything else in the heavens,
however, the Moon changes its shape regularly.

Sooner or later the question must have arisen, Why does
the Moon change its shape?

Undoubtedly, man's first thought would be that what
seemed to happen *did* happen: that, every month, a new
Moon was born from the fires of the Sun.

Some unnamed Sumerian might have had his doubts,
however. The complete and careful study of the Moon's
position in the sky as compared to the Sun must have made
it quite clear that the luminous portion of the Moon was
always the portion that faced the Sun.

It would appear that as the Moon changed position relative to the Sun, progressively different portions were illumi-

nated, and this progressive change resulted in changes of phase as seen from the Earth.

If the phases of the Moon were interpreted in this fashion, it appeared that the Moon was a sphere that shone only by light reflected from the Sun. Only half the sphere was illuminated by the Sun at any one time, and this illuminated hemisphere shifted position to produce the succession of phases.

If any proof were needed to substantiate this, it could be found in the manner in which, at the time of the crescent Moon, the rest of the Moon's body could sometimes be made out in a dimly red luminosity. It was there but was simply not being illuminated by the Sun.

By Greek times, the fact that the Moon shone only by reflected light from the Sun was accepted without question. This meant that the Moon was *not* an intrinsically luminous body, as all the other heavenly bodies seemed to be. It was a *dark* body, like Earth. It shone by reflected light, like Earth. (In fact, the dim, red glow of the dark Moon at the time of the crescent resulted from the bathing of that part of the Moon in earthlight.)

Then, too, the Moon's body, unlike that of the Sun, showed clear and permanent markings, dark splotches that marred its luminosity. This meant that, unlike the other heavenly bodies, the Moon was visibly imperfect, like the Earth.

It was possible to suppose, then, that the Moon, at least, was a world as the Earth was one; that the Moon, at least, might bear inhabitants as Earth did. Even in ancient times, then, the Moon (and the Moon alone) gave man the notion of a multiplicity of worlds. Without the Moon, the notion might never have arisen before the invention of the telescope.

Aristotle, to be sure, did not put the Moon in a class with the Earth, but considered it to be composed of ether. One might argue that the Moon was closer to Earth than any other heavenly body was, and therefore absorbed some of the imperfections of earthly elements, developing stains and losing the capacity for self-illumination.

But then Greek astronomy advanced further. About 250 B.C., Eratosthenes of Cyrene used trigonometric methods for calculating the size of the Earth. He came to the conclusion that the Earth had a circumference of twenty-five thousand miles and therefore a diameter of eight thousand miles. This was essentially correct.

In 150 B.C., Hipparchus of Nicaea used trigonometric methods to determine the distance to the Moon. He decided the distance of the Moon from the Earth was about thirty times the diameter of the Earth. This, too, was essentially correct.

If the work of Hipparchus and Eratosthenes was combined, then the Moon was 240,000 miles from Earth, and to appear to be its apparent size, it had to be a little over two thousand miles wide. It was a *world!* Whatever Aristotle said, it was a world in size at least.

It is not surprising, then, that by the time Claudius Ptolemy was publishing his grand synthesis of Greek astronomy, Lucian of Samosata was writing a popular romance involving a trip to an inhabited Moon. Indeed, once the Moon was recognized as a world, it was an easy further step to assume that other heavenly bodies were worlds as well.

Yet it is only the Moon—*only* the Moon—that is close enough to Earth for its distance to be estimated by trigonometric methods based on unaided-eye observations. Without the Moon, it would have been impossible to gain any knowledge whatever of the distance and size of any heavenly body prior to the invention of the telescope. And without the nudge of knowing the Moon's distance and size, might there have been quite the urge to explore the heavens even after the telescope was invented and used for military purposes?

Then, in 1609, Galileo did press the telescope into astronomic service for the first time.

Galileo studied the heavens and found that, through his telescope, the planets, which seemed to be dots of light when viewed by the unaided eye, appeared to be distinctly formed spheres of light. What's more, Venus, at least, was so located with respect to the Earth as to show phases like those of the Moon; phases, moreover, plainly related to its position with respect to the Sun.

The conclusion seemed inevitable. All the starlike planets: Mercury, Venus, Mars, Jupiter, and Saturn; were worlds like the Moon. They appeared as mere dots of light because they were so much farther from us than the Moon was.

This in itself was not fatal to the Aristotelian view, for it could be argued that the planets (and the Moon), however large they were, and however non-luminous, were nevertheless composed of ether.

What really destroyed the ethereal concept once and for all, however, was Galileo's observation of the Moon. (Indeed, he looked at the Moon first of all.) On the Moon, Galileo saw mountains, and dark, smooth areas he interpreted as seas. The Moon was clearly, *visibly,* a world like Earth: imperfect, rough, mountainous.

It is no wonder, then, that with this second blow dealt by the Moon, the concept of the plurality of worlds took another giant step forward. The seventeenth century saw the beginning of a set of novels dealing with manned voyages to the Moon that grew steadily more sophisticated and have not ceased right down to the present day.

Of course you might say that Galileo would have demonstrated the plurality of worlds, by telescope, even if the Moon had not existed, and that the resistance of the Aristotelians would have broken as telescopes improved and as other tools were invented.

Suppose that were the case: Science-fiction writers might then have dreamed of flights to Mars or Venus instead of to a non-existent Moon. . . . But dreams are only dreams, after all. Would man have attempted to make space flight a *reality* if the Moon had not existed?

The Moon is less than a quarter of a million miles from us. Venus, on the other hand, is 25 million miles away even when it is at its closest (at intervals of a year and a half). It is then a hundred times as far from us as the Moon is. Mars at its times of closest approach is farther still. Every thirty years or so, when it is particularly close, it is 35 million miles away.

It takes three days to reach the Moon. It would take at least half a year to reach Venus or Mars.

It has taken heroic measures for men to reach the Moon. Would it have been reasonable to expect them to have made the many-times-multiplied heroic measures necessary to reach Venus or Mars from scratch?

No, it is the Moon—the Moon *only*—that made space flight possible. It did so first by letting us see that there are other worlds than our own and then by offering us an easy steppingstone by means of which we can sharpen our techniques and from which, as a base, we can eventually make the much greater assault on the more distant worlds.

The triple triumph of the Moon, then, is that it made it possible for man to exist; it made it possible for him to develop mathematics and science; it made it possible for him to transcend Earth and conquer space.

If, then, in accordance with the line of argument in chapter 1, I concluded that it would have been of great use to man to have Venus possess a Moon like ours, in this chapter I deny any desire to lose our own.

What would have been ideal would have been for *both* planets to be Moon-accompanied.

three

MOON OVER BABYLON

One morning recently I was in upstate New York, having given a talk at a local university the night before. I wanted to get an early start home and was a little disappointed that the gas station immediately next to the motel was closed, although it was already 8:45 A.M.

I muttered something about it, with a sigh, to the lady behind the desk at the motel office as I paid my bill, and she said with a sharp note of surprise, "It's not open?"

"Afraid not," I said.

"Well, it should be," she said, her face setting into angry lines. "My son runs it, and he's going to hear from me."

Uneasy at being the unwitting cause of a family tempest, I sought a mollifying excuse and hastily said, "Oh, well, it's Sunday morning."

"That makes no difference," she snapped back at me. "We're Seventh-Day Adventists."

"Ah, yes," I said, grinning. "*Yesterday* was Sunday, wasn't it?"

She looked surprised for a moment, then laughed and said, "Yes, yesterday was Sunday." With the laugh, her anger evaporated. And since her son showed up at just about that time anyway, I got my gas and all was well.

But that reminded me of our seven-day week and of some of its peculiarities, so if the Gentle Reader will hold still for a moment . . .

As we all know, the year is made up of twelve months, each with anywhere from twenty-eight to thirty-one days in an irregular arrangement. There is a total of 365 days in the year three times out of four, and 366 days on the fourth occasion.

The result is a calendar that varies from year to year in an intricate pattern. This makes inevitable the clear waste of effort that comes from having to prepare and distribute new and different calendars each year. What is worse, the pattern of the year produces confusion in the details of calendar dating from year to year, resulting in personal annoyance and business expense.

And the villain in the piece is neither day nor month, but the week.

The day, the month, and the year are all fixed by astronomical cycles. The day is the period in which the Earth rotates about its axis; the month is the 29.53-day period during which the Moon circles the Earth and goes through its cycle of phases; the year is the 365.25-day period during which the Earth revolves about the Sun and the seasons go through the cycle. The actual calendar we now use is a rough approximation intended to force these not-quite-commensurable units into line so that there are exactly twelve months to the year and, as aforesaid, twenty-eight to thirty-one days to the month.

And where does the week come in?

The Moon goes through the cycle of its phases in 29.53 days, and there are four moments in the cycle when the phase detail is sufficiently remarkable to get a name of its own: When the Moon is just about a perfect disk of light, it is "full Moon," and when it is so close to the Sun in the sky that it can't be seen as anything but, at most, the tiniest sliver of crescent, it is the "new Moon." In going from the new Moon to the full Moon, and again from the full Moon to the new Moon, there is a point at which exactly half the Moon's visible disk is lit. Both are "half Moons." It is customary, though, to call the half Moon during the period when the visible Moon is moving toward the full, the "first quarter," because it comes after the cycle is one-quarter done. The half Moon in the stage of the waning Moon is, for analogous reasons, the "third quarter."

The time of the new Moon was, of course, celebrated as the beginning of each month in a strictly lunar calendar such as the Babylonians had. In such a calendar, the full Moon would invariably come in the middle of the month, and it might receive a certain amount of homage too. The Babylonians did, indeed, seem to have a full-Moon festival, which they called *sappatu*.

The Babylonians were the cultural leaders of the Near East through all the period prior to the conquests of Alexander the Great, and undoubtedly their way of life had its effect on other peoples. A form of the word *sappatu* entered the Hebrew language and, by way of that, it entered the English language too, in the form of "Sabbath."

During the period prior to the Babylonian exile of the Jews, the term "Sabbath" may have meant strictly the full-Moon festival, and it is sometimes used in the pre-exilic books in what appears to be a kind of antonym to the new-Moon festival. As one example, when a woman wished to go to the wonder-working prophet Elisha after her son had died of sunstroke, her husband said to her, "Wherefore wilt thou go to him today? it is neither new moon nor sabbath." (2 Kings 4:23)

Perhaps there were some ceremonies marking the two half-Moon phases as well, so there were a total of four lunar festivals each month, which might have come to be called four Sabbaths.

As it happens, these four points in the cycle of phases of the Moon are equidistant in time. The time lapse from one point to the next, from new to first quarter, from first quarter to full, from full to third quarter, and from third quarter to new again, is in each case just one-fourth of the lunar month, or about 7.38 days.

For the purposes of popular celebrations, it is difficult to handle fractions of a day. The nearest whole number is 7, and the tendency would be to have the lunar celebration come every seven days. If you do that, you have a seven-day period built into the calendar. We call it "week" from a primitive Teutonic word meaning "change" (of the Moon's phase, of course). The connection is clearer in German, where *Woche* means week and *Wechsel* means change.

Of course, the seven-day week doesn't match the Moon's phases exactly. If we start with the New Moon at noon on day 1, then the first quarter is around 9 P.M. on day 8, full Moon is about 6 A.M. on day 16, and third quarter is well after 3 P.M. on day 23. If the phase changes are celebrated every seven days without fail, the celebration falls on days 1, 8, 15, and 22, and the last two are a day off.

In fact, by this system you will be celebrating the next new Moon a day and a half early, and if you continue the seven-day period inflexibly, the third new Moon will be celebrated three days too early, and so on.

There are two alternatives from which the Babylonians might have chosen:

1) They might have made the period of the week flexible so as to keep it in a close match to the phases of the Moon. They could have had some pattern of 7-day weeks and 8-day weeks that would add up to an average of a 7.38-day week. For instance, in one month the weeks could have a 7, 8, 7, 8 pattern and in the next a 7, 8, 7, 7 pattern. If months continue to alternate in this way, the week would continue about thirty years before falling out of line with the phases of the Moon. There is precedent in this too, for the Babylonians developed a flexible month, which sometimes had twenty-nine days and sometimes thirty days, and a flexible year, which sometimes had twelve months and sometimes thirteen months, in order that the calendar might continue to match the seasons.

2) They might on the other hand have kept the week inflexible, making it a steady 7-day period indefinitely, and forsaken the attachment of the week to the lunar phases. The new Moon, the full Moon, and the quarters would then have fallen on any day of the week, and what had begun as a lunar period of time would then have taken on an independent existence.

Apparently the Babylonians decided on the second alternative, which is surprising in view of their record with regard to the month and the year.

In seeking a reason for the inflexibility in connection with this particular period of time, we must probably fall back on the nature of the number 7.

The Babylonians were the great astronomers of pre-Greek days, and they well knew that there were seven bright bodies in the sky that moved against the background of the fixed stars. These were the Sun, the Moon, Mercury, Venus, Mars, Jupiter, and Saturn. (For the last five we use the names of Roman gods; the Babylonians used the names of their own gods.)

The coincidence of seven days to a phase change and seven planets in the sky seems to have been too much for the Babylonians and they couldn't help but match up each of the seven days with a particular planet. In that case, an eight-day week with no eighth planet would mean an impossible anomaly. In the hard choice between the planets as a group and one of their number, the Moon, the planets won out. Since the Babylonians very likely named each day of the week after a different planet, that further helped make the week an inflexible seven days in length.

When the Jews were in Babylonian exile, in the sixth century B.C., there would have been a strong tendency to go along with the week as a unit of time. It would be difficult to live and work in Babylonia and not do so. Undoubtedly the carefully religious among them could not bring themselves to use pagan names for the weekdays and so they simply numbered the days of the week, as the first day, the second day, and so on. Throughout the Bible, in both the Old Testament and the New, the days of the week have no names, only numbers.

Even if the Jews in exile did not go along with the Babylonian religious rites, they would have to suspend business every seventh day. (It is difficult not to suspend business when the vast majority is doing so—or vice versa—as Jews have found out on many occasions since.)

To do so, and yet to avoid making such suspension honor what they considered idolatrous worship of Sun, Moon, and planets, the Jews had to make the week have some significance in their own religious system. It was during the Babylonian exile that the first thirty-four verses of the biblical Book of Genesis achieved their modern form. In those verses God is pictured as creating the world in six days and resting on the seventh. This gives Judaistic significance to the week and the fact that the seventh day of the week is a day of rest. (The word Sabbath is from a Semitic word for "rest.")

When parties of Babylonian Jews returned to Judea, they brought back with them the newly elaborated notion of the Sabbath and used it as an important distinction between themselves and those who were then living in the land.

Despite the fact that the Bible, as put into its final form during the Babylonian exile and afterward, places the institution of the Sabbath at the very creation, there is virtually no mention of it in the early historical books, of Judges, I and II Samuel, and I and II Kings, the material of which is pre-exilic. It is only in the postexilic books that it becomes really important from a ritualistic standpoint. Thus, in the postexilic book of Nehemiah, Nehemiah can report Sabbath-breaking as shocking evidence of backsliding: "In those days saw I in Judah some treading wine presses on the sabbath. . . ." (Nehemiah 13:15)

Thereafter the Jews attached ever greater importance to the Sabbath. During the day of Seleucid persecution, in the second century B.C., some were content to die or to lose battles rather than violate it.

The earliest Christians were, of course, Jews, and while many of the elaborate Judaistic tenets of the first century were abandoned in the course of the spread of Christianity through the Roman Empire (notably the necessity for the rite of circumcision), the week and the notion of the Sabbath were not.

Eventually, when the Roman Empire made Christianity the state religion, the week was adopted in the West as an official part of the calendar—*and not until then*. It was the Emperor Constantine I, the first Christian Emperor (though he was not actually baptized till he was on his deathbed) who, in the fourth century, made the week an official part of the Roman calendar.

Undoubtedly, though, the week as a mystical period must have entered the West earlier than that. Astrologers in the West used a system for dedicating the days to the planets (and through them to the gods) that they probably borrowed from the Babylonians. It worked as follows:

Suppose you list the planets in order of increasing speed of motion against the stars: Saturn, Jupiter, Mars, Sun, Venus, Mercury, Moon. Then imagine the planets in charge of successive hours of the day in that order.

Thus, the first hour of the first day would be Saturn, the second hour Jupiter, the third Mars, and so on. After seven hours one would have worked his way through the list, and the eighth hour would be Saturn again; the fifteenth and twenty-second likewise. The twenty-third would be Jupiter, the twenty-fourth would be Mars, and the twenty-fifth, which would be the first hour of the *second* day, would be the Sun.

If the planet that rules the first hour of a particular day is associated with the day as a whole, then the first day becomes that of Saturn and the second that of the Sun. If you continue matching the planets with the hours according to this system, you will find that the first hour of the third day is associated with the Moon and that the next days of the week are associated with Mars, Mercury, Jupiter, and Venus, in that order. The eighth day is dedicated to Saturn again, and the cycle begins over.

When the week was introduced as a Christian institution, it turned out that the day of the week that had astrologically been associated with Saturn was the same day that by Jewish tradition was the seventh day (the Sabbath). The day associated with Saturn was therefore put at the end. The Roman week thus began with the day associated with the Sun. It went as follows: 1) dies solis (Sun), 2) dies lunae (Moon), 3) dies Martis (Mars), 4) dies Mercurii (Mercury), 5) dies Jovis (Jupiter), 6) dies Veneris (Venus), and 7) dies Saturni (Saturn).

The Romance languages follow this for the second through fifth days inclusive. In French these days are lundi, mardi, mercredi, jeudi, and vendredi. In Italian they are lunedì, martedì, mercoledì, giovedì, and venerdì. In Spanish, they are lunes, martes, miércoles, jueves, and viernes.

In English and German it is the Teutonic gods who are celebrated. We have Sunday and Monday for the first two days of the week, while the Germans have Sonntag and Montag. The third, fourth, fifth, and sixth days are for Tiu, Woden, Thor, and the goddess Freya, who is the Norse Venus. We have Tuesday, Wednesday, Thursday, and Friday. The Germans have Freitag for the sixth day and use their versions of the names of gods, Dienstag and Donnerstag, for Tuesday and Thursday. Wednesday, which commemorates the chief god of the Teutonic pantheon, is lost out in German, where it is simply Mittwoch, which means, sensibly enough, "mid-week."

Since the Roman dies Saturni is the Sabbath of the Jewish tradition, that affects the name of the day in the Romance languages. The seventh day is sabato in Italian, and sábado in Spanish, while in French and German it seems to be a kind of compromise between Saturn and Sabbath, being samedi and Samstag, respectively. (In German the seventh day is also called Sonnabend, meaning "Sunday eve.")

It is strange that English should remain so paganishly adherent to Saturn over the Sabbath, but we call the seventh day "Saturday."

The early Jewish Christians celebrated the Sabbath as did the Jews generally, and on the seventh day too. How-

ever, just as the Jews had once been anxious to distinguish
themselves from the surrounding Babylonians, so the early
Christians were anxious to distinguish themselves from the
surrounding non-Christian Jews.

To do so, they fixed on the one point in their doctrine
that was absolutely distinct: the crucifixion, resurrection,
and Messiah-hood of Jesus. By tradition, Jesus was cruci-
fied on a Friday and was resurrected on the third day,
which was Sunday. The early Christians, therefore, in addition to celebrating the Sabbath on the seventh day, also
celebrated the Resurrection on the first day, which they
called the Lord's day.

For that reason, the Romans of the Christian empire
called the day not only dies solis, but also dies Dominica,
and that, too, has lingered, since the first day is domingo in
Spanish, domenica in Italian, and dimanche in French.
English and German stolidly continue to commemorate the
Sun, however, with Sunday and Sonntag.

As Christianity became more Gentile and less Jewish,
the emphasis shifted more and more from the seventh day
to the first day, and Sunday became not only the Lord's
day but came also to attach to itself all sorts of sabbatical
customs. It became the weekly day of rest, the day when
worldly business must cease, the day when church atten-
dance was desirable—or even compulsory—and so on.

Naturally there is an inconsistency here. The creation
story of Genesis makes it quite clear that it is the seventh
day of the week that is the Sabbath. "And on the seventh
day God ended his work which he had made; and he rested
on the seventh day from all his work which he had made.
And God blessed the seventh day, and sanctified it. . . ."
(Genesis 2:2–3)

Nor is there any question that the seventh day is the one
we call Saturday. Calendars in use in the United States universally begin the week with Sunday as the first day and
end it with Saturday as the seventh day.

Some Christians worried about reserving for the first day
rituals of worship that God had seemed to reserve for the
seventh. In 1844 a group of Christians organized themselves into a sect of Adventists; that is, a sect that expected
the not-too-long-delayed, and perhaps momentary, second
Advent (appearance) of Jesus. Because they also felt that

they ought to adhere to the literal word of Genesis 2:2–3, they insisted on celebrating the Sabbath on the seventh day, not on the first: on Saturday, not on Sunday. They therefore called themselves "Seventh-Day Adventists" (like the lady behind the motel desk, to whom I referred in the introduction to this chapter).

Nor are these the only Christians who celebrate Saturday as the Sabbath. There are Seventh-Day Baptists too, I believe, and perhaps still other sects.

All these "Seventh-Day" sects are lumped, together with the Jews, as "Sabbatarians," and these create a problem. In a society like the twentieth-century United States, religious observances are fairly loose. Anyone can observe any day he wishes as a Sabbath, or observe no day at all.

Nevertheless, as part of the tradition from an older and tighter time, Sunday is treated legally as a day different from other days. Businesses close on that day, even if they don't close on any other. In fact, some businesses are required to close by law.

But, then, what about Sabbatarians, who feel compelled to close their businesses on Saturday for religious reasons and are forced by law to close them on Sunday too, though that day has no significance at all for them? Where's justice for Sabbatarians?

Or what about the fact that once we have a Sabbath on *any* day and establish a principle of rest on a fixed day of the week, with everybody taking off like a bunch of robots, the habit easily spreads to two days a week, and even three. Then a person like myself, who observes no specific day of rest at all, but who is quite likely (when permitted) to work steadily and industriously seven days a week, finds he can receive no mail on Sunday and cannot reach his editors on either Saturday *or* Sunday. Where's justice for non-Sabbatarians?

These difficulties, however important for individuals, are trivial, of course, for the world in general.

What is much more important for the world is that the week, which originated in Babylonia for what would now seem to us to be trivial reasons* and which came down to

---

* Come on, who *cares* what the phase of the Moon is? Do you yourself care, or even know, what the phase of the Moon is this very night?

us through a variety of improbable turns of history, now
creates endless confusion.

Consider: It is usually important to know what day of
the week a particular date is. If a particular date is a Sunday, you may not accept some invitation that you would if
it were a Tuesday. You might hesitate to visit a restaurant
without a reservation on a Saturday night, but not on a
Wednesday night. A particular week night may be poker
night; a weekday, your girl's day off or ladies' day at the
ball park. The list is endless.

Yet, given a date at random, you can't tell without considerable figuring (or without consulting a calendar) what
day of the week it is.

There is only one word to describe this situation: stupid-
ity, because it doesn't have to be.

Let me give you the basic reason why weekdays can't be
predicted without a great deal of trouble. There are 365
days in a year (366 days in a leap year) and 7 ×
52=364. This means that in an ordinary year there are
fifty-two weeks—plus one day left over. In a leap year
there are fifty-two weeks—plus two days left over.

Day 1 of an ordinary 365-day year may fall, let us suppose, on a Sunday, so that it is the first day of the first
week of that year. In that case, the next to the last day of
the year, day 364, would be the last day of the fifty-second
week and would fall on a Saturday. This means that January 1 (day 1) would fall on a Sunday, and December 30
(day 364) would fall on a Saturday. But, then, that still
leaves day 365, which is December 31, which would fall on
a Sunday.† Then January 1 of the next year falls on a
Monday.

If the year were a leap year with January 1 on Sunday,
day 364 would be December 29 (because February 29
would have gotten in as day 60, pushing March 1, which is
ordinarily day 60, into the day-61 position, and so on all
the way to the end). Then there would be two more days,
December 30 and 31, falling on Sunday and Monday, respectively, and January 1 of the next year would fall on
Tuesday.

---

† Check a calendar if you don't see this at once and you'll discover
that in any ordinary 365-day year, January 1 and December 31,
first and last of the year, fall on the same day of the week.

This is true of any date of the year, not just January 1. Any date will be one day later in the week than it was the year before, and sometimes two days later if a February 29 has worked its way in between.

To give you an arbitrary example: Consider the date October 17, 1971. That fell on a Sunday. In 1972, October 17 fell on Tuesday (February 29 came between). Then, in succeeding years, October 17 falls on Wednesday, Thursday, Friday, Sunday, Monday, Tuesday, Wednesday, Friday, Saturday, Sunday, Monday, Wednesday, Thursday, Friday, Saturday, Monday, Tuesday, Wednesday, Thursday, Saturday, Sunday, Monday, Tuesday, Thursday, Friday, Sunday.

It is not until 1999, twenty-eight years after 1971,* that October 17 falls once again on a Sunday in the year before a leap year, so that the pattern starts repeating. If you can memorize this 28-member pattern, then you would have a scheme for telling the weekday of any date of any year since the establishment of the Gregorian calendar (which was 1752 in Great Britain and the American colonies). You can do this, however, only if every fourth year is a leap year without fail.

As it happens, under the Gregorian calendar there are three occasions every four centuries when the fourth year is *not* a leap year. The next occasion will be 2100 A.D., and every time such an occasion arises, the 28-member pattern has to be slightly revised.

So the question at hand is this: How can this sort of nonsense (together with a few other problems not quite as infuriating) be eliminated from our calendar?

This can be done easily, as a matter of fact, and I will show you how in the next chapter.

---

* No secret to the twenty-eight. There are seven days in the week, and a leap year comes every four years. Since seven and four are mutually prime, the pattern does not repeat for 7×4=28 years.

four

THE WEEK EXCUSE

Over the past few years I have appeared on television talk shows now and then. I have not appeared often enough to become a national celebrity by any means, but it has been often enough to give some people an uncertain feeling of quasi-recognition when they see me.

The recognition, such as it is, is aided by the sideburns and long hair I now affect, which give me a rather leonine look. Add to that a kind of ferocious expression I naturally fall into when thinking—which is generally all the time—and I suppose I become a trifle hard to forget.

At any rate, I was going down on an elevator recently when an elderly lady was the only other person on board. She fixed me with a hard glance and then, using the privilege of age, said abruptly, "You're someone famous. I know it. What's your name?"

I said, trying to smile pleasantly, "I'm Isaac Asimov, ma'am."

And she said blankly, *"Who?"*

So much for fame! You would think that events like that would teach me my place and make me less eager to advance my own revolutionary notions in this field or that. Somehow they don't.

For instance, I want to follow the previous chapter with one devoted to a discussion of calendar reform, and in the process I intend to give you *my* notions on the subject, which I consider better than those of anyone else in the world. How's that for humility?

Calendar reformers object seriously to the calendar we all now use and some of us love. First and foremost, there is the difficulty (as I explained in chapter 3) that, every year, the calendar changes. There are seven different ordinary 365-day years, since January 1 can (and periodically does) fall on each of the seven different days of the week. In the same way, seven different leap years are possible. Since a leap year comes every fourth year, the calendars are different each successive year in a complex pattern until a period of twenty-eight years have passed. After that, the pattern starts repeating.

Thus the calendars for 1901, 1929, 1957, 1985, 2013, 2041, 2069, and 2097 are all identical. All are ordinary years in which January 1 falls on a Tuesday. In all of them, July 4 is on a Thursday and Christmas is on a Wednesday. (There are superficial differences, of course. There was no "Armistice Day" listed as a holiday in 1901 or 1973, for instance, but there was in 1935.)

In this 28-year pattern there are twenty-one ordinary years, three beginning on each of the weekdays, and seven leap years, one beginning on each of the weekdays. If you save calendars for each of twenty-eight successive years, you will then have a "perpetual 28-year calendar." You can paste all twenty-eight in order on the wall and move from one to the next each year, coming full circle after twenty-eight years and repeating.

This will work as long as every fourth year is a leap year without fail. There are no failures between 1900 and 2100, but in general three out of every four even-century years are not leap years, so there are then seven ordinary years in a row, as from 1897 to 1903 inclusive.

To get a real perpetual calendar that will fit the Gregorian system we now use, you will need twenty-eight hundred successive calendars, from, say, 1601 A.D. to 4400 A.D. After that, things repeat exactly from 4401 A.D. to 7200 A.D. and so on.

This, you will agree, is not exactly a practical notion, especially since, after a number of cycles, the present Gregorian calendar will get a day out of phase with the Sun so that a leap year will have to be subtracted.

Surely we can do better than that. Let's think about it.

The simplest thing we might do is to just number the days. We might begin at some convenient time and number them consecutively and without limit. We won't run out of numbers, which are infinite, and if we consider days *only*, and don't worry about weeks, months, or years, we don't need a calendar at all. We just remember that we were born on day so-and-so, married on day so-and-so, made a killing on the stock market on day so-and-so, etc. The big advantage, aside from the abolition of calendars altogether, would be the fact that you could always tell the number of days between two events by simple subtraction.

Such a system may sound utterly unthinkable to you, too mathematical and depersonalized. Yet we do exactly this in the case of the years. We are simply numbering them indefinitely and we are now up to nearly two thousand in our figures. This has meant depersonalization too, for there was a time when all the years were identified as the one in which So-and-So was archon or consul, or the such-and-such year of King So-and-So.

The advantage of simply numbering the years was, however, so great that all the little personal touches used to identify them (which, however endearing and human, were endlessly confusing when it came to keeping orderly records) were abandoned. Of course there is the question of when you begin the count. You have to find some important landmark on which the world will generally agree. In the case of the years, such a landmark was found in the birth of Jesus.

Not only are years numbered by this system, but days too, believe it or not. Back in the late-sixteenth century a French scholar, Joseph Justus Scaliger, suggested that the days be numbered, and as day 1 he chose January 1, 4713 B.C. by the Gregorian Calendar.* He called these numbered days "Julian days" in honor of his father, Julius Caesar Scaliger.

Astronomers use the Julian day right now, for they find it convenient in their calculations to deal with days only. Thus it happens that I am writing these words on Julian day 2,441,252.

But there's the trouble. We can stand the infinite numbering of years, since we're still in four-digit numbers, which can be handled, and we won't add a fifth digit for over eight thousand years. If we number the days, however, we are already in seven digits, and that is no good. Even

---

* Why that day? Well, Scaliger counted backward and found that on that day a number of important astronomical cycles such as the solar year, the lunar month, the saronic period of eclipses, and so on, all started together.

someone as devoted to numbers as I am must admit that seven-digit identification of individual days is a bit much.

Besides, the cycle of seasons (one year to a complete cycle) is too important to world economy and to personal human affairs to be ignored. We have to have the year.

But, in that case, why not combine the year and the day, giving each numbers and nothing more? Each year would have days numbered from 1 to 365 (or 366 if a leap year). We could speak of 72, 1944, or 284, 1962, or 366, 1984, and uniquely and unmistakably identify each date. To be sure, you will still have six or seven digits to deal with, but you would be thinking of days and years separately, which makes a psychological difference.

In such a day-year numbering, you still wouldn't need a calendar. In fact, you need a calendar in our present system only when the question of the day of the week comes up. In consulting a calendar, you ask yourself one of only two varieties of question: 1) What day of the week is the twenty-eighth of next month? or 2) What is next Tuesday's date?

If you did not care on what day of the week any date fell, you would simply never consult a calendar.

But we can't get rid of the week. It is too deeply ingrained in our way of life. What would we do without the weekend, for goodness' sake?

So we must keep the week and we must have a calendar in which all the days of the year are arranged in seven columns.

Suppose the year were *exactly* 364 days long. In that case, we would have those 364 days arranged in seven columns, each of which was fifty-two items long. If day 1 were on a Sunday, days 8, 15, 22, 29, 36, . . . 358 would all be on Sunday; days 9, 16, 23, 30, 37, . . . 359 would all be on Mondays; and so on. Day 364 would be on Saturday and that would end the year, so day 1 of the next year would begin on a Sunday and the whole thing would start all over.

In such a case, a single calendar, with all the days numbered and divided into fifty-two complete weeks, would do for every single year in perpetuity (barring changes in the lengths of the day and the year over the aeons).

But the year is not 364 days long, but about 365¼ days

long, so every year has at least 365 days and sometimes 366.

Can we ignore those extra days and pretend that 364 days make up a year? What's a day or two here and there? But if we try to do this, then the year gets out of whack with the seasons. If the vernal equinox is on March 21 this year, it would be on March 22 the next year (or March 23 if the next year is a leap year) and so on. After 292 years, the vernal equinox (and every other astronomical landmark of the seasons) would have made a complete cycle, coming back to March 21.

This can be done. The ancient Egyptians ignored leap years, letting their year fall a quarter day behind the Sun each year, so the seasonal landmarks made a complete cycle of the year every 1,460 years. They refused to change this even though they knew it was happening and knew how to keep it from happening. Tradition, you know.

Well, down with tradition. Let's keep a 364-day year without abandoning days 365 and 366. All we need do is refuse to assign those extra days to any day of the week.

Suppose we consider day 365 to be a day that is assigned to no weekday. It just comes at the end, counting as a holiday to be called "Year Day." In leap years there is also day 366, which is still another holiday, to be called "Leap Day," without a day of the week. Thus, after Year Day each year (and after Leap Day too, in leap years) we go on to day 1 of the next year, which is still a Sunday, even though in this case eight days (or nine in leap year) have elapsed since the previous Sunday, which was day 358. In such a calendar, days 365 and 366 can be placed in parentheses to the right of the seven columns somewhere and not be allowed to intrude on the week.

While this calendar of years, weeks, and days only (no months, you'll notice) had never been seriously suggested—and even I don't suggest it seriously—all repeating calendars that have been suggested on an annual basis have to make use of a Year Day and a Leap Day that are not assigned any day of the week. Only so can we keep the seven-day week from throwing the calendar out of line and making each year different from the one before.

But it is on this rock that calendar reform founders. There are many influential religious bodies that will not hear of any day not being associated with a day of the week. The Sabbath must be celebrated every seven days without fail, and if, once a year, two Sundays (or two Saturdays if you're a Sabbatarian, or two Fridays if you're a Muslim) are eight or nine days apart, the religious skies will, apparently, fall.

If you want my own opinion, I consider this week excuse for opposing calendar reform a weak excuse.* Without trying to make an actual list of the myriad compromises various religions have made in the interest of expediency, I merely suggest that Jesus said, "The sabbath was made for man, and not man for the sabbath." (Mark 2:27)

It is possible, then, that someday those who view the Sabbath as returning with the endless tick of a metronome will give way in the interest of sanity.

Taking an entire year as the unit has its difficulties, because that includes the complete cycle of seasons but ignores the individual seasons. I am accustomed, for instance, to four seasons of sharply different characteristics, each with its own effect on agriculture, business, transportation, vacation, consumption—variety generally. It is therefore useful to keep track of the individual seasons in the calendar.

It would seem natural to use the months for the purpose. The month was originally adopted in order to mark the cycle of the phases of the Moon and had nothing to do with the seasons at all. Still, they are there.

Traditionally there are twelve months, through the accident of the length of the cycle of lunar phases. Unfortunately, however, twelve equal months in a 364-day year (the only kind of year that makes sense in a repeating calendar) are each 30 1/3 days long, or 4 1/3 weeks long. In other words, the months of a 12-month year cannot be made even with either days or weeks.

Oddly enough, though, a 13-month year would be perfect in this respect, since 364=13×28, and 28=7×4. In a 13-month year, each month would be just four weeks long and, of course, twenty-eight days long. Each month would look like:

* No, I'm not ashamed of myself at all.

S	M	T	W	T	F	S
1	2	3	4	5	6	7
8	9	10	11	12	13	14
15	16	17	18	19	20	21
22	23	24	25	26	27	28

This is not an utterly strange month in appearance. Three times every twenty-eight years, February looks like that. Indeed, February 1970 looked like that.

If *every* month looked like that, the arrangement would quickly be memorized. We would come to understand that the 17th was always on a Tuesday and the 13th always on a Friday (sorry!), the 1st always on a Sunday, and so on. After a while, we wouldn't need a calendar at all.

But what do we do about the thirteenth month? One possibility was suggested in the International Fixed Calendar, which for a while, some decades ago, achieved some favorable publicity. In it, the thirteenth month (named Sol) was placed between the sixth and seventh, June and July. In this calendar, Year Day appeared as December 29 and Leap Day as June 29—neither, of course, being assigned a day of the week.

It is not possible to make a calendar containing days, weeks, and months any simpler than the International Fixed Calendar, and it is a shame that it possesses so serious a disability as to be useless. Thirteen months cannot be evenly divided by four, so there are not a whole number of months per season. In the International Fixed Calendar, there are three months and one week per season, and that introduces an unevenness that outweighs all the uniformities.

A 12-month year, however, would have the advantage of being evenly divisible into the four seasons, three months to a season. In a 12-month year it is impossible to have each month look exactly like its predecessor and successor, as in the International Fixed Calendar, but this disadvantage is considered trivial in comparison with its season exactness.

Keeping the seasons, then, how do we make the calendar as simple and as repetitive as possible? Since there are fifty-two weeks in a 364-day year, there are thirteen weeks per season. Thirteen weeks contain ninety-one days, and these can be distributed through three months in as nearly equal a fashion as possible by giving the first month thirty-one days and the other two thirty days each. Here is the way the three-month period would look:

S	M	T	W	T	F	S	
1	2	3	4	5	6	7	January
8	9	10	11	12	13	14	April
15	16	17	18	19	20	21	July
22	23	24	25	26	27	28	October
29	30	31					
			1	2	3	4	February
5	6	7	8	9	10	11	May
12	13	14	15	16	17	18	August
19	20	21	22	23	24	25	November
26	27	28	29	30			
					1	2	March
3	4	5	6	7	8	9	June
10	11	12	13	14	15	16	September
17	18	19	20	21	22	23	December
24	25	26	27	28	29	30	

Again, this is all the calendar we would ever need, for if this represented a three-month period, the fourth month would begin all over again precisely like the first. Thus, if the top month were January, the middle month February, and the bottom month March, the same three-month calendar could be used for April, May, and June, then again for July, August, and September, and finally for October, November, and December—year after year after year.

Such a perpetual three-month calendar is called the "World Calendar," and there are active movements in its favor. In the World Calendar, Year Day is on December 31, and Leap Day on June 31, and both are without weekday assignments.

Another advantage of the World Calendar is that the months are familiar in form: there is no three-month sequence in our ordinary calendar that is exactly like that of the World Calendar (there are no two 30-day months in a row), but individual months are alike. August 1971 is exactly like the top month of the three-month sequence, September 1971 like the middle month, and September 1972 like the bottom month.

Undoubtedly the World Calendar is, of all the repeating calendars, the best yet, in the sense that it requires the least modification of the existing system. Nevertheless there are some improvements I would like to suggest that do require some further modification but end in what I consider the simplest and most rational calendar possible that takes both weeks and seasons into account.

First, there are four natural points, from the astronomic viewpoint, at which the year could begin: the two solstices and the two equinoxes. These are not equally spaced through the year, because the Earth's orbit about the Sun is not perfectly circular, but we can place them on December 21, March 21, June 21, September 21 of our present calendar without being out more than a day or two.

Each might serve as a starting point for the year. On December 21 the Sun is at its lowest noonday point as seen from the Northern Hemisphere, while the same is true on June 21 for the Southern Hemisphere. On March 21 the renewal of plant growth is about to begin in the Northern Hemisphere, and the same can be said of September 21 in the Southern.

In choosing among the four, however, it makes sense to give preference to the Northern Hemisphere, for the large majority of the human race live there.

As between December 21 and March 21, the former is the start of the upward spiral of the Sun and the latter of vegetation, and the former is the sharper fact. Besides, December 21 is closer to the year's beginning we use now. Consequently I advocate December 21 as the beginning of the year, since that will make successive three-month periods fit the seasons most accurately.

The simplest way to bring about a December 21 beginning is to choose some year and, on December 20, drop eleven days from the calendar and call the next day January 1.

If dropping eleven days is too drastic a change (although it has been done in previous history: the British Empire, including the American colonies, dropped eleven days in 1752), I have another suggestion. Let us adopt the World Calendar and, for a while, omit both Year Day and Leap Day. Each ordinary year, we will move the days of the year one day backward with respect to the Sun, and two days backward in leap years. If we were to adopt the

World Calendar on January 1, 1979, for instance, and omit all Year Days and Leap Days, then January 1, 1988, would fall on the winter solstice (December 21, 1987, by our present calendar). Thereafter the date would stay on the winter solstice indefinitely, if Year Days and Leap Days were appropriately placed.

Once that was done, a second modification would involve the elimination of the months. The months have no real relation to the seasons; they relate, irrelevantly and inaccurately, to the Moon. The World Calendar restricts the variations in connection between date and weekday, but not altogether. The 5th of a month can never be on a Monday, Wednesday, Friday, or Saturday, but it could be on a Sunday, Tuesday, or Thursday. Any other date could be on any of three weekdays, depending on the month it is in. Who needs that?

Why not abandon the months altogether and keep only the seasons? In that case, each season of each year, year in and year out, would have the following calendar.

S	M	T	W	T	F	S
1	2	3	4	5	6	7
8	9	10	11	12	13	14
15	16	17	18	19	20	21
22	23	24	25	26	27	28
29	30	31	32	33	34	35
36	37	38	39	40	41	42
43	44	45	46	47	48	49
50	51	52	53	54	55	56
57	58	59	60	61	62	63
64	65	66	67	68	69	70
71	72	73	74	75	76	77
78	79	80	81	82	83	84
85	86	87	88	89	90	91

The above table, repeated exactly four times each year, would be the only calendar you would ever need to have.

You could begin by noting that any day of the season whose number is exactly divisible by 7 is a Saturday; if there is a remainder of 1 it is a Sunday, a remainder of 2 a Monday, and so on. Eventually you wouldn't need to do any division; you would just remember the whole thing—

and if you didn't, you could always look at the calendar: always the same one.

This calendar, which is original with me as far as I know, I call the World Season Calendar, and it is the simplest possible calendar that preserves both weeks and seasons. Its disadvantage is that it looks "funny." Imagine a month with ninety-one days. But think! Just by the use of the number alone, you could tell how early or late in the season it is. A date of the 5th is always early in the season—any season—while the 40th is always midseason and the 83rd late season.

Another simplifying step would be to eliminate the names of the season. The names are parochial anyway. What are spring and summer in the United States are fall and winter in Argentina, and vice versa. And there are many regions of the Earth where the four seasons don't really fit, where there are one or more wet seasons and dry seasons, or, as in Hawaii, no true seasons at all.

Why not just give the seasons letter designations? These letters have no connotations. We'll call the first season of the year A. This would be winter in the United States, summer in Argentina, a wet season perhaps in Ghana, not much different from any other season in Hawaii. Then there will follow B, C, and D.

By the World Season Calendar, my birthday would be on A-2, or if I really want to keep it on the correct day, allowing for the change in New Year's from January 1 (Gregorian) to December 21 (Gregorian), it would be on A-12. (Don't forget, you don't count Year Day on any day of the week. Year Day is D-92, and Leap Day, when it occurs, is B-92.)

If you wish, you can amuse yourself by building up a conversion table from Gregorian to World Seasonal, allowing for the fact that December 21 Gregorian is January 1 World Seasonal. You will then find it is perfectly simple to rewrite histories in order to give all dates as World Seasonal. . . . And can you think of anything simpler that takes both weeks and seasons into account? I can't.

B

ABOUT OTHER SMALL WORLDS

five

THE WORLD CERES

Some years ago, a friend called me to say that he had just come across an article that had mentioned me (because of my popularizations) as "the Leonard Bernstein of Science."

I was just about flattered out of my seat at that, but I remembered my pose of brash self-esteem just in time and managed to gather my wits together long enough to respond stiffly, "Quite wrong! Bernstein is the Isaac Asimov of music."

Since then, however, I have listened to and watched Bernstein's appearances on television with a pleased and proprietary air, and yesterday (as I write this) I heard him lecture on, and conduct, a series of tone poems called *The Planets,* by Gustav Holst. In the process, Bernstein, for the benefit of his young audience, ran through the list of planets.

It struck me, as I listened, that he had left out a planet. It was not his fault; everyone leaves it out. I leave it out myself when I list the nine planets, because it is the four-and-a-halfth planet.

I'm referring to Ceres, a small but respectable world* that doesn't deserve the neglect it receives.

Ceres was discovered on January 1, 1801, by the Italian astronomer Giuseppe Piazzi. Its orbit lies between those of Mars and Jupiter, and it is a surprisingly small world, only a few hundred miles across. Still, there is no rule that says a planet has to be larger than a certain size, and despite its smallness, Ceres would certainly have entered the list of planets if Piazzi's discovery had remained as it was.

---

* While I was wondering whether I ought to do an article on Ceres, I thought of the title for this piece, and after that there was no holding me.

Within six years, however, three more small planets were discovered with orbits that were, like that of Ceres, between the orbits of Mars and Jupiter.

Should all four have been placed in the list of planets? The list of sizable planets was seven at the time (Neptune and Pluto had not yet been discovered); to make it eleven by the addition of these four would have given the small worlds extraordinary prominence.

And even if astronomers could have brought themselves to make the addition, there came in 1845, the discovery of a fifth such planet. After that, new discoveries came thickly. By 1866, eighty-eight small planets were known between the orbits of Mars and Jupiter, and as of now, over sixteen hundred are known, with thousands more surely remaining to be discovered.

It would simply make no sense to place all these bodies in the list of planets, and so none of them were.

Quite early on, when only four of the small planets were known, the German-English astronomer William Herschel had suggested that they be called "asteroids" (from a Greek word meaning starlike), because they were so small that in the telescopes of that time they showed up as points of light, as the stars do, rather than as tiny spheres, as the other planets do.

The suggestion was accepted, and it became easier and easier each year to speak of the asteroids as something quite distinct from planets. People will rattle off the names of the planets in order, from Mercury to Pluto, and then say, "And, of course, there is the asteroid belt between Mars and Jupiter."

But can't we even take *one* asteroid as representative of the rest and include it in the list? The largest one? Ceres?

The trouble is that size is usually interpreted in terms of diameter, and in terms of diameter Ceres doesn't seem to be outstandingly large. It has a diameter of about 480 miles, but the second-largest asteroid has a diameter of about 300 miles and the third-largest, a diameter of about 240 miles. Then there are six more asteroids with diameters of 100 miles, and no less than twenty-five asteroids with diameters over 60 miles. It is a smooth progression, with Ceres first in line but not particularly predominating.

But suppose we consider volume instead, which increases as the cube of the diameter. Ceres has a volume of

57,000,000 cubic miles, and this happens to be equal to the volume of the next fifteen largest asteroids *put together*.

The total mass of all the thousands of asteroids, discovered and undiscovered, is often estimated to be about one-tenth the mass of our Moon. If so, one-tenth of the total asteroidal mass is concentrated within the single world of Ceres. Viewed in that fashion, Ceres certainly does predominate.

Add to this the fact that Ceres had a nearly circular orbit, and one that is just about in the average position for all the asteroidal orbits known, and there can be no further doubt. It would seem perfectly fair to consider Ceres, in size and position, as thoroughly representative of the asteroids and to include it in the list of planets. Perhaps we could list it, in fifth place, as "Ceres, etc."

Once we begin to establish outposts on other worlds of the solar system, Ceres may well gain considerably in importance. Let's reason it out.

From the scientific standpoint, one of the most important reasons for going out into space is to establish an astronomical observatory beyond the Earth's atmosphere, or any atmosphere. For that purpose, an airless world would be wanted.

We could build such a world for ourselves in the form of a space station, but this would inevitably be in the neighborhood of the Earth. Such a space station could make important Earth studies, but surely the chief yearning of astronomers would be to explore the distant reaches of space. For that, it would be ideal if there were no nearby object blotting out half the sky or periodically drenching the astronomical station with radiation.

With that in mind, there are no decent airless bodies in the inner solar system that would suit the purpose. Mercury is too close to the Sun; the satellites of Mars are too close to Mars. Even the far side of the Moon is probably not completely ideal for the exploration of deep space, with intense solar radiation present half the time.

There are, of course, the occasional asteroids that venture inside the orbit of Mars and are therefore called "Earth grazers." All are airless and none are associated with a planet. All of them, however, tend to get as close to the Sun as the Earth does, or, in almost every case, considerably closer. This could give them specialized value. The asteroid Icarus approaches closer to the Sun than even Mercury does, and an astronomical station within its tiny body might be invaluable for the study of Venus, Mercury, and the Sun. None of them, however, would be better adapted to the study of deep space than the Moon would be.

In the outer reaches of the solar system there are a number of airless bodies that have the merit of being far from the Sun and the demerit of being far from Earth and correspondingly hard to reach and supply.

Pluto may be airless, but it is farthest of all and, whatever its advantages, there would be an overwhelming tendency to look for something closer. Most of the satellites of the outer planets are airless, but, again, they are near their planets. They are useful as bases for the study of those planets but not ideal for the study of deep space.

Of all the outer-planet satellites, those of Jupiter are closest, and of them, the four outermost are from 13 to 15 million miles from the planet, on the average. (Jupiter-VIII travels outward to a 20-million-mile distance from Jupiter but swoops in to within 8 million miles too.) These outermost satellites are small and are probably captured asteroids.

But if we're going to deal with asteroids, why not move to the asteroid belt itself? There we will find bodies 200 million miles closer to ourselves than Jupiter's satellites are, yet bodies that are not near any large object. The asteroids are the nearest *isolated* airless bodies that we can reach.

And if we choose among them, why not choose Ceres? It is never within 100 million miles of any body larger than itself, and it is itself large enough to have at least some gravity: 3.5 per cent that of the Earth. I consider it quite conceivable that the day may come when Ceres will be the astronomical center of the solar system.

Now let's consider Ceres as a world.

It is small, of course, but not as small as it looks. The surface area of Ceres is about as large as Alaska and California put together, and that's not bad at all. Plenty of room not only for astronomical stations but also for tourist accommodations.

And what will Ceres be like as a tourist world? I'm not sure how much it will be engineered, or to what extent recreational facilities can be designed to make use of the low (but not zero) gravity. But of one thing we can be sure: the sky won't change, and we can try to imagine right now what Ceres' sky would be like and what might be the most interesting astronomical sights for the layman looking upward with nothing more than his unaided eyes.

For one thing, there will be the Sun. The average distance of Ceres from the Sun is 257 million miles. Ceres is 20 million miles closer to the Sun at perihelion and 20 million miles farther at aphelion, but that is not a very considerable difference. To the unaided eye, the Sun would not change its appearance significantly in the course of the Cerean year (which, by the way, is 4.6 Earth years long).

Ceres is 2.8 times as far from the Sun as the Earth is, and that means that the Sun would appear to have a diameter of about 11' of arc, or about one third of its diameter as seen from Earth. This means it will look considerably smaller than it does to us on Earth but that it will still be visible as a distinct globe.

Its apparent area in the sky of Ceres would be only one-eighth that of its area in our own sky, and that means it would deliver only one-eighth the light, the heat, and the radiation of all kinds.

Each portion of the Sun's globe, as visible from Ceres, would, however, be just as bright as the same portion visible from Earth. The lesser brightness of Ceres' Sun would be not due to the fact that it is dimmer per given area, but just that there is less area. In fact, even though the radiation is diminished to one-eighth by the time it reaches Ceres, the fact that there is no Cerean atmosphere means that the Sun's hard radiation is not blocked off. Hard ultraviolet, X rays, charged particles, and so on would reach the surface of Ceres in greater quantity than they reach the surface of the Earth after so much has been absorbed by Earth's atmosphere.

Since no one will go out onto Ceres' airless surface without a spacesuit, a leaded and tinted faceplate will undoubtedly be used to minimize the danger of solar radiation. Even then, tourists on Ceres will probably be warned quite emphatically that they must not be fooled by the dimness of the light into looking too long directly at the Sun.

An important question is, How fast does Ceres rotate? After all, if Ceres whirls too rapidly, its usefulness as an astronomical observatory is diminished, for astronomers will be forever chasing the various objects as they hasten across the sky.

Unfortunately it is difficult to determine the periods of rotation of the various asteroids. Nor can one make a reasonable guess merely from the diameter, for, in general, size has not much to do with period of rotation. The period depends not only on size but on the tidal influence of the gravitational fields in the vicinity and on electromagnetic interactions that may have taken place aeons ago.

Icarus, for instance, which may have a diameter of just under one mile, seems to rotate in two hours or so. Eros, which is fifteen miles long (it is brick-shaped), appears to rotate in a little over five hours.

A recent estimate is that Ceres rotates in just over nine hours. Let us assume, for simplicity's sake, that the axis of rotation is not tilted but is at right angles to the plane of revolution about the Sun and that Ceres rotates in the usual direction, from west to east.

If these assumptions are correct, then everything in Ceres' sky will seem to drift from east to west, at 2.7 times the rate it does in Earth's sky. The Sun, for instance, will rise in the east, set in the west four and a half hours later, rise again four and a half hours after that, and so on.

Anything else of interest in Ceres' sky besides the Sun? Certainly nothing else that will appear as a visible globe.

Ceres has no satellite and is near no planet. You may think that the asteroid belt is thickly strewn with bodies that will be hovering all about Ceres, but if you do, you are wrong. It is doubtful if at any time there will be any object more than a mile or two across within ten million miles of Ceres. One of the other large asteroids might occasionally come close enough to be seen with the unaided eye, but it will always appear as a starlike point ("asteroid" indeed), never particularly bright, and certainly never globular in shape.

But what about the planets? The real, large-sized planets?

Four of these, Mercury, Venus, Earth, and Mars, lie closer to the Sun than Ceres does. This means that from

Ceres they will always be seen as evening stars and morning stars, never departing farther than a certain distance from the Sun. The closer to the Sun the planet is located, the closer it hugs the Sun as seen from Ceres.

This is the case with Venus as seen from Earth (see chapter 1). Our Venus never gets farther than about 47° from the Sun, either to the east or to the west. When it is at "maximum elongation" to the east of the Sun, it appears 47° high in the western sky at the time of sunset. When it is at maximum elongation to the west of the Sun, it appears 47° high in the eastern sky at the time of sunrise.

In the former case it is the evening star and continues to sink toward the horizon in the twilight, setting three hours after sunset. In the latter case it is the morning star, rising three hours before sunrise and continuing to move higher in the sky till sunrise, when the glare wipes it out. When Venus is not at maximum elongation, it sets less than three hours after sunset or rises less than three hours before sunrise.

None of the four inner planets, as seen from Ceres, has a maximum elongation equal to that of Venus from Earth. The maximum elongation of Mars is about 36.9°, of Earth 22.2°, of Venus 15.2°, and of Mercury 9.7°. As the Sun moves from eastern to western horizon in four and a half hours, it drags all these planets with it. Those to its west rise and set earlier than the Sun; those to the east rise and set later than the Sun.

On Earth, thanks to the light-scattering of the atmosphere, planets near the Sun simply cannot be seen when the Sun is in the sky. On airless Ceres there is no light-scattering: the sky remains black and the planets visible even when the Sun is in the sky. However, it won't be pleasant to inspect parts of the sky in the Sun's neighborhood, and because of the sunlight and its effect on the iris, other, lesser objects in the solar neighborhood will seem dim and washed out. Once the Sun sets, the stars and planets will all seem to brighten and it will be then that sky watching will be pleasant and easy.

Let us now suppose a very rare configuration, one in which Mercury, Venus, Earth, and Mars happen all to be east of the Sun and all at maximum elongation.

When the Sun sets and the tourists come out to look at the sky, each of these planets will be lined up in the west if

we assume the tourists to be located more or less at Ceres'
equator. Mercury will be a tenth of the way up from the
horizon toward the zenith, Venus a sixth of the way up,
earth a quarter of the way up, and Mars two-fifths of the
way up.

All the planets will be sinking, and, one after the other,
these will set. Still assuming a nine-hour Cerean rotation,
Mercury will set 6 minutes after the Sun, Venus 4 minutes
after Mercury, Earth 5 minutes after Venus, and Mars 10
minutes after Earth. Anyone watching that string of pearls
go down would have a vivid sensation of the sky turning
(or, perhaps, of Ceres rotating). I wonder if he'd get dizzy.

If all the planets were lined up to the west of the Sun,
then they would all rise before the Sun in reverse order,
Mars coming first, then Earth, Venus, and Mercury. Finally, 6 minutes after Mercury, the Sun would come up.
There would be no preliminary dawn either, since there is
no atmosphere. One minute the sky would be black and the
next there would be a tiny bit of liquid fire on the eastern
horizon.

(The phenomenon of a sunrise without dawn can be
seen from the Moon and would be more spectacular on the
far side, with no Earth in the sky. On the Moon, though,
sunrise is slow and it takes a whole hour for the Sun to lift
its entire globe above the horizon after the first appearance
of its upper edge. On Ceres, assuming that 9-hour rotation,
the smaller Sun would be entirely above the horizon seven
seconds after its first appearance. Wow!)

Of course the chain of four planets would be a once-in-a-
long-while deal. At almost all times, one or more of the
four planets would be to the east and one or more to the
west, and at varying distances.

How bright will the chain of planets seem? The brightness of each planet will vary according to its position with respect to Ceres and the Sun. At maximum elongation, each
planet will be seen as a "half planet." If it is moving around
toward the far side of the Sun, the phase will grow toward
the "full planet," but the size of the planetary globe will
shrink. If it is moving around toward the near side of the
Sun, the size of the planetary globe will increase, but the
phase will shrink to "crescent planet." At some point,
where the planet is in a thick-crescent phase, the area of

lighted portion will be at its maximum and the planet will be at its brightest.

Mercury would be only about one-fifteenth as bright seen from Ceres as it would seem from Earth at the corresponding phase, because, of course, it is farther from Ceres than it is from Earth. It would gain a little, however, by the fact that it is not obscured at all by any atmosphere on Ceres. On the whole, it would have a magnitude of 1.4 (though I warn you that my calculations are rough and I don't guarantee any of my magnitude figures very rigorously).

It would still be bright, as bright as what is roughly called a first-magnitude star. Strictly speaking, it would be less bright than Mercury as seen from Earth, but in actual practice it would seem brighter. Seen most easily immediately after sunset or immediately before sunrise on either Earth or Ceres, Mercury would have the advantage on Ceres of being seen in a totally black sky. On Earth, Mercury is usually seen in twilight or dawn, with horizon haze acting as additional obscuration.

In the case of the other inner planets, Venus would have a magnitude of −0.4, Earth one of +0.3, and Mars 2.0.* The four evening/morning stars would all look like bright stars and would not be very different in brightness. Venus and Earth would be somewhat brighter than Mercury and Mars but not enough so to keep tourists from considering the evening/morning stars as quadruplets.

Not one of them, however, would be as bright as Venus appears to be from Earth. Venus had, to us here, a magnitude, at its brightest, of −4.3.

And what about the other planets, the ones farther out: Jupiter, Saturn, Uranus, Neptune, Pluto?

They would not be tied to the Sun but could be seen at any time of the night and at any height in the sky; even at the zenith (if one were at Ceres' equator and there were no axial tilt). The closer any of these planets is to the zenith at midnight under these conditions, the closer it would be to Ceres and the brighter it would appear.

We'll start with Jupiter. When Jupiter is at zenith in Ceres' midnight sky (which it is every seven and a half

---

* Remember that the lower the magnitude, the brighter the object.

years) it is as close as 220 million miles to Ceres. It then shines with a magnitude of −4.1, and is almost as bright as Venus appears to us on Earth when it is at its brightest. For a year or so at a time, Jupiter is the brightest object in the Cerean sky—except, of course, for the Sun.

Saturn at its brightest will have a magnitude of −1.3, and it, too, will then be brighter than any of the Cerean evening/morning stars. It will be at its brightest for a several-month period every five and a half years.

When we come to the planets beyond Saturn, however, it is scarcely worth bothering. Those are not really much closer to Ceres than they are to Earth. Ceres can be 150 million miles closer to any outer planet than Earth can ever be, but 150 million miles isn't much where distances in the billions of miles are involved.

Uranus, which has a maximum brightness equivalent to a magnitude of 5.7 when seen from Earth, will seem, at intervals of five years, to brighten to 5.1 as seen from Ceres. This additional brightness is more due to the airlessness of Ceres than to Uranus' closer approach to that body. Uranus would be visible as a dim star when seen from Ceres, but it is also visible as a dim star when seen from Earth.

As for Neptune and Pluto, they would be as invisible to the unaided eye from Ceres as from Earth.

Anything else of interest in Ceres' skies? What about the satellites of the planets? If our Moon were alone in the sky of Ceres (Earth having set or not yet risen), it could have a maximum brightness equivalent to a magnitude of 4.7. It would seem brighter than Uranus and could be made out as a dim evening/morning star. Unfortunately Earth is in its neighborhood, and the two are never separated by more than 5' of arc as seen from Ceres. Earth's seventy-times-greater brightness overwhelms the Moon, which is not likely to be made out by the unaided eye.

The fate of the Moon as seen from Ceres is precisely that of the Jovian satellites as seen from the Earth. The four large satellites of Jupiter: Io, Europa, Ganymede, and Callisto, have magnitudes of 5.3, 5.7, 4.9, and 6.1, respectively. They would be visible to the unaided eye as faint objects if Jupiter were not present with its three-thousand-times-brighter glare.

As seen from Earth, the maximum separation of these four satellites from Jupiter varies from 1' of arc for Io to 10' of arc for Callisto. Unfortunately Callisto, the farthest and therefore the most likely to be seen through Jupiter's glare, is also the dimmest. Consequently the large satellites of Jupiter are not seen with the unaided eye, although even slight help will reveal them; they were easily seen with Galileo's original, very primitive telescope.

Seen from Ceres, the satellites of Jupiter are both brighter and farther separated from their planet. The magnitude of the four satellites as seen from Ceres are Io 3.7, Europa 4.1, Ganymede 3.3, and Callisto 4.5. Any of them, alone in the sky, would be easily visible as objects of middling brightness.

Their maximum separation from Jupiter, as seen from Ceres, would vary from 2' of arc for Io, to 18' of arc for Callisto. It seems to me, then, that it ought to be possible to make out Callisto, for it would be separated from Jupiter by as much as three-fifths the width of the full Moon as seen from Earth. Ganymede would be separated from Jupiter by never more than 10' of arc, but, as a third-magnitude obect, it might be visible too.

Naturally the two satellites would be visible only under favorable conditions: when Jupiter is at or near its time of close approach to Ceres and when Ganymede and Callisto are at or near their time of maximum separation.

Indeed I suspect that one of the prime sights pointed out to visiting tourists at appropriate seasons would be the satellites of Jupiter. It would not be a spectacular sight, but even on Ceres it would be an unusual one—and from Earth an impossible one.

six

THE CLOCK IN THE SKY

Years ago, at a party, I was introduced to a tallish fellow with unruly hair and a somehow pointed face. The words of the introduction were "John Updike—Isaac Asimov."

I thought furiously. There was no hint in the introduction as to whether it was *the* John Updike, the writer. If it was he, I felt I had better say something appropriately modest, as befitted a second-class writer greeting a first-class one. If it were some other John Updike, a used-car dealer, for all I knew, it would be incredibly embarrassing to be caught pulling my forelock.

Updike (for it was he, the writer) had no such problem, of course; anyone with the name Isaac Asimov has to be the writer. So while I was still hesitating, he said, with a distinct note of awe in his voice, "Say, how do you write all those books?"

I was left with the grim feeling that I had arrogantly let him make the first advance. Nothing I could do after that helped.

I made up my mind to get in the appropriately humble remarks *first* the very next time I met a well-known writer. Three days later, only three, I saw Max Shulman, the humorist, at another party. I had never met him before but recognized him from photographs I had seen of him.

I hastened toward him and began with ingratiating humility, "Mr. Shulman, may I introduce myself? My name is Isaac Asi—"

And he said, with a distinct note of awe in his voice, "Say, how do you write all those books?"

I gave up. I want to be humble but the world won't let me—and it keeps asking me the same question, too.

In science, the question I get asked more than any

other—over and over—in person—by phone—by letter—is "How can you be *sure* things can't go faster than light?"

"Well, I've answered this question in various places many times and I won't go into it here. The previous explanations didn't stop the question and another one won't either.

Instead, I'll take up another aspect of the matter. How was the speed of light determined in the first place? In fact, what made people think that light had some definite speed in the zeroth place?

If in ancient times people thought at all of the notion of a speed to light, it must have been with the feeling that the speed was infinite. If light appeared, it appeared everywhere at once. If the clouds broke and the Sun pierced the veil that hid its glory, you didn't see light making its way down the avenue of the atmosphere, hitting a mountain peak first and rolling down the mountainside like a stream of water. It hit the valley as quickly as the peak.

What must first have shaken the notion of the infinite speed of light was the matter of sound. Light and sound were the two great avenues to the outside world. The eye saw and the ear heard, and both sound and light were casually assumed to do their work honestly. If you saw something in the distance, it was really in the place you saw it at the moment you saw it. And if you heard something in the distance, it was really in the place you heard it at the moment you heard it.

At moderate distances this was true enough for practical purposes, but as distance increased, the two senses fell noticeably out of step. Sound suffered a delay. If you watched a man chopping wood, for instance, the sight of contact of ax and wood and the sound of contact should have come together—and did, if you were close. At a distance, however, the sound came after the sight, and the greater the distance the greater the lag.

It was clear from that alone that whether the speed of light was infinite or not, the speed of sound was clearly *not* infinite. It took time for sound to travel; that was abundantly clear to the senses. And if sound traveled at a finite speed, why not light as well?

If the speed of sound was not infinite, it was nevertheless quite large. In the lapse between the sight of a distant action and its accompanying sound, nothing material known to the men of the pre-industrial age could possibly have covered the distance. Sound clearly traveled hundreds of miles an hour.

(It wasn't till about 1738 that the speed of sound was measured with reasonable precision. French scientists set up cannon on hills some seventeen miles apart. They fired the cannon upon one hill and timed the interval between flash and sound on the other hill. Then they fired the other cannon and timed the interval between flash and sound on the first. The time lapse in the two cases was averaged in order that the effect of the wind might be canceled—for it was known that sound was carried by the motions of air molecules. With the distance between the cannon known, and the time lapse measured, the speed of sound could be calculated. It turns out that the speed of sound in air at 0° C.—the speed goes up with temperature and is different in other media—is 740 miles an hour, or 331 meters per second.)

Since sound lagged markedly behind the light, it was clear that light had to travel at speeds much greater than mere hundreds of miles per hour. The speed of light should therefore be much harder to measure than that of sound.

Nevertheless, with a kind of gallantry above and beyond the call of duty, the Italian scientist Galileo tried to measure the speed of light in the early 1600s.

The method he used was as follows:

Galileo placed himself on an elevation and had an assistant climb to another elevation about a mile away. Both carried shielded lanterns. The idea was that Galileo would unshield his lantern. As soon as the assistant saw the flash of light that followed the unshielding, he was to unshield his own light.

Galileo reasoned thus. He would unshield his light, and the beam would take a certain time to travel to the other peak. When it came, the assistant would flash his light, and again it would take a certain time to travel back to Galileo. The time between the moment that Galileo flashed his light and the moment that he saw his assistant's light would represent the time it took light to travel from one elevation to the other elevation and back.

Knowing the distance between the elevations, and measuring the time lapse, Galileo would then have put himself into the position of being able to calculate the speed of light.

There *was* a short time lapse, and for a moment things looked hopeful, but then Galileo tried other distances, expecting that the time lapse would increase in proportion to the distance—and it did not. It stayed the same, however short or long the distance between the lanterns was. We can be quite sure that if Galileo and his assistant were standing six feet apart, there would be just the same time lapse between Galileo's flash and his sight of the assistant's flash as when they were a mile apart—or ten thousand miles apart.

It was clear that the interval of time Galileo was measuring did not represent the time it took for light to travel from A to B and back to A, but only the time it took his assistant to realize he had seen a flash and to then make his muscles move so as to produce the return flash. Galileo was measuring the speed of human reaction, and not the speed of light at all.

From the fact that there was no change in the time lapse with distance, Galileo had to conclude that the time it took the light beam to travel did not contribute perceptibly to the result. The speed of light could not be measured in this fashion, because it was so much greater than that of sound. The speed of light might even be infinite, for anything Galileo could tell from his attempt at measurement.

If light traveled *very* quickly, then even if its speed was not infinite, no earthly distance might suffice to produce a perceptible delay in light propagation. Heavenly distances might, though. If someone could climb into the sky instead of going to another hill, and turn a star on and off on command, the interval between the command and seeing the star go on (or off) would represent the time it took for light to make the round trip.

Alas for the brilliant idea. No one in Galileo's time knew how far away any heavenly body (except the Moon) was. Even if the distances of the heavenly bodies were known, no one could reach them (not even the Moon). Even if someone could reach them, how communicate over such long distances and give the command to turn a star off? And even if one could communicate, how would one turn a star off?

Moonshine! Moonshine!

—Except that that (or almost that) is exactly what happened. The speed of light was first determined by a method that was precisely analogous to turning a star on and off at a signal. And it began with a discovery by Galileo. And it *was* moonshine; literally moonshine.*

First, Galileo's discovery:

In 1609 he had received rumors that far off in the Netherlands somebody had placed lenses at either end of a hollow tube and had succeeded in making distant things appear nearer. Galileo needed no further hint. In almost no time he had a similar device of his own—a telescope.

Immediately, he turned it on the heavens. He saw mountains on the Moon, and spots on the Sun, and crowds of invisible-stars-made-visible in the constellations.

On January 9, 1610, he looked at Jupiter; through the telescope it seemed like a small globe rather than a mere dot of light. Near it, on either side, and in the same straight line, were three small, starlike objects. On January 13 he saw a fourth.

He watched them night after night, and it became clear that each one of them was moving back and forth from one side of Jupiter to the other, each one moving a fixed distance to either side. It was impossible not to realize what one was seeing. Jupiter was being circled by four smaller bodies, each in its own orbit. And all four orbits were being seen nearly edge on from Earth.

Galileo announced his discovery at once, and the contemporary German astronomer Johannes Kepler named the small bodies that were circling Jupiter "satellites." This was from a Latin term for hangers-on that constantly circled some rich man and flattered him in order to be invited to his dinners.

The four satellites were named after characters in the Greek myths who were closely related to Jupiter (or Zeus, to be more accurate). These were, in order of increasing distance from Jupiter: Io, Europa, Ganymede, and Callisto. These names were suggested by a German astronomer, Simon Marius, who claimed he had seen the satellites before

---

* And people ask me why I prefer writing non-fiction to fiction! I couldn't possibly get away with these ridiculous flights of fantasy in fiction.

Galileo had. Marius' claim was disallowed—but his names were kept.

Galileo's discovery was important for two reasons. First, it was a case of finding new members of the solar system, members that were unknown to the ancients; and that had never happened before. This alone shook the common notion among the intellectual establishment of the time that the Greek philosophers had brought all knowledge to its final pitch.

Then, too, in 1610 there were still some, among the educated ignoramuses, who refused to budge from the ancient position that all heavenly bodies, without exception, circled the Earth. Here at least were four bodies that clearly and visibly circled a body other than Earth. They circled Jupiter.

The only way to deny this was to refuse to look at them, and some great thinkers of the day actually did just that. They refused to look through the telescope, reasoning that since the satellites were not mentioned in Aristotle, they weren't there, and that to look at them would merely unsettle the mind.

In Galileo's time there were no decent methods for measuring intervals of time accurately. It was not until 1656 that the Dutch scientist Christian Huygens devised a method for having the hands of a clock driven by the even motion of a swinging pendulum.

(This was based on the discovery, over half a century before, that a pendulum swings with an even periodicity, independent, to a certain extent, of the size of the swing. This basic discovery was made by you-know-who.*)

The pendulum clock invented by Huygens was the first timepiece that could reasonably be expected to keep time to the nearest minute for days on end.

Or could it? Could one be sure?

Until quite recently, mankind had to depend for the ultimate determination of time on periodic motions in heaven. There was the rotation of the Earth relative to the Sun (the day), the revolution of the Moon about the Earth relative to the Sun (the month), and the revolution of the Earth about the Sun (the year).

* Galileo.

The shortest of these usable periodicities was the day, and for anything less than the day there was nothing in the sky that would serve as an ultimate check.

But what if some new and shorter heavenly period were found by means of telescope? Surely the heavenly motions—not being man-made—would be completely accurate, and even the best man-made clocks, even Huygens' pendulum clock, could be profitably checked against them.

The four satellites of Jupiter seemed just the thing. Io, Europa, and Ganymede passed behind Jupiter every revolution, since the orbits were seen nearly edge on. Callisto, the farthest out of the four, could sometimes be made out above or below the globe of Jupiter as it passed behind, but it was usually eclipsed too.

In general, Io was eclipsed every 1¾ days, Europa every 3½ days, Ganymede every 7¼ days, and Callisto every 16⅔ days. The moment of eclipse could be detected with considerable precision, and as the moments were separated by irregular intervals, you could get measurements of all sorts of time periods from 1¾ days on down to a few minutes.

Using the best timepieces available, the intervals between successive eclipses of the different satellites were measured, and with that as a start, and taking all sorts of refinements into consideration, the times of future eclipses for each were calculated.

Once that was done, there was every reason to think that an accurate clock in the sky was available for short periods of time. Any clock being used could always be checked against the configuration of the satellites of Jupiter and be pushed a little ahead or a little behind in accord with what the four satellite hands of the Jupiter clock indicated.

Except that peculiar things began to happen. The observatory clock gained, slightly but steadily, and then after some months of this it began to lose again. In fact, if it was watched long enough, it gained, then lost, then gained, then lost, in a slow but very regular period. Nor did it matter how carefully the satellite observations were made and remade and how meticulously the calculations of future eclipse moments were made. The clocks persisted in this slow, regular swing of gaining and losing. What's more, if different clocks were involved, they all gained and lost si-

C

ABOUT CARBON

seven

THE ONE AND ONLY

These essays can complicate my life. Writing them on any subject I choose makes me sound like an authority on everything. For instance, a couple of years ago I touched on astrology in one of my articles. The consequence was that I was instantly pinpointed as an expert on the subject, and one who wasn't afraid to speak out against astrology, too (something apparently not easy to find).

So a newspaper reporter, about a month ago, invaded my office with a tape-recording device, turned it on, and proceeded to ask me questions. I obliged and talked quite forcefully on the subject of rationalism versus mysticism— with myself, as all my Gentle Readers know, on the side of rationalism.

When we were through and the reporter was packing up, I said on impulse, "I will give you a practical example of the difference between mysticism and rationalism. A mystic would accept the fact that that little object has recorded our voices just because you say so. A rationalist would say, 'Let me hear the voices before I believe.' "

The reporter smiled. He said, "I have recorded hundreds of interviews, and this tape recorder has never failed me."

"I'm sure of that," I said, "but just to humor my rationalism, play it back and let's make sure."

So, still smiling, he played it back. He had done something wrong; no voices were recorded. (So help me, it's a true story.)

He was chagrined, of course, but not a tenth as chagrined as *I* was. Had I let it go, he would have gone on home and not discovered the flaw for days, and it would then have been too late to do anything. As it was, just because of my inane desire to show how rational I was, I had to go through the entire interview a second time.

Oh, well, it turned out to be a pretty good interview.

But it got me to thinking how mystical even rationalists are. It is impossible to check everything personally; it is impossible to make sure that everything is personally understood by our own personal brain. We have to accept many things on faith for sheer lack of ability to do otherwise, and sometimes we repeat certain catch phrases so often that they become unquestionable.

And then—as in the case of the tape recorder that had never failed in hundreds of interviews—it becomes fun, once in a while, to question them.

For instance, chemists divide chemistry into two sections, "organic" and "inorganic," the former dealing with compounds containing the carbon atom, the latter dealing with compounds containing any or all the remaining 104 kinds of atoms, excluding only the carbon atom.

Is this not a strangely unequal division? Yes, it is, but not in the way it might seem.

As it happens, there are more molecules containing the carbon atom, *far* more, than there are of all the remaining 104 elements as they combine among themselves in any conceivable fashion with only the restriction that they avoid the carbon atom. And any additional discoveries can only increase the disproportion still further in the direction of carbon.

What's more, the carbon-containing compounds, some with small molecules (which, in a few cases, possess the characteristics of inorganic molecules), some with middle-sized ones, some with large ones, and some with giant ones, are the basis of life (which is why this class of compounds is called "organic").

Those of us who aren't chemists may have heard of this, and if so, we have had to accept it without question. Carbon atoms can form chains and rings of all sizes and complexities, and on this fact rests the complexity and versatility of life. We accept that.

But is carbon indeed the only element with atoms capable of combining into compounds various enough, complex enough, delicate enough, versatile enough, to possess the amazing properties we associate with life? Couldn't some other element do it too, with a little encouragement perhaps? How does it happen that carbon is so different from all other elements?

Fair enough. Let's look into the matter.

There are 105 known elements all together, each with its own variety of atoms. We are asking ourselves which of these 105 different types of atoms can form chains and rings among themselves of all kinds, large and small, that are versatile enough to be the basis of life.

Can we eliminate any offhand?

To begin with, we can eliminate all those elements lacking stable isotopes and possessing only radioactive atoms. After all, if radioactive atoms are bound into chains and rings, those chains and rings can't possibly maintain themselves. Sooner or later, one of the atoms will emit an extremely energetic particle. What is left of the atom will recoil energetically and break any chain or ring of which it is part. It is hard to see how life can be built up out of molecules that change in random ways at random intervals.

That removes twenty-four elements from the list of possibles and leaves eighty-one stable elements; eighty-one elements, that is, that include at least one non-radioactive isotope, the atoms of which can conceivably form chains and rings.

As it happens, though, of the eighty-one elements, five (the noble gases: helium, neon, argon, krypton, and xenon) are made up of atoms that do not link up with each other under any circumstances.* In elementary form, these noble gases exist as single atoms. We certainly cannot have chains or rings of these elements, and we therefore eliminate them. That leaves us with seventy-six stable elements other than the noble gases that are still candidates to serve as the basis of life.

Atoms of these seventy-six elements can link together by sharing electrons with each other. The nature of this sharing depends on how many electrons a particular atom has that are available for donation to a shared pool, and how much room each atom has for accepting shares of electrons. Many types of atoms have very few electrons to donate, but appetites for the acceptance of many. Under such conditions, the most stable situation for the element is one in which a great many atoms get together so that all can

---

* That's right. I have not forgotten the noble-gas compounds. Atoms of krypton and xenon will attach to *other* kinds of atoms—fluorine and oxygen, for instance. Two krypton atoms or two xenon atoms will not link up, however, under any laboratory conditions, nor will a xenon and a krypton.

share in the few electrons available. You then have an orderly array of atoms with a few electrons moving about almost freely from atom to atom, each giving each atom a small share of itself.

The presence of these mobile electrons makes it possible for a conglomeration of atoms of that particular element to carry an electric current and to conduct heat with great ease. It also lends the element other properties we associate with metals. In fact, any element made up of atoms that tend to share a few mobile electrons *is* a metal.

In order to share the mobile electrons, the atoms of a metal must stick closely together; they are said to be held together by a "metallic bond."

The metallic bond can be powerful indeed; it can take a great deal of energy to pull the atoms of a metal apart against the stickiness associated with the desire to stay near those mobile electrons. The easiest way to add energy to the atoms is to raise their temperature, and one measure of the tightness with which atoms cling together is the level of the boiling point—the temperature at which the atoms are torn apart and sent tumbling into independent motion as a gas. Tungsten has a boiling point of 5,927°C., the highest of any element. The surface of the Sun is just barely hot enough to keep tungsten gaseous.

The metallic bond works best, however, where many atoms are clinging together. It will produce the equivalent of giant molecules but not small ones, and living tissue needs small molecules as well as large ones. Let us, therefore, eliminate all metallic elements from consideration.

That represents a major reduction in the possibilities, for it eliminates fifty-eight elements and leaves us with the eighteen stable nonmetals, excluding the noble gases, as the remaining candidates for serving as the basis of life.

In these eighteen elements the ability to donate an electron and the ability to receive one are well balanced. Two atoms of such an element can each donate an electron to form a two-electron pool in which each can share. The participation in such a shared pool results in greater stability than would be the case where the two atoms move independently. In order to keep the shared pool, the atoms must remain in close proximity, and the result is a "covalent bond" holding the two atoms together.

multaneously, even though by any other criteria they seemed to be neither gaining nor losing.

By 1675, by which time the Italian-French astronomer Giovanni Domenico Cassini, had made observations of Jupiter's satellites with unprecedented accuracy, it could only be concluded that it was the clock in the sky that was unreliable. If you took averages of the intervals between eclipses and used that average as what "ought to be," it turned out that the eclipses were sometimes ahead of time by quite a few minutes and sometimes behind time by quite a few minutes. They switched from early to late to early to late in a gradual and periodic fashion, and no one knew why.

Until, in 1675, a Danish astronomer, Olaus Roemer, considered the problem.

In 1619, Kepler had worked out an accurate model of the solar system, with all the planetary orbits in place. Astronomers had learned how to handle the model, and Roemer knew quite well the relative positions of Earth and Jupiter at any given time.

Roemer used Cassini's observations and calculations and decided to match particular eclipses with the planetary positions.

It turned out that the eclipses came earliest when Earth and Jupiter were on the same side of the Sun, and when, in fact, they were as close together as they could get.

Earth, being closer to the Sun than Jupiter is, moves considerably faster in its orbit than Jupiter does. Earth therefore races ahead of Jupiter, and, curving in its orbit, moves away from it. And as the distance between Jupiter and Earth increases, the timing of the satellite eclipses grows steadily later.

When Earth and Jupiter are on directly opposite sides of the Sun and are as far apart as possible, the eclipses come latest. (Of course, when Earth and Jupiter are on opposite sides of the Sun, Jupiter is too close to the Sun, in Earth's sky, to observe. The results of observations when Jupiter *can* be seen, however, made Roemer quite certain as to what was happening while Jupiter was skulking in the vicinity of the solar blaze.)

Then, as Earth continues to race on and begins to approach Jupiter again, the timing of the eclipses begins to grow earlier.

What it amounts to is that the eclipse time when Earth is at maximum distance from Jupiter was, by Roemer's calculations, 22 minutes later than when Earth is at minimum distance from Jupiter.

To Roemer, there seemed a possible solution. Suppose light traveled at some very rapid but finite speed. When a satellite passed Jupiter, its light was cut off, but an observer on Earth didn't see the cutoff instantly (as he would if the speed of light were infinite). Instead, the beam of light continues traveling toward Earth at its finite speed and it is only at some time after the actual moment of eclipse that the cutoff reaches the observer and the satellite's light winks out.

When Jupiter and Earth are closest together, light from Jupiter and its satellites travels to Earth at its orbital near-point to Jupiter. When Jupiter and Earth are farthest apart, on opposite sides of the Sun, light from Jupiter travels to the Earth's orbital near-point and then must travel, *in addition*, the complete width of Earth's orbit to get to Earth's position at the far-point.

If it takes light about twenty-two minutes to cross the full width of Earth's orbit, then the behavior of the satellite eclipses is explained. Allow for the finite speed of light, and everything falls into place; the eclipses come on the dot, never too early and never too late by an instant.

The question is, How fast must light travel to speed across the full width of Earth's orbit in twenty-two minutes?

When Kepler had devised his model of the solar system, he hadn't known its scale. He'd known none of the interplanetary distances. If he had known one—only one—he could have calculated all the rest. But he hadn't known that one.

In 1671, however, Cassini had managed to determine the parallax of Mars. From that, he calculated the distance of Mars from Earth at that moment of time. From that and from the relative position of Earth and Mars in Kepler's model at that moment of time, which was also known, he could calculate all the other planetary distances.

Cassini's measurement of the parallax of Mars was just a little bit off (though it was an excellent piece of work for first time out); his calculations showed the average distance of the Earth from the Sun to be 87,000,000 miles.

The full width of Earth's orbit (from one spot on it to the Sun and then on to a spot at the opposite side) was twice that, or 174,000,000 miles.

If light managed to cross 174,000,000 miles in twenty-two minutes, then it must be traveling at a little over 130,000 miles per second.

And that was excellent too, first time out. Since Cassini's time, we have refined the measurements of the scale of the solar system. We know that the distance from the Earth to the Sun is just a hair under 93,000,000 miles on the average, and we also know that light crosses Earth's orbit in a little over sixteen minutes, not twenty-two. So we know that the speed of light is 186,282 miles per second. Still, considering the state of the art in Roemer's day, we can only accept his figure with considerable satisfaction.

When we think of the speed of light, which is pretty near a million times the speed of sound, we need not wonder that Galileo's manful attempt failed. The time lapse involved in the passage of light over an earthly distance is minute enough to ignore. It takes light (or anything else traveling at the speed of light: say, radio waves) less than one-sixtieth of a second to go from New York to Los Angeles.

For distances beyond Earth, however, the time lapse becomes perceptible. It takes anywhere from 1.28 to 1.35 seconds for light to reach us from the Moon (depending on which part if its orbit the Moon is in and how far it is from us). And, more or less as aforesaid, it takes light an average of 8.3 minutes to reach Earth from the Sun and 16.6 minutes to cross the entire width of Earth's orbit.

The speed of light, though it seems incredibly large by any ordinary standard, begins to wear an aura of finitude indeed when still longer distances are involved: It takes light over five hours to travel from the Sun to Pluto, over four years to travel from Alpha Centauri to ourselves, and over a billion years to travel from the nearest quasar to ourselves.

Considering that the speed of light is now known to be a fundamental constant of the universe, it is distressing to have to report that its first announcement created no great stir and drew mixed reactions. Roemer announced his calculation of the speed of light at a meeting of the Academy of Sciences in Paris in 1676. Huygens was favorably impressed, and so was Isaac Newton. The influential Cassini, however, was not. It was his observations and calculations that had been used, but that cut no ice with him. He was almost pathologically conservative, and Roemer's work was too far out for him.

Under the weight of Cassini's displeasure, Roemer's determination of the speed of light was allowed to pass out of astronomical consciousness for half a century.

Then, in 1728, an English astronomer, James Bradley, determined the speed of light from another kind of astronomical observation altogether. Although the two methods were completely independent, Bradley's figure was in the same ballpark as Roemer's figure, and after that, there was no forgetting.

Roemer took his proper niche in the history of science and has not been lost sight of again.

. . . But now, before I leave, let me make two points:

1) Roemer's method of determining the speed of light was almost like a cosmic repetition of Galileo's experiment, and did what I had earlier suggested, in jest, to be impossible. A star, or at least the starlike points of the satellites, were turned on and off; not by any man-made device, to be sure, but by Jupiter and by the facts of celestial mechanics—and that did just as well. And the notion *was* moonshine, for it was moonshine (the light of the moons of Jupiter) that did the trick.

2) Although the speed of light is nearly a million times the speed of sound, it is light whose speed was determined first—and by sixty years.

The simplest way of representing such a covalent bond is to place a dash between the symbols for the elements to which the atoms belong, as X—X.

Particular atoms, depending on the number and arrangement of the electrons they possess, can form different numbers of covalent bonds with other atoms. Some can form only one, some two, some three, and some as many as four. Among the eighteen elements with which we are still dealing, all classes are represented; they are listed in Table 1. In each class the elements are listed in order of increasing atomic weight.

Table 1
Stable Non-Metals Capable of Forming Covalent Bonds

1 bond	*2 bonds*	*3 bonds*	*4 bonds*
Hydrogen	Oxygen	Boron	Carbon
Fluorine	Sulfur	Nitrogen	Silicon
Chlorine	Selenium	Phosphorus	Germanium
Bromine	Tellurium	Arsenic	Tin
Iodine		Antimony	

(You may notice that some of the elements in Table 1 are commonly considered metals: tin, for instance. However, there are no sharp boundaries in nature, and tin has pronounced non-metallic properties as well.)

Let's consider those elements that form only one covalent bond—hydrogen, for instance. Two hydrogen atoms, each represented by the chemical symbol H, can be linked so: H—H.

Where only hydrogen atoms are involved, that is *all* that can happen. Each hydrogen atom in the H—H combination has used up its only covalent bond and can form no covalent link with any other atom. This means that if a large mass of hydrogen atoms are brought together under ordinary conditions of temperature and pressure, they pair up in these two-atom combinations, or hydrogen molecules, very often written simply as H_2, and nothing else.

The hydrogen molecules are held together by very feeble attractions called "Van der Waals forces," after the Dutch physicist who first considered them in detail. These are enough to hold the molecules together and keep hydrogen liquid, or even solid, but only at very low temperatures. Even at a temperature as low as $-253°C$. (only twenty degrees above absolute zero) there is enough intensity of heat to counter the Van der Waals force and send hydrogen molecules spinning off independently into gaseous form. Thus, $-253°C$. is the boiling point of liquid hydrogen.

We can't expect hydrogen atoms to form, by themselves, then, any chain made up of more than two atoms. No matter how important hydrogen atoms may be to life, they cannot form the skeleton of complex molecules. . . . So we eliminate hydrogen.

As a matter of fact, the situation is the same for any one-bond atom. Fluorine, chlorine, bromine, and iodine all form two-atom molecules and nothing more: F_2, Cl_2, Br_2 and I_2.

To be sure, the larger the mass of the molecules, the stronger (in general) the Van der Waals forces between them and the higher the boiling point. Thus, the fluorine molecule has nineteen times the mass of the hydrogen molecule, and liquid fluorine therefore has a boiling point of $-188°C$., which is sixty-five degrees higher than that of hydrogen. Chlorine, with molecules more massive still, has a boiling point of $-35°C$., bromine $58°C$., and iodine $183°C$. At ordinary temperatures, fluorine and chlorine are gases, bromine is a liquid, and iodine is a solid.

Whether gas, liquid, or solid, none of these one-bond elements can possibly form a chain of atoms, linked by covalent bonds, that is longer than two atoms. All five one-bond elements are eliminated as possible bases for life.

Let's pass on to the elements with atoms capable of forming two covalent bonds each. You can imagine a chain of oxgen atoms, for instance, looking like $-O-O-O-O-$ and so on, with any number of oxygen atoms in the chain. This gives us our first glimpse of a possible chain of atoms: short, middle-sized, long, or giant. The only trouble is that it doesn't happen.

To understand that, we have to consider bond energies. We can measure the energy we must pour into a two-atom combination in order to break the covalent bond between the atoms. Or we can measure the energy liberated when those two atoms abandon independence and form a covalent bond. By the law of conservation of energy, those two energy measurements must be, and are, equal, and that is the energy content of the particular covalent bond.

Bond energies are usually given in units of "kilocalories per mole," but it is not necessary to hug that unit to the chest. We are just going to compare one bond energy with another, and, for that, the number alone is sufficient.

For instance, the energy of the covalent bond between two oxygen atoms ($O-O$) is 34. (This varies somewhat with conditions, but 34 is a good representative value.)

This property is additive. That is, suppose you imagine four oxygen atoms at the points of a square, each attached to its two neighbors by a bond: $\begin{matrix} O-O \\ | \quad | \\ O-O \end{matrix}$ There would be four bonds all together, and the total bond energy would be $4 \times 34 = 136$.

Suppose, however, that two oxygen atoms used both their bonds for mutual attachment. The oxygen atoms are then linked by a "double bond" thus: $O=O$. In that case the bond energy becomes 118. This is not equal to twice the bond energy of a single bond, but to about 3.5 times as much.*

This means that if four oxygen atoms are combined into a four-atom molecule with four single bonds, the total bond energy is $4 \times 34 = 136$, but if they are combined into two two-atom molecules with two double bonds, the total bond energy is $2 \times 118 = 236$.

The natural tendency is for atoms to take up those configurations that place bond energies at maximum. (This is similar to the natural tendency of balls to roll downhill.) Consequently when oxygen atoms are brought together, all without exception form the two-atom, double-bonded molecule, usually written O_2, and neither atom in the molecule has any covalent bonds left over to do anything else with. Only Van der Waals forces hold them together, and the boiling point of liquid oxygen is $-183°C$.

This eliminates oxygen from consideration at once, but

---

* Why? In a way, it doesn't matter why. This is a measured fact and must be accepted whether we know why or not. However, there exists a mathematical treatment called quantum mechanics which explains the why of many atomic facts of life. But please, if you love me, don't ask me to go into quantum mechanics.

does it mean we can eliminate the other two-bond elements similarly?

Not quite. In general, the larger the atoms, the less closely they can approach, center to center, in forming a covalent bond, and the smaller the bond energy. The oxygen atom, which is the smallest of the two-bond atoms, can form a spectacularly energetic second bond. A similar but larger atom such as sulfur, selenium, or tellurium cannot. The second bond, if formed, would not be particularly energetic, and there is nothing to force the atoms into a double-bonded situation in place of a single-bonded one.

Sulfur, for instance, can easily form a chain or ring of atoms. In liquid sulfur the molecule is made up of a ring of eight sulfur atoms.

However, the sulfur chain or ring, just by existing, uses up all the valence bonds available to the sulfur atoms under ordinary circumstances. (Oxygen or fluorine atoms can force the sulfur atoms to donate additional electrons and form additional covalent bonds, but these are limited effects that would not lend the chains or rings sufficient versatility for the requirements of life molecules.)

So we eliminate all the two-bond elements, after all, and go on to the three-bond ones.

If we consider nitrogen, its situation is very much like that of oxygen. The single bond between two nitrogen atoms has a bond energy of 38, but a double bond between them raises that energy to 100, two and a half times that of a single bond.

And suppose the nitrogen atom used all three of its covalent bonds for the attachment to another nitrogen atom, forming a "triple bond." Now the bond energy becomes 225, which is more than twice as high as the double bond and *six* times as high as the single bond.

When nitrogen atoms are brought together, therefore, they form the two-atom, triple-bonded molecule at once, and the nitrogen molecule that results, usually symbolized N_2, can form no further valence bonds. The molecules are held together by Van der Waals forces, and the boiling point of liquid nitrogen is $-196°C$.

Nitrogen is eliminated as a possibility, but, again, the larger atoms of the same sort—phosphorus, arsenic, and antimony—must be considered separately. They can form singly bonded chains. (Phosphorus vapor, for instance, contains molecules made up of four phosphorus atoms.)

We can imagine a phosphorus chain— —P—P—P—P—
| | | |

— with a third valence bond available at every phosphorus atom. This third valence bond could be attached to still other phosphorus atoms, or to other kinds of atoms, and molecules of all stages of simplicity and complexity can be conceived. This means we cannot eliminate phosphorus from consideration as a possible skeleton for life molecules. Nor can we eliminate arsenic and antimony at this point.

Boron, the remaining three-bond atom, does not belong to the nitrogen family, but it has the capacity for forming chains too.

That leaves us with the final group of elements, the four-bond ones. Of these, carbon has the smallest atom. Can we follow the lead of oxygen and nitrogen and consider two carbon atoms attached by all four bonds, forming the molecule C_2 with a quadruple bond?

No, we can't. A quadruple bond does not exist, and carbon atoms can be linked together only by single bonds, double bonds, and triple bonds. In any of these cases the carbon atom will still have covalent bonds available for attachment elsewhere. Even if two carbon atoms are attached by a triple bond, each has a fourth bond left over. It would seem, then, that carbon chains are not only possible but almost unavoidable.

But which is the bond of choice in the case of carbon atoms? The bond energy of a single bond between carbon atoms is 82, that of a double bond is 146, and that of a triple bond is 200. Notice that two single bonds have a total energy of 164 and three single bonds a total energy of 246. Carbon atoms therefore achieve the greatest bond energies if they link up by way of single bonds only.

The energy differences aren't enormous. Carbon atoms connected by double bonds or triple bonds can and do exist, and sometimes special conditions increase the bond energies to the point where they are particularly stable. In most cases, however, double and triple bonds are comparatively unstable and can be altered to single bonds with little effort.

The typical situation in the case of the carbon atom can therefore be expressed most simply by presenting it as a chain of indefinite length, $-\overset{|}{\underset{|}{C}}-\overset{|}{\underset{|}{C}}-\overset{|}{\underset{|}{C}}-\overset{|}{\underset{|}{C}}-$, with each carbon atom possessing two additional valence bonds for attachment to other atoms. The two additional bonds can be attached to other carbon atoms, forming branched chains, or to other places in the chain, forming rings.

This offers all the chances for complexity I mentioned earlier in connection with the phosphorus atom, compounded to a much higher level since there are two spare bonds per atom rather than one. The situation is the same for the other members of the carbon family: silicon, germanium, and tin.

We have now reduced the number of elements that can conceivably serve as the basis of life from the total number of 105 to a mere eight. Of these eight remaining candidates, four are three-bonded (boron, phosphorus, arsenic, and antimony), and four are four-bonded (carbon, silicon, germanium, and tin).

How can we judge among them? Is there any way we can show that some are more hopeful candidates than others? What are the criteria?

In the first place, we can say that the four-bonded atoms are surely superior to the three-bonded ones, since the former can clearly produce more complicated molecules, all things being equal.

In the second place we might consider the single-bond energies for each of these eight elements. It would seem fair to consider that the stronger the bond energies, the more stable the chains and rings built up of their atoms and the more likely these will do as the basis for life. In Table 2 I give the energy of the single bond connecting two atoms of each candidate element.*

If we consider Table 2, we see at once that by the two criteria I've mentioned, carbon is clearly the best candidate

---

* The only bond energy I couldn't find in my library was that for boron, so I was forced to make a rough estimate from other data I could dig up. I am often asked why I don't research my articles outside my library when my library falls short, and that thought may be occurring to you right now. My answer is a simple one: I consider that cheating.

for the position of serving as a basis of life. It is four-bonded, and it has a considerably stronger bond than any of the others, so it forms the most stable and complicated chains by far.

But that only means that carbon is the best of a number of possibilities, and that's not enough. Is there any way we can show that it is the only possibility altogether?

Table 2

Element	Bond Number	Bond Energy
Carbon	4	82
Boron	3	69 (?)
Silicon	4	53
Phosphorus	3	51
Germanium	4	38
Tin	4	34
Arsenic	3	32
Antimony	3	30

All right; let's approach the situation from another direction: The three most common types of atom in the universe are, in order, hydrogen, helium, and oxygen. Helium forms no covalent bonds, so we can forget it. It seems to me, then, that every sizable planet that exists is going to have either a preponderance of hydrogen (and helium) or a preponderance of oxygen.

If it is a large, cold planet like Jupiter, it is bound to have a preponderance of hydrogen simply because there is so much of the gas. If it is a smaller, warm planet like Earth, and fails to retain most of the available hydrogen (and helium) as it forms, it will then have to have a preponderance of oxygen (though not necessarily as free oxygen in the atmosphere, of course). It's one or the other.

In that case, it is not enough to talk about chains and rings of atoms of a particular element as though that element exists in isolation. What would happen to those chains and rings if atoms of other elements were present? What would happen, in particular, if atoms of hydrogen or oxygen, one or the other, were present in large excess?

If atoms of a particular element form stronger bonds with either oxygen or hydrogen or both than they do among themselves, then they aren't likely to form long chains or rings of themselves.

Consider silicon, for instance. It is four-bonded and has a bond energy that is fairly strong, even if not as strong as carbon's. (In science fiction the possibility of "silicon-life" has often been considered.) The silicon-silicon single bond has an energy of 53, but the silicon-oxygen bond has an energy of 88 (66 per cent stronger) and the silicon-hydrogen bond has one of 75 (42 per cent stronger).

In the presence of a large excess of either oxygen or hydrogen, silicon atoms simply would not attach themselves to one another. They would hook onto either oxygen or hydrogen instead. On Earth, which is oxygen-excessive, you do not find silicon-silicon bonds in nature. Ever! Every silicon atom found in the Earth's crust is attached to at least one oxygen atom.

We can go through the entire list of elements in Table 2 from the bottom up and show that all are more likely to exist in combination with oxygen than with themselves and that complicated chains and rings of them are not at all likely to exist in nature.

Until we come to carbon. What about carbon?

The carbon-carbon single-bond energy is 82. The carbon-hydrogen bond is 93 (or 13 per cent stronger), while the carbon-oxygen link is 85 (or only 4 per cent stronger).

The difference is there, but it is not great. Carbon in the presence of oxygen *will* form carbon-oxygen bonds (and therefore burn), but only if it is heated sufficiently. Carbon in the presence of hydrogen *will* form C—H bonds (so that coal can be converted to petroleum), but only with considerable difficulty.

Neither change goes either easily or quickly. Carbon atoms will as soon link together with each other as with hydrogen or oxygen. Carbon *will* form chains, then, both long and short, straight and branched; and rings, both simple and complex; even in the presence of an excess of hydrogen or (as on Earth) oxygen.

We might still speculate on various elements serving as the basis of life in combination (silicon, oxygen, and phosphorus, for instance), but these possibilities are highly speculative and unlikely.

It we stick to the reasonable, then, carbon is the only

element capable of permitting the formation of molecules, both simple and complex, of the kind characteristic of life. Not just the best, but the only.

The one and only.

eight

THE UNLIKELY TWINS

A little over a year ago (as I write this) I was urged by two estimable ladies at Walker & Company to write a satire on the sexual "how-to" books that were, and are, infesting the nation. Much against my better judgment, I let myself be talked into it, and one weekend in April 1971 I sat down and dashed off something called *The Sensuous Dirty Old Man*. (A case of typecasting, I suppose, except that I'm not *really* old.)

It was published under the transparent pseudonym of "Dr. A.," and I was under the impression that nobody was going to know I wrote it.

Fat chance! The "secret" was announced in a press release even before the book was published, and pretty soon I found myself on television in my role as sensuous dirty late-youth man. And now it is out in paperback with the "Dr. A." followed by my full name in parentheses.

Since the book is *not* grimy, it never made the best-seller lists. On the other hand, since it *is* funny, it sells pretty well. And because it is *not* grimy and *is* funny, I'm not in the least ashamed of it.

One thing, though, is that I'm getting (and expect to continue to get) a rash of speaker introductions that include ". . . and among his umpty-ump books are *Asimov's Guide to the Bible* and *The Sensuous Dirty Old Man*."

The incongruous coupling is always good for a laugh, which, of course, is why they do it.

Incongruous couplings are amusing, or disturbing, in science too, and since I discussed carbon in the previous chapter, I will now go on to talk of it in connection with a pair of particularly unlikely twins.

Carbon is one of the elements known to the ancients, because its chemical properties are such that it can exist free in nature, and because it is solid and therefore easily recognizable. There are nine such elements all together, and of these, only two are non-metals; carbon is one and sulfur is the other.

Carbon actually exists as a mineral and can be dug out of the earth. In one of its less common forms it is a black, flaky substance that can be used for making marks. While solid enough to stick together in a chunk, tiny pieces will rub off when it is passed over some surface. Pieces of such carbon (mixed with clay) are used as the "lead" in pencils, and it is therefore called graphite from a Greek word meaning "to write."

The ancients did not, however, come across carbon in the form of graphite to begin with. It is much more likely that their first experience with carbon came in connection with wood fires. If the pile of burning wood was large and insufficiently aerated, the wood inside the pile would not burn completely. Atoms in the wood other than carbon (chiefly hydrogen atoms) would combine readily with oxygen. It was molecules of hydrogen combined with carbon that produced the vapors and dancing flame. Carbon atoms in themselves combine with oxygen not at all readily, and when the hydrogen-containing compounds are consumed and the flame dies down, wood that had been charred blackly into carbon may be left behind.

In Latin this black stuff was called *carbo*, from which we get our word carbon. In English the word coal originally meant any glowing ember, and when such embers ended up charred into a black substance or when such a black substance could form an ember, it was called charcoal.

The value of charcoal was that it would burn if it was well exposed to air, but unlike wood, would release no vapors to speak of and yield no flame. It merely glowed, and the result was that it delivered a particularly high temperature over a particularly long period of time. The high temperature was especially valuable in the smelting of iron, and charcoal making became an important industry. (Since it was prodigiously wasteful of wood, it accelerated the disappearance of forests in those areas where metallurgy was important.)

Over geologic ages, whole forests have slowly undergone a kind of natural charring by heat, pressure, and insufficient oxygen, so thick seams of carbon are commonly found underground. This is "coal" (because it will form a coal in the old sense if heated).

Some forms of coal are more nearly pure carbon than others are. If coal is heated without access to oxygen, the non-carbonaceous portion is driven off, and what is left is called coke.

Another form of carbon that must certainly have been noted in earliest times is the soot deposited out of the smoke and vapor of burning wood or oil. This is composed of carbon fragments left behind when the inflammable hydrogen-containing compounds burn, with the hydrogen seizing the oxygen so avidly that the carbon atoms are sometimes crowded out. This soot, mixed with oil, formed the first inks, so that carbon is the secret of both pen and pencil.

All these forms of carbon are black and brittle. Graphite is visibly crystalline, while the other forms are not. Charcoal, coal, coke, and soot, in all their various forms, are, however, made up of crystals of microscopic or submicroscopic size, and these are always identical to those in graphite. It is perfectly fair, therefore, to lump all the forms of black carbon together as "graphite."

To be sure, although carbon has been known in elementary form since prehistoric times, its recognition as an element in the modern, chemical sense did not take place until chemists understood what elements were—in the modern, chemical sense.

It was not till the eighteenth century that chemists developed a clear notion of elements, and it was only then that it was realized that graphite was an element, being made up of carbon atoms only.

Now we change the subject, apparently. Since ancient times, occasional pebbles were discovered that differed from all others in being extremely hard. They could not be scratched by anything else: rocks, glass, or the sharpest metal. The pebbles, on the other hand, could scratch anything else.

The Greeks called them *adamas* or, in the genitive case, *adamantos*, from words meaning "untamable," since there was nothing else that could make an impression on them. This became "adamant" in English, a word still used to signify the characteristic of unchangeability. However, the word also underwent gradual distortion, including the loss of the initial "a," and became "diamond," which is what we now call those hardest of all pebbles.

In the early days of chemistry, chemists developed a furious desire to know the composition of all things, diamonds included. Diamonds were, however, hard to handle just because they were "untamable." Not only could they not be scratched, but they remained untouched by almost all chemicals and were not affected by even considerable heat.

What's more, chemists weren't too anxious to expose diamonds to the chance of chemical or physical vicissitudes. A diamond couldn't possibly change into anything as valuable as itself, and who wanted to buy a diamond and then destroy it?

What was needed was a rich patron, and as it happened, Cosimo III, Grand Duke of Tuscany, who ruled from 1670 to 1723, was well-to-do and interested in science. He presented a couple of interested Italian scholars with a diamond about 1695, and the scholars put it at the focus of a strong lens. The concentrated solar rays lifted the temperature of the diamond to a level higher than that of any flame available to the experimenters. . . . And the diamond disappeared completely.

That was their report; naturally it was met with considerable skepticism. Nevertheless the number of chemists willing to repeat the experiment was confined to those willing to risk a diamond, and it was eighty years before the experiment was repeated.

In 1771 a French chemist, Pierre Joseph Macquer, obtained a flawless diamond and heated it to temperatures approaching 1,000°C. The diamond was by then red hot, yet there seemed to be a still brighter glow around it. The temperature was maintained, and in less than an hour the diamond was gone.

Was the diamond simply vanishing in some mysterious way, or was it burning? If it was burning as other things burned, a supply of air would be necessary. A jeweler named Maillard therefore packed diamonds into all sorts of non-combustibles, sealed the whole system tightly, and then heated it strongly enough to make the diamond disappear. This time it did not disappear. The conclusion was that diamonds burned in air just as so many other things did—provided they were heated sufficiently.

About this time, the French chemist Antoine Laurent Lavoisier was working out the fundamentals of modern chemistry, and he was to make it quite clear that ordinary burning in air involved a combination with oxygen of whatever it was that was burning. The burning object turned into an oxide, and if it seemed to disappear it was because the oxide was a vapor. It could be concluded, then, that diamond oxide was a vapor.

One ought to trap and study the vapor if one wanted to find out something about diamond. In 1773, Lavoisier, Macquer, and a couple of others heated a diamond under a glass bell jar, using a giant burning glass. The diamond disappeared, of course, but now the diamond-oxide vapor was trapped inside the bell jar. It could be studied, and was found to have the same properties as carbon dioxide obtained by burning charcoal.

By the time Lavoisier had completely worked out his oxide theory, he had to conclude that diamond and graphite both yielded carbon dioxide and that both were therefore forms of pure carbon.

The incongruity of placing diamond and graphite in the same cubbyhole was so extreme as to cause laughter—or indignation. Scientists found it hard to believe. Diamond (once it was properly cut—with other diamonds) was transparent and beautiful, while graphite was black and dull. Diamond was the hardest substance known; graphite was soft and so slippery that it could be used for a lubricant. Diamond did not conduct an electric current; graphite did.

For a generation, chemists remained doubtful, but more and more experimentation finally made the fact incontrovertible. Graphite and diamond were two different forms of carbon. In 1799, for instance, a French chemist, Louis-Bernard Guyton de Morveau, heated diamond strongly in the absence of air (so it would not burn) and actually observed it change into graphite.

Naturally, once diamond was successfully turned to graphite, there arose a furious interest in the possibility of doing the reverse: of turning graphite into diamond. Throughout the nineteenth century, attempts were made, and for a while it was believed that the French chemist

Henri Moissan had succeeded, in 1893. He actually presented diamonds he had prepared, one being a thirty-fifth of an inch in diameter and, apparently, flawless.

The work could not be repeated, however, and it is now known that diamonds couldn't possibly be formed by the methods Moissan used. The usual theory is that Moissan was victimized by an assistant who hoaxed him and then dared not own up to it when the hoax was taken seriously.

Carbon is not unique in this twinship. There are other cases of elements existing in different forms. Ordinary oxygen consists of molecules each of which contains two oxygen atoms. However, ozone (discovered in 1840) consists of molecules each containing three oxygen atoms. Oxygen and ozone are "allotropes" (from a Greek word meaning "variety") of oxygen.

There are allotropes of sulfur, phosphorus, and tin, too, and in every case it is a matter of the atoms of the element being present in any of two or more different arrangements.

Well, then, aren't diamond and graphite just one more case of allotropy? Yes, but in no other case are allotropes of an element so distinct in properties, so radically different, as are diamond and graphite. Is it possible that such opposites can be produced merely by rearranging the atoms?

Let's go back to the carbon atom. It has four bonds; that is, it can attach itself to four different atoms in four different directions. The bonds are in the directions of the vertices of a tetrahedron.

You can perhaps see this without a three-dimensional model (two-dimensional drawings are of doubtful help) if you imagine the carbon atom sitting on three of its bonds as though it was a flattish three-legged stool, while the fourth bond is sticking straight up.

If a series of carbon atoms are attached, one to another, to form a chain, such a chain is usually written in a straight line for simplicity's sake: $-C-C-C-C-$. Actually it should be written zigzag to allow for the natural angle ($109.5°$) at which the bonds are placed.

By following the natural angle of the bonds, it is easy to produce a ring of six carbon atoms, but that ring isn't flat. Seen in profile, the two ends curl up, or one end curls up while the other curls down. Ignoring that, we can write the six-carbon "cyclohexane ring" as follows:

Notice that each carbon atom has four bonds all together. Two are used up in joining to its neighbors in the ring, but the remaining two are available for use in other ways.

In the case of each carbon atom, however, one of those two spare bonds can be added to those forming the ring. In that case, each carbon atom is joined to one of its neighbors by a single bond and to the other by a double bond to form a "benzene ring":

Ordinarily, as I explained in the previous chapter, a double bond between carbon atoms is less stable than a single bond. You would expect that it would be easy to convert the benzene ring into a cyclohexane ring—but it isn't. Quite the reverse! The benzene ring is more stable than the cyclohexane ring, despite the double bonds.

The reason for this is that the carbon atoms in the benzene ring are in a plane; the benzene ring is perfectly flat. Furthermore, the benzene ring is symmetrical. The flatness and the symmetry add to the stability of the ring for reasons that require the use of quantum mechanics, and if you don't mind, we'll leave out the quantum mechanics in these chapters.

Of course, the benzene ring as I drew it above is not entirely symmetrical. Each carbon atom has a single bond on one side and a double bond on another, and surely this represents an asymmetry. Yes, it does, but this business about single bonds and double bonds arose before chemists had learned about electrons. Nowadays we know that the bonds consist of shared electrons and that the electrons have wave properties.

If the single bonds and double bonds are taken literally, it would seem that two carbon atoms separated by a single bond share two electrons, and two carbon atoms separated by a double bond share four electrons. This would be so if the electrons were particles—but they are waves.

Because of the flatness and the symmetry of the benzene ring, the electron waves stretch over the entire benzene ring and distribute themselves equally among all the atoms. The result is that each carbon atom is attached to each of its neighbors in precisely equal fashion (which is what makes the benzene ring so stable). If we wanted to be simplistic, we would say that the six connections in the benzene ring consist of six "one-and-a-half" bonds.

We could therefore picture the benzene ring as follows, in order to show the equivalence of the bonds and make the molecule entirely symmetrical:

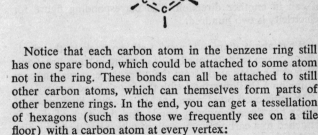

Notice that each carbon atom in the benzene ring still has one spare bond, which could be attached to some atom not in the ring. These bonds can all be attached to still other carbon atoms, which can themselves form parts of other benzene rings. In the end, you can get a tessellation of hexagons (such as those we frequently see on a tile floor) with a carbon atom at every vertex:

If you imagine a large number of such flat tessellations, one stacked over another, then these tessellations will hold together not by ordinary chemical bonds but by the weaker Van der Waals forces, which I mentioned in the previous chapter.

Each carbon atom in a hexagon is 1.4 angstroms from its neighbor (an angstrom is a hundred-millionth of a centimeter). One tessellation is, however, 3.4 angstroms from the one below. The greater distance in the second case is an expression of the weaker force of attraction.

As it happens, pure graphite consists of just such stacks of tessellations of carbon atoms. Each flat layer of hexagons holds firmly together but can be easily flaked off the flat layer beneath. It is for this reason that graphite can be used for writing or as a lubricant.

Then, too, the electrons that stretch all over the benzene rings have some of the properties of the mobile electrons that help form metallic bonds (which I mentioned in the previous chapter). The result is that graphite can conduct an electric current moderately well (though not as well as metals).

Heat and electricity can travel more readily along the plane of tessellation than they can travel from one plane to another. This means that heat can travel through a graphite crystal in one direction a thousand times more easily than it can in another direction. The corresponding figure for electricity is two hundred.

What about diamond, now? Let's go back to the single carbon atom with its four bonds pointing in four directions, each at the same angle from the other three: a carbon atom sitting on a shallow tripod with the fourth bond upward.

Imagine each bond connected to a carbon atom, each of which has three remaining bonds, and that each of *these* is attached to a carbon atom, each of which has three remaining bonds, and that each of *these* is attached to a carbon . . .

The result is an "adamantine" arrangement, a perfectly symmetrical arrangement of carbon atoms in three dimensions.

This means that all the carbon atoms are held equally well in four different directions. No atom or group of atoms is particularly easy to break off, so diamond won't flake. You can't write with it or use it as a lubricant.

Quite the reverse. Since, in every direction, carbon atoms are held together by strong, single bonds, and since these are the strongest bonds to be found in any substance solid at ordinary temperatures (as I explained in the previous chapter), diamond is usually hard. It scratches rather than being scratched and, far from lubricating, would quickly ruin anything at all rubbing against it.

Furthermore the electrons in diamond are all held firmly in place. Their waves are confined to the spaces between adjacent atoms, so diamond is a poor conductor of heat and electricity.

About the only thing that isn't easy to explain is why diamond is transparent and graphite is opaque. That comes down to quantum mechanics again, so I won't try.

The next question is this: If you start with a large quantity of carbon atoms and let them combine, what arrangement will they take up spontaneously: the graphite arrangement or the diamond arrangement?

Well, it depends on conditions.

On the whole, the benzene ring is so stable that, given a reasonable choice, carbon atoms will happily form these flat hexagons. (While carbon atoms in the benzene ring are separated by 1.4 angstroms, those in the adamantine arrangement are separated by 1.5 angstroms.) Under most conditions, then, you can expect graphite to be formed.

Diamond, however, has a density of about 3.5 grams per cubic centimeter, while graphite, thanks to the large distance between tessellations, has a density of only about 2 grams per cubic centimeter.

If, therefore, carbon atoms are placed under huge pressure, the tendency to have them rearrange themselves into a form taking up less room eventually becomes overwhelming, and diamond is formed.

But if at ordinary pressure graphite is the form of choice, how is it that diamonds exist? Even assuming they were formed in the first place under great pressure deep in the bowels of the earth, why do they not turn to graphite as soon as the pressure is relieved?

There's a catch: The carbon atoms in diamond would indeed be doing what comes naturally if they shifted into the graphite configuration. They are held so tightly by their bonds, however, that the energy required to break those bonds and allow the shift is enormous. It is as though the diamond were on top of a hill and perfectly ready to roll down it except that it is at the bottom of a deep pit on the top of that hill and must be lifted out of the pit before it can do any rolling.

If the temperature of a diamond is raised to nearly 2,000°C. (in the absence of oxygen, so as to prevent burning), it is lifted out of the pit, so to speak. The atoms are shaken loose and take up the preferred graphite configuration.

To do the reverse—to turn graphite into diamond—you need to have not only very high temperatures to knock the atoms loose, but *also* very high pressures to convince them they ought to take up the denser, diamond pattern.

Moissan's facilities in 1893 were absolutely incapable of delivering the simultaneous heights of temperature and pressure required, so we know he could not really have formed synthetic diamonds. In 1955, scientists at General Electric Company managed to form the first synthetic diamonds by working with temperatures of 2,500°C. combined with pressures of over 700 tons per square inch.

One last item before I let you go for this chapter. Carbon has a total of six electrons, boron five, and nitrogen seven. If two carbon atoms combine (C—C), they have twelve electrons all together. If a boron atom and a nitrogen atom combine (B—N), they also have twelve electrons all together.

It is not surprising, then, that the combination of boron and nitrogen, or "boron nitride," has properties very much like that of graphite (though boron nitride is white rather than black and does not conduct electricity). Boron nitride is made up of hexagons in which boron and nitrogen atoms alternate at the corners, and from these hexagons, stacks of tessellations are built up.

If boron nitride is subjected to the high-temperature, high-pressure combination, its atoms also take up the adamantine arrangement. The result is a denser and harder form of boron nitride, a form called "borazon." (The "-azon" suffix comes from "azote," an old name for nitrogen.)

Borazon (again, not surprisingly) is almost as hard as diamond. In fact, it has an important advantage over diamond in being non-combustible. It can be used at temperatures at which diamond would combine with oxygen and disappear.

Borazon may therefore well replace diamond for industrial uses, but somehow I don't expect to see borazon engagement rings for a while.

D

ABOUT MICRO-ORGANISMS

nine

THROUGH THE MICROGLASS

I have just come back from a two-week stint at a writers'
conference in Bread Loaf, Vermont, where I had a very
good time. Among the assets of such a place are all the
young ladies who are anxious to learn to write, and my
attitude toward them was much noted and widely admired
for its suavity.

And then, toward the end of the stint, one of the young
ladies, to whom I was being very suave indeed, giggled and
said, "Oh, Dr. Asimov, you're so levatious."

That stopped me cold. We were sitting on a bench and
my arm had been resting comfortably about her waist, but
now a cloud passed over the sun of my being. I had never
been called "levatious" by anyone, let alone by a mere slip
of a girl, and I was disturbed. Chiefly I was disturbed because I didn't know the meaning of the word.

"Levatious?" I said. "What's that?"

She said, "Oh, you know, Dr. Asimov. The way you go
around olging the girls."

From the way she pronounced "ogling," I learned the
system by which she handled words. She got the first letter
and the last letter right and let all the intermediates take
care of themselves.

"By levatious," I said, "do you mean lascivious?"

"That's the word," she said happily, clapping her hands.

I was at once lost in thought. I had never considered
myself lascivious, merely suave. On the other hand, I
thought, I might very well be levatious, at that. It *sounded*
right: a combination of "laughing" and "vivacious." What's
more, it was clearly from the Latin *levare*, meaning "to
raise," as one's spirits. And indeed, many girls at Bread
Loaf had said to me, "Oh, Dr. Asimov, your laughing vi-
vacity raises my spirits."

But while I was puzzling all this out, the young girl who had started it all managed to get away.

This shows that words mean even more to me than girls do, which is as it should be for a writer. And it is not surprising, then, that in most of the segments of knowledge that interest me I constantly find myself hung up on words.

Take microbiology (from Greek words meaning "the study of small life"), for instance . . .

In 1675 the Dutch microscopist Anton van Leeuwenhoek became the first man to see tiny living things under his lenses: creatures that were too small to see with the unaided eye and yet were indubitably alive.

He called them "animalcules," meaning "little animals." But not all the tiny organisms visible under a microscope are active and animal-like in nature; some are green and passive and are clearly plantlike. Today we call all these microscopic organisms "micro-organisms," a perfectly general term of completely transparent meaning.

Micro-organisms come in various sizes, and some are small indeed. In 1683 Van Leeuwenhoek detected tiny objects at the very limit of the resolution of his lenses, objects that eventually proved rather less advanced than either the animal or the plant micro-organisms.

It took another century for microscopy to advance to the point at which these tiny objects could be seen clearly enough to be studied in some detail. The Danish biologist Otto Friedrich Müller was the first to divide these tiny creatures into groups and to attempt to classify them into genera and species. In a book by him published in 1786 (two years after his death) he referred to some as "bacilli," from a Latin word for "little rod," since that was their shape. Others he referred to as "spirilla," because they were shaped like tiny spirals.

In the course of the nineteenth century, other terms were introduced: The German botanist Ferdinand Cohn applied a new name to rodlike micro-organisms that were rather stubbier than bacilli. He called them "bacteria," from a Greek word for "little rod." The Austrian surgeon Albert Christian Theodor Billroth called those varieties that looked like little spheres "cocci," from a Greek word for "berry."

Now for some general terms:

Those one-celled micro-organisms clearly animal in nature, sharing properties with the cells that make up large animals such as ourselves, were "protozoa," from Greek words meaning "first animals." Those one-celled micro-organisms that were clearly plantlike in nature and were very much like those cells found in large strands of seaweed were called "algae," from the Latin word for "seaweed."

But what about those particularly small micro-organisms, the bacilli and the rest? What general name would cover all of them? Scientists have finally settled on "bacteria" (the singular is bacterium) for the purpose, and the study of these organisms is called bacteriology.

The general public, however, used another name, one that is still popular.

In Latin, any tiny speck of life that can develop into a larger organism was a *germen*, or "germ." Tiny seeds were the best examples of this that the ancients knew, and when a seed begins its development, we say it "germinates." What's more, we still speak of "wheat germ," for instance, when we mean the portion of the wheat kernel that is the actual bit of life.

It seemed reasonable, then, to refer to these tiny micro-organisms as "germs" too. Somewhat less common is "microbe," from Greek words meaning "small life."

Actually none of these terms are perfect. "Germ" and "microbe" are too general, since there are small bits of life other than those creatures we commonly call by those names. "Bacteria," on the other hand, is too specific, since it was originally used for only one variety of those creatures we commonly call bacteria. . . . It's no use, though; no one listens to us logalators.*

In the mid-nineteenth century the French chemist Louis Pasteur was the outstanding chemist/biologist/bacteriologist in the world. He had explained the mystery of racemic acid, for instance, and he had learned how to prevent the souring of wine through gentle heating, or "pasteurization." In a very dramatic experiment in public he had, in 1864, shown that bacteria were alive in the fullest sense of the word. They did not arise out of inanimate mat-

* This one you can look up for yourselves.

ter, but only out of preexisting bacteria. (A fascinating story, but that's for another day.)

Consequently, in 1865, when the silkworm industry in southern France was being ruined by a mysterious sickness that was killing the silkworms, the call went out for miracle-man Pasteur. No one else would do. So Pasteur traveled south.

He studied the silkworms, and the mulberry leaves they fed on, with his microscope. He found that a tiny micro-organism infested the sick silkworms and the leaves they fed upon, while healthy silkworms and their leaves were free of it.

Pasteur's solution was simple, but drastic. All silkworms and all mulberry leaves infested with this micro-organism must be destroyed. A new beginning would have to be made with healthy worms; and with the micro-organism absent, all would go well. Any reappearance of the disease must be met with new destruction at once before it could spread far.

The silk industry followed orders and was saved.

But this got Pasteur to thinking about diseases that could be spread from one organism to another. Surely this silk-worm infestation by micro-organisms could not be unique. Wasn't it reasonable to suppose that infectious diseases were always associated with some micro-organism and that the infection consisted in the passing of a micro-organism from a sick person to a healthy one?

This notion of Pasteur's has been called, ever since, the "germ theory of disease," and the phrase is a good one. Though the first micro-organisms to be studied in connection with disease were bacteria, it has been found that disease agents can be both more complex and less complex than bacteria; the more general term "germ" is just right.

And for that reason I will refer to pathogenic (disease-producing) micro-organisms as germs in the rest of this article.

To dream up a germ theory of disease was fine, but its validity had to be demonstrated.

First, a germ of some kind had to be detected in organisms sick of a certain disease, and must not have been found in organisms without the disease.

Second, the germ had to be isolated and allowed to multiply under conditions that would give the experimenter a pure culture, one with no other organisms in it.

Third, a small quantity of this culture, when introduced into a healthy organism, had to produce the disease.

Fourth, the germ had then to be isolated from the newly sick organism and prove capable of producing the disease in still another organism.

The work of the German physician Robert Koch fulfilled these requirements for a number of different diseases; this placed the germ theory of disease on a firm footing. No sane person has since questioned it.

The germ theory led directly to the conquest of infectious diseases. It came to be understood, for the first time, exactly why one should wash one's hands before eating, why one should not place the outhouse too near the well, why one should boil water if suspicious of its origins, why one should develop good sewage systems, and so on. In short, it was no longer possible to equate personal and public hygiene with effete decadence and to suppose dirt to be a mark of sturdy masculinity—or even saintliness.

Then, too, once diseases were studied from the new angle, it was found that organisms developed substances that could counter the bad effect of germs. Such substances could be deliberately developed in animals subjected to the germs. The substances could then be isolated and injected into human beings to help them fight off a disease. Or else weakened germs could be placed in human beings and, without hurting the body, cause it to form a substance capable of fighting off the germs even in their full strength. In other words, techniques of immunization were developed.

One of the diseases tackled by Pasteur from the standpoint of the germ theory was rabies. It is a disease that affects the nervous system, and animals that have the disease show such peculiar behavior that they seem mad. (A "mad dog" is one with rabies, and should more appropriately be called a "rabid dog.") For one thing, such animals become unreasonably aggressive and bite without cause. They seem to be raging, or raving, and the word "rabies" is from the same Latin root as those two words.

Naturally with the nervous system primarily affected, there is loss of muscular control. When a rabid human being tries to swallow, his throat muscles begin to contract uncontrollably and painfully. Sometimes the mere sight of water, producing, as it does, the thought of swallowing, brings about the agony. For that reason, rabies is sometimes called "hydrophobia," from Greek words meaning "fear of water."

Although the disease is not common, it is much feared, because it is prolonged, exceedingly painful, and almost surely fatal once established. The cry of "Mad dog" and the sight of such an animal in an advanced stage of the disease, with saliva frothing about his jaws, will send everyone running, and quite justifiably, too, for if a bite breaks the skin and the saliva enters the victim's blood stream, he has very likely had it.

There was no question that rabies was a communicable disease, and Pasteur initiated a program designed to isolate the germ in order to find a way of combating it. This involved a kind of bravery that was in itself mad (when viewed by a timid soul like myself). It was necessary to begin with the saliva of a rabid dog, which meant that such dogs had to be trapped, held down, and samples of the saliva removed. Working with angry cobras would have been no more dangerous.

Pasteur got his samples, and when the saliva of rabid dogs was injected into the blood stream of rabbits, they eventually became rabid.

It was slow work, however. The rabies germ, after injection into the blood stream, took from weeks to months really to establish itself. A human being, once bitten by a rabid dog, rarely took less than two weeks to begin to show symptoms, and that period of fearful waiting added to the horror of the disease.

Pasteur had to work out some scheme for cutting down on the waiting period if he were to make progress. Since the first symptoms of the disease seemed to be those that would be expected of a nervous disorder, it seemed possible that the delay was an expression of the time it took the germ to pass out of the blood and into the nervous system. It would only be after the germ had well established itself in the nervous system that the symptoms would appear. What, then, if the saliva from rabid dogs were injected directly into a rabbit's brain? Then, once the disease was well established, the brain and spinal cord would surely be far richer sources of the germ than saliva would be.

All this turned out to be correct. Pasteur, beginning with a sample of saliva from a rabid dog, began to multiply the germ by injecting it into a rabbit brain and then passing it from one rabbit to another by way of the nervous system.

Eventually he had a large supply of the germ-containing material and was less dependent on rabid dogs and their saliva froth. What's more, as the germ passed from one rabbit to another, it seemed to become adapted to the new species and became less and less infectious to dogs.

Pasteur naturally began to wonder if the infectiousness could be reduced generally. He had weakened (or "attenuated," from Latin words meaning "to thin out") germs in connection with other diseases by subjecting them to unfavorable conditions. What about this one?

Pasteur began to dry infected spinal cord in the presence of mild warmth. On each successive day, he injected a preparation of the dried cord into a rabbit and noted whether rabies appeared and how badly. Clearly the germ in the preparation was being damaged, for the virus was less and less deadly each day. After two weeks, it did not produce rabies at all.

Could the attenuated germ, however, stimulate the body to form a substance that could fight off even strong and virulent germs? It might seem, considering the deadliness of rabies once established, that the body had no defense; but, once established, it might very well be that the germ overwhelmed the defenses. There could be many cases of minimal infection in which the disease was fought off before it could establish itself and the symptoms did not appear and the whole affair was passed off without notice.

Pasteur tested the possibility by injecting his attenuated preparation of rabies germ into a healthy dog and then waiting a good long time to see if the disease would develop. When it was clear that no rabies was produced, the question was whether the dog had developed an anti-rabies defense just the same. To test this, the dog was put into a cage already occupied by a rabid dog. The rabid dog attacked at once and there was a battle royal. The healthy dog was finally rescued, but only after it had been battered and thoroughly bitten. It *still* did not develop rabies.

But what about men? How could one dare perform the necessary experiments on human beings, even on condemned criminals? The possibility of accidentally inflicting rabies on any human being was unbearable to someone like Pasteur.

On July 4, 1885, however, a nine-year-old Alsatian boy, Joseph Meister, was bitten severely and repeatedly by a rabid dog. The wounds were treated with carbolic acid, but this was known to be useless against the disease and it seemed wise to bring the boy to Louis Pasteur.

Once the disease established itself in the boy's nervous system it would be too late, but there was a period of grace, and Pasteur prepared to work quickly. Here, at least, an experiment seemed advisable, since if Pasteur did nothing, the boy would surely die in agony.

Pasteur therefore began by injecting the most attenuated rabies preparation, and then a somewhat less attenuated one, and then a still less attenuated one, and so on, trusting that the body would develop massive defenses before the real germs got their grip on the nervous system. After eleven days, young Joseph was getting virtually the straight stuff. The boy did *not* get rabies, and Pasteur was more the miracle man than ever.

(Joseph Meister's end, by the way, was tragic. He grew to manhood and eventually became gatekeeper at the Pasteur Institute, the research institution named for the great man who had saved him and on whose grounds Pasteur was buried. Aged sixty-four, Meister was still gatekeeper in 1940, when the Nazis took Paris. Out of curiosity, some Nazi official ordered Meister to open Pasteur's crypt. Rather than do so, Meister killed himself.)

In all his work on rabies, Pasteur had consistently failed to fulfill the very first requirement of the germ theory of disease. He had not detected any germ in any of his preparations, at least none connected with rabies. Any germ he did detect turned out to be incapable of producing the disease. (One germ he detected and discarded was studied by the German physician Albert Fraenkel in 1886 and shown to be the germ that caused pneumonia.)

Strictly speaking, this absence of any detectable germ might be taken as evidence that the germ theory was wrong. Pasteur, however, did not accept that for one moment. It was clear to him that all his work with rabies made sense if he supposed that there *was* a germ. The fact that he didn't see one didn't mean that one didn't exist; it just meant that he didn't see one.

There's nothing either mystical or puzzling about what I have just said. Under the circumstances, the statement is perfectly logical. Micro-organisms come in a variety of sizes. Some are so large that they can be made out as clearly visible specks by the unaided eye under favorable conditions. Others are smaller, and still smaller, right down to the stage where they can barely be made out by a good microscope of the kind available to Pasteur.

What a monumental coincidence it would be if the smallest micro-organisms happened to be just large enough to be made out under Pasteur's microscope and there were no micro-organisms at all that were smaller still. Such a coincidence would, in fact, be quite unbelievable, and Pasteur did not believe it. He was certain that there were micro-organisms too small for his microscope to make out and that it was one of those too-small germs that caused rabies.

But must one depend on eyes only? Is there some way of detecting a small germ besides actually seeing it?

Suppose, for instance, one filtered a preparation that seemed to contain no germs at all but was capable of producing a disease when injected into a healthy animal. Suppose one used as a filter something that possessed very tiny holes. If the holes were too tiny to let the germs through, but large enough to let water molecules through, then the fluid emerging from the filter would no longer be capable of producing a disease. The material left behind in the filter, if washed out, would be capable of transmitting it. A germ would, in this way, be detected even if it were not seen.

A filter of that kind that would hold back objects as small as the average germ was devised by a French bacteriologist, Charles Édouard Chamberland. It was a hollow cylinder with the bottom closed off by unglazed porcelain. Because of its appearance it was called a "Chamberland candle."

The first to use such a filter in an attempt to remove a

germ from a liquid preparation containing it was Russian bacteriologist, Dmitri Alexeievich Ivanovski. He was working with tobacco plants suffering from a disease that produced a mottled mosaic pattern on the leaves; this was called tobacco mosaic disease.

If the leaves were mashed up, a juice could be extracted that would produce the disease if placed on healthy tobacco plants. By the germ theory of disease, one would expect to find a germ in the juice, and it would be this germ that transmitted the disease.

Ivanovski, however, could not find any sign of a germ in the juice that transmitted the disease. He wasn't content, however, to dismiss the matter by saying that the germ was too small to see. Less imaginative than Pasteur, he assumed that the fault lay somehow in himself, and it occurred to him to use some method other than eyesight to trap the germ.

In 1892 he forced the fluid that carried the disease through a Chamberland candle and found that what came through could *still* transmit the disease to healthy tobacco plants.

This could be interpreted as supporting Pasteur's insight: The germ passed through a filter capable of holding back ordinary germs and was therefore smaller than ordinary germs and too small to be seen in a microscope.

Unfortunately Ivanovski could not shake free of his inability to accept something too small to see in a microscope. His interpretation of the results was that the Chamberland candle he used was defective. Therefore, although he is sometimes considered to be the first to demonstrate the existence of subbacterial forms of life, his claim to that fame is a tarnished one, since he himself missed the significance of his work.

In 1898, though, the experiment was tried again, this time by a Dutch botanist, Marinus Willem Beijerinck (pronounced "buyer ink"). He also was working on tobacco mosaic disease, and he also used an extract capable of communicating the disease but in which he could see no germ. He also forced it through a filter of unglazed porcelain and ended with a fluid still capable of communicating the disease.

Unlike Ivanovski, however, Beijerinck assumed no flaws in the filter. He flatly maintained that he had demonstrated the existence of a germ too small to see in a microscope and small enough to pass through the pores in unglazed porcelain.

Beijerinck had called his disease-carrying fluid a "virus," from a Latin word for a poisonous plant extract (like the juice of the hemlock, which killed Socrates). After all, the fluid from diseased tobacco plants was a kind of poisonous plant extract. Since the tobacco-mosaic-disease virus passed through a filter but was still a "virus," Beijerinck called it a "filtrable virus." It is Beijerinck who ought to get the credit, then, for discovering subbacterial disease agents.

Beijerinck, having opted for smallness, now went to the extreme in that direction and maintained that the filtrable virus was a kind of living fluid; that is, a form of life with particles of the same order of complexity as those of water or other common liquids.

This, however, proved to be wrong, and the evidence came by way of still finer filters. The British bacteriologist William Joseph Elford abandoned unglazed porcelain and used collodion membranes instead. These could be prepared by methods that would give them pores of any size. Membranes could be prepared with pores small enough to stop objects considerably smaller than ordinary bacteria.

In 1931 Elford forced filtrable viruses through membranes capable of stopping objects only a hundredth the diameter of an ordinary bacterium. When a filtrable virus passed through such a membrane, the fluid that emerged was non-infecting. The germ had been trapped. It was much smaller than an ordinary germ, but it was still much larger than a water molecule. The filtrable virus was *not* a form of liquid life.*

The term "filtrable virus," applied by Beijerinck to the disease-carrying fluid, was now shifted to the infectious agent itself. The term was shortened to "virus," and this is now universally accepted as the term for something that is much smaller than a bacterium and yet is alive enough to transmit a disease.

But what are the viruses? Just ultrasmall bacteria? Or do

---

* Outmoded theories, alas, live on in science fiction sometimes. I remember reading and enjoying a story by Ralph Milne Farly treating of viruses in Beijerinck fashion. The story, actually called "Liquid Life," appeared in the October 1936 *Thrilling Wonder Stories,* five years after Elford's demonstration.

they have properties all their own that make them a new form of organism altogether?

Well, if I end a chapter with a question, you can be sure that the next chapter will deal with the answer.

RECYCLE
BOOKS RECORDS
PH 408-286-6275

···· 2·08·90 ·

···· ···· 1 ····75 ·
···· 13 ····05 ·
···· ···· ·····80 TOL
···· ···· ·····1.00 CASH
3904A00 ·····20 CNG

ten

DOWN FROM THE AMOEBA

I was at a party last week. Most of us, including myself, were in the basement with the drinks and (in my case) the hors d'oeuvres. Upstairs, virtually alone, was the young lady who had been kind enough to accompany me. A quiet, sensitive creature, she had to withdraw every once in a while.

Later she said to me, "I was half asleep, when suddenly I became aware of the rapid, quavering, cracked voice of an old, old man downstairs. That shocked me awake, because I knew there was no old man at the party. I listened, but I couldn't make out the words. Then the voice stopped and there was a roar of laughter. I relaxed, because I knew it was you telling the joke about the eighty-eight-year-old rabbi."*

That tells you two things about me. First, it shows I'm a darned good storyteller. Modesty forbids me to say this, but I never listen to Modesty.

The second thing is that I tend to repeat myself. If I hear a joke I like, I spend at least a month telling it to everyone I meet, which means a close companion is bound to hear it twenty-seven hundred times—hence can identify it from a distance on the basis of the tiniest of clues.

This rather strong reminder of my tendency to repeat myself made me a little self-conscious. After all, this chapter you are now looking at represents my 173rd monthly article for *The Magazine of Fantasy and Science Fiction* (roughly seven hundred thousand words, for goodness' sake); there is bound to be overlapping here and there. This chapter and the previous one deal with micro-organisms, for instance. Have I ever dealt with them be-

---

* No, I won't tell you the joke about the eighty-eight-year-old rabbi. It's too long, and it verges on the improper.

fore? I went over my list of *F & SF* essays and it turns out that there were some comments about micro-organisms in two essays I wrote eleven years ago.

But the overlap isn't much. The approach and detail are quite different now, and it's been a long time. So I will go on, with my conscience in a state of chemically clean purity.

In those early essays, for instance, I discussed the sizes of micro-organisms, and I am going to do so now again, but for a different purpose.

Let's start with the one specific micro-organism that everyone has heard of if he's heard of any: the amoeba. An average amoeba is about 1/125 of an inch in diameter, but no one uses inches in making such measurements. If we switch to the metric system, we might use millimeters, each one of which is equal to about 1/25 of an inch. The diameter of the amoeba can then be said to be one-fifth of a millimeter, or, if you prefer, 0.2 millimeter.

It would be better, however, to use the micromillimeter (usually, but imperfectly, called the millimicron) as the unit of measure, and still better to give it its present name of "nanometer." Since there are a million nanometers in the millimeter, we can say that the amoeba has a diameter of 200,000 nanometers.

The juxtaposition of 1/125 of an inch and 200,000 nanometers is just right. The diameter is the same, expressed either way, but 1/125 shows the amoeba to be quite small on the ordinary scale, and 200,000 shows it to be quite large on the submicroscopic scale. Since we are going to stay submicroscopic, let's stay with the nanometer as a unit and avoid the boredom induced by repeating it each time, by taking the word as understood.

The amoeba is composed of a single cell; I won't define "cell" any further than to say it is a blob of living matter enclosed in a membrane. The outsizeness of the amoeba cell becomes apparent when I tell you that every one of the fifty trillion or so cells in your body is smaller than the amoeba. The largest human cell (occurring in the female only) is the ovum, which has a diameter of about 140,000. An average human cell is more likely to have a diameter of about 55,000.

The difference in size is even more extreme if we consider volume rather than diameter. An amoeba is nearly four times the diameter of the average body cell, and that gives it roughly fifty times the volume. Yet the amoeba is no more completely alive than the body cell, merely for being larger, than a man is more completely alive than a mouse.

Still we might reasonably suppose that there comes a time when a cell becomes so small that it can no longer be completely alive. There just isn't enough room in it to hold all the necessary paraphernalia of life, we might argue.

Consider, for instance, the red blood cells, of which there are roughly five million per cubic millimeter of blood. These are among the smallest cells of the human body, disk-shaped and with a long diameter of only 7,500. They *don't* have all the paraphernalia we usually associate with life.

The typical cell has a nucleus, a small body more or less in the center of the cell, and all else is "cytoplasm." The red blood cell has no nucleus and is essentially a bag of cytoplasm. Since it is the nucleus that contains the machinery for cell division, the red blood cell, lacking a nucleus, can never divide. It does its work, carrying oxygen molecules from the lungs to the body cells, until it wears out (after about three months), and then it is dismantled. The body doesn't run out of red blood cells, however, because more are continually being formed from precursors that *do* have nuclei.

It can be argued, and often is, that the red blood cell, although alive (since it metabolizes), is not a complete cell. In fact it is sometimes denied the name and called a red blood "corpuscle."

Nor is the red blood cell the smallest living unit in the body. The smallest of all (and present only in the male) is the sperm cell, which has a diameter of about 2,500, so that half a million of them would fit into a single amoeba.

The sperm cell is little more than half a nucleus and nothing else. With half a nucleus it can't divide, and with only a smidgen of cytoplasm (in which the energy-producing apparatus of the cell exists) it can't stay alive long. It has just enough energy to make that mad race for the ovum (if one is in the vicinity) and, if superlatively lucky, enter and fertilize that ovum. If no ovum is present or if some other candidate gets in first, the sperm cell dies.

In view of that, can one consider a sperm cell a complete cell? Perhaps not. After all, its sole purpose is to join another cell to become complete. And sheer size has nothing to do with it. The human ovum, which I mentioned before as the largest cell in the body, also contains but half a nucleus, and cannot divide until a sperm enters and adds the other half.

Disregarding size, then, ought we to define a "complete cell" as one that has a complete nucleus together with enough cytoplasm for adequate energy production so that it is able to divide?

If we do that, what do we do about the nerve cells and muscle cells in a human body? Both types of cells are so specialized that they have lost the capacity to divide even though both have perfectly good nuclei and perfectly adequate cytoplasm. Each nerve cell and muscle cell can live over a century, and many do or the human being couldn't. It would be silly not to call them cells just because they don't divide, and in fact no physiologist denies them the name.

But if we don't insist on cell division as the criterion for a complete cell, by what right do we deny that a red blood cell is complete? It doesn't have a nucleus, true, but it does what it is supposed to do, efficiently, for three months, and it is unfair to ask more.

Let me suggest a different criterion for a complete cell, then:

The characteristic chemical substances of cells are the large molecules of nucleic acids and proteins. Certain proteins called "enzymes" catalyze specific reactions within cells. Without those enzymes in working order, a cell can't carry out the chemical reactions characteristic of life, and, at best, can live only in a kind of suspended animation for a while.

As for the nucleic acids, they see to it that the proper enzymes are formed in the first place.

Without nucleic acids, a cell must make do on the enzymes already present while those enzymes last. With nucleic acids, a cell can live a long time, because the nucleic acids can replace themselves and make enzymes too, by building them out of small molecules absorbed from the outside world. If it is not too specialized to undergo division, a cell with nucleic acid, and its descendants, can live indefinitely.

Let us define a complete cell, then, as one that has all the large molecules (enzymes and nucleic acids) that it needs for its normal functions; or, if it doesn't have enough of either or both, one that can build up what it needs out of the small molecules in its environment.

An incomplete cell would be one that lacks some of the large molecules it needs and cannot make them out of small molecules. Such a cell can only lie in suspended animation and eventually die unless it succeeds in somehow making use of the large molecules in another cell, different from itself. An incomplete cell, in other words, can function only if, for at least some part of its life, it is parasitic on a completed cell.

By this definition, the red blood cell is complete, but the ovum and the sperm are each incomplete. Each of the latter two is a half cell doomed to only a limited life span until such time as they unite and become a complete cell, each depending in part on the large molecules of the other to make the fuller life possible.

The mutual parasitism of ovum and sperm is, however, a one-shot thing. Once combined, the "fertilized ovum" that results is permanently complete. Are there, on the other hand, fragments of life that are permanently incomplete, that parasitize complete cells without in any way becoming complete themselves through the process?

If such there are, we might suspect they would have to be smaller than the ordinary cells making up multicellular creatures such as ourselves. The human sperm cell, with a diameter of 2,500, is already so small that it can only hold half a nucleus and almost no cytoplasm. Anything that size or smaller (it might be reasoned) would have to be incomplete for simple lack of room for the minimum number of large molecules required for total cellular functioning.

This naturally brings us to the world of the bacteria, all of which are smaller than the human sperm. The largest bacteria are perhaps 1,900 in diameter; 1,000 might be considered average. And aren't they parasites? At least, most of us think of bacteria as living ruthlessly on other living things, especially on ourselves.

But that is wrong. Most bacteria are saprophytes, living

on the dead remnants of living things. Even those that are parasitic, in the sense that they flourish within living organisms, live on the small molecules present in these organisms—in the intestines, where they usually don't bother us, and sometimes in the blood, where they usually do.

Despite their small size, bacterial cells are complete. They need only a supply of small molecules; out of those, they can manufacture all the large molecules they require. In some respects their chemical versatility is greater than that of the larger cells that make up our bodies.

It is for this reason that bacteria, even those which are parasitic, can be cultured in the laboratory on artificial media containing the small molecules they need. It is because they can be so cultured, and therefore studied in isolation, that late-nineteenth-century medicine made its start toward conquering bacterial diseases.

But how can bacterial cells be complete when they are so tiny and so much smaller than the sperm cell, which is only half a nucleus? The smallest known bacterium is the pleuropneumonia organism, which has a diameter of only 150. Some 2,000 of them can be squeezed into a space the size of a human sperm cell.

That sounds paradoxical, but we mustn't judge, from the size of the nucleus needed to contain all the control paraphernalia for an organism the size and complexity of a human being with its tens of trillions of co-operating cells, the size of one needed to run a tiny blob of matter much smaller than any one of those cells. We might as well argue that, since a heart is necessary to the functioning of any mammal, no mammal smaller than the human heart (a mouse, for instance) can possibly exist. The mouse has a heart too, after all, but a much smaller one than we have.

Similarly, a bacterial cell has nuclear matter too, but it needs far less than our cells do. I say "nuclear matter," because the bacterial cell has no distinct nucleus but does have the nucleic acids usually found within the cell nucleus. These nucleic acids are located in bits throughout the bacterial cell. In this respect, bacteria resemble certain very simple plant cells called blue-green algae, which are like bacteria structurally except that they are somewhat larger and possess chlorophyll.

Bacteria and the blue-green algae apparently represent a very primitive stage in evolution. As cells grew larger and more complicated, the increasing quantity of nuclear matter necessary for enzyme manufacture was gathered into a compact nucleus so that cell division could take place flawlessly. Still, the mere fact that bacteria and blue-green algae are more primitive in this respect does not mean that such cells are less than complete, any more than the fact that an earthworm is more primitive than you are makes it any the less a complete organism.

This brings us to Howard Taylor Ricketts, an American pathologist who, about seventy years ago, tackled Rocky Mountain spotted fever, a serious disease that killed 20 per cent or more of those who contracted it.

Ricketts was able to show that it was primarily a disease of ticks and of the small animals whose blood they fed on. Sometimes cattle ticks would have it; it was from those that human beings were most likely to catch the disease. Ricketts managed to locate the micro-organism that caused the disease and showed that it was transmitted from tick to mammal and back to tick.

He then went on to study the even more widespread and serious disease typhus, which was produced by a similar micro-organism, one that primarily infested the body louse and was spread from human to human by the bite of that intimate little creature.

While studying typhus in Mexico City, Ricketts managed to contract the disease himself and died of it on May 3, 1910, at the age of twenty-nine. Mexico observed three days of mourning on his behalf. The organism of the type that causes Rocky Mountain spotted fever and typhus are called rickettsiae in his honor, and the diseases themselves are examples of "rickettsial diseases."

The rickettsiae look like small bacteria, with typical diameters of 475, *but* they cannot be cultured on artificial media, the way other bacteria can. Rickettsiae remain in suspended life outside cells and can grow only *inside* the cells of the creatures they infect.

They apparently lack certain key enzymes necessary for growth and reproduction and cannot make them out of small molecules. Inside the cell they infect, they can make use of the necessary enzymes present in that cell for their own purposes.

The rickettsiae, then, are examples of true incomplete

cells, cells that parasitize complete cells and do not in the process become complete themselves.

Nor is it just a matter of size. A typical rickettsial cell has some thirty times the volume of a pleuropneumonia organism and therefore can be supposed to have room for thirty times as many of each variety of large molecule. However, at least one key large molecule must be totally missing in the rickettsial cell, while none are *totally* missing from the pleuropneumonia organism, so the former is an incomplete cell and the latter a complete one.

What, then, of the viruses I talked about in the previous chapter? William Elford, as I said, filtered a suspension of the virus and held back the infective agent. He showed that viruses must be particles with a diameter of about 100—at least the one he worked with was. As it turns out, some are larger, almost half the diameter of a rickettsial cell. Others, however, are considerably smaller. The tobacco necrosis virus, for instance, has a diameter of only 16.

Twenty-five thousand of the tobacco necrosis virus particles can be squeezed into a volume equal to that of a rickettsial cell, nearly four million into the volume of a human sperm cell, two trillion into the volume of an amoeba. Such a tiny virus has indeed only about fifteen times the volume of an average protein molecule.

Surely the viruses must be incomplete cells that, like the rickettsiae, can live only within the cells they parasitize, but, being much smaller, cannot be detected either in or outside the cell by any ordinary microscope.

In fact, are they alive at all? Surely there must be a limit to how small an object can be and still be alive! The virus particles are so small they can contain very few molecules by ordinary cellular standards. How can there possibly be enough to give them the complex properties of life?

To be sure, viruses grow and multiply with ferocious speed once within a cell, and it is quite logical to assume that they are reorganizing the material they find into their own structure and doing so efficiently. Isn't that enough to make them alive? What more can any living organism do?

And yet there are no sharp boundaries in nature, and if we stop to think about it, we must realize that, in the course of the gradual evolution of large molecules out of small in the primordial ocean, there must have been a period when there were molecules or systems of molecules not complex enough to have gained all the properties we associate with life, yet complex enough to have gained some of them.

If there was this time of sublife, might it not be that the viruses are remnants that have survived to the present? In that case, might they belong to a special class of objects neither quite living nor quite non-living?

Where can we draw the line? Are the viruses the simplest form of life, the most complex form of non-life, or on the boundary line?

We switch to Wendell Meredith Stanley, who, when he was an undergraduate at Earlham College, in Indiana, played football with great skill and whose ambition it was to be a football coach. However, while visiting the campus of the University of Illinois, he was so incautious as to get into a discussion with a professor of chemistry. This opened his eyes to a new interest, and he never became a football coach. He got his Ph.D. at Illinois, studied in Europe, and in 1931 went to Rockefeller Institute, in New York.

Rockefeller Institute was abuzz at the time with a novel biochemical feat, the crystallization of enzymes.

In a crystal, the component atoms, ions, or molecules are arranged with great regularity. It is this regularity that gives the crystal its properties. Naturally, the larger and more complex a potential constituent particle happens to be, the more difficult it is to get a number of them to take up the necessary regular positions.

Nevertheless, by obtaining a sufficiently pure solution of a particular protein, even its molecules can be forced into crystalline position. In 1926 an enzyme named urease had been crystallized by James Batcheller Sumner, and this was the final proof that enzymes were proteins. In 1930 John Howard Northrop, at Rockefeller Institute, had crystallized the well-known digestive enzyme pepsin.

With all the excitement concerning the crystallization of hitherto uncrystallized biological materials, some of it at the very institution in which Stanley was working, it occurred to him to try to crystallize a virus.

The tobacco mosaic virus seemed a good one to work with. A plant host was easier to work with than an animal host, and tobacco plants could be grown in the Institute's

greenhouse. Stanley grew them, infected them with tobacco
mosaic disease, harvested them, ground up the leaves,
worked with the juice, went through all the steps known to
concentrate and purify proteins.

Eventually, in 1935, from one ton of tobacco plants, he
isolated a few grams of tiny white needles that represented
the crystalline virus.

Stanley's discovery made the front page of the New York
Times, and eventually, in 1946, Sumner, Northrop, and
Stanley shared the Nobel Prize for Medicine and Physiol-
ogy.

The virus crystals showed all the tests for protein, so the
virus was essentially protein. So far, so good. The crystals
would keep at low temperature, as proteins would, and
even after a considerable period of storage they remained
infective. In fact, a given weight of the crystallized virus
was hundreds of times as infective as the typical solutions
that had been worked with.

The fact that the virus could be kept for periods of time
without losing infectivity (dying, in other words) was no
real argument that the virus was not alive. Certain bacteria
can form spores that can remain in suspended animation
longer and withstand harsher conditions than a virus crystal can, yet no one denies that the bacterial spore is alive.

No; it was the fact that viruses could be crystallized that
seemed to argue that they were not living things. Stanley
himself led the fight in favor of the view that viruses, being
subject to crystallization, could not be living.

But is that so? Until 1935, crystals, to be sure, had been
associated entirely with non-living substances. They were
most common in the field of inorganic substances, where
any pure compound could be crystallized, usually without
trouble. Even organic crystals were made up of simple molecules that might be associated with life and might be
found in living tissues, yet could not themselves be considered alive by any stretch of the imagination.

To take it to the pre-1935 extreme, the crystallized enzymes of Sumner and Northrop were made up of arrays of
molecules that were unusually large and complex but that
were still *not* living, by any reasonable criterion.

The moment a virus was crystallized, then, it could be
argued, and was, that a virus was *not* a living organism but
a *non*-living protein molecule.

This seemed reasonable, for it was difficult to conceive of a crystallized organism. Can you imagine a crystalline humanity, for instance?

And yet there was a difference between a virus and a non-living protein molecule. Some protein molecules had as powerful an effect on an organism as a virus would. Some protein molecules killed quickly in very small quantities.

But there was one thing no non-living protein molecule could do that a virus could. The non-living protein molecule could not make more of itself. A small quantity of protein might affect an organism, but then a small quantity of extract from that organism could not affect a second organism in the same way. In the case of the virus, however, infection could go from one organism to another to another to another indefinitely.

Besides, what is the magic of crystallization that separates it from life? The key characteristic of a crystal is the orderly arrangement of its constituent particles, but why cannot those particles be living if they happen to be simple enough in structure? Sufficient simplicity to crystallize and sufficient complexity to be alive are not really mutually exclusive as far as any law of nature is concerned. The two properties were just *assumed* to be mutually exclusive, because until 1935 nothing had been known to possess both. But suppose viruses *do* possess both?

To show that this is not ridiculous, let us be a little more liberal in what we consider crystals and ask again, as I did before, if we could imagine a crystalline humanity. Well, we can! I've seen samples myself!

Columns of soldiers marching along an avenue in review make up a sort of human crystal. The properties of a mass of ten thousand men, in regular rank and file, marching in step, are completely different from the properties of a mass of ten thousand men moving at will as a disorderly mob. Indeed the almost inevitable success of a trained army battalion against an equal number of equally armed civilians is partly the result of the fact that the properties of crystalline man are more suitable to organized warfare than those of mob man.

For that matter, a squadron of aircraft flying in close formation has crystalline properties. Just imagine those same aircraft suddenly breaking formation and taking up random directions. The result could be instant disaster. It requires the crystalline properties of formation to make such close-quarters flight safe.

To my way of thinking, then, the fact that viruses can be crystallized is irrelevant to the larger problem of their living, or non-living, nature. We must look for other evidence, and in 1937, two years after the crystallization, Frederick C. Bawden and Norman W. Pirie, two English biochemists, showed that viruses are *not* entirely protein.

. . . But that's another story—next chapter's story.

eleven

THE CINDERELLA COMPOUND

There is an organization that has computerized scientific citations. In a particular field of science, they will go through the pertinent papers and study the earlier papers to which each refers, and then those to which those earlier papers refer, and so on. Some papers are cited more often than others, and it is possible to work out a network with the help of the computer, that will show the key references: the great watersheds that turn the current of science in a new direction.

Naturally the organization wanted to know if by merely counting and organizing references they were getting a true picture of the advance of science. Therefore they planned to compare their results with the picture presented in some book about the field that gave the historic overlook as seen through the eyes of a keen-eyed scientist. In that way, the computer would be matched against the judgment and intuition of a qualified human expert.

I found out about this because, a number of years ago, the organization wrote to tell me about it. They had decided to use molecular biology as their field for testing (that being just about the most exciting branch of science in the quarter century following World War II), and the book they were planning to use as their standard of comparison was *The Genetic Code*, published in 1962, and written by—all together now—Isaac Asimov.

Naturally I turned green, but before you all die of suspense, let me tell you there was a happy ending. The diagram drawn from my book and the diagram worked out by the computer matched very closely.

They shouted with triumph, because they thought it showed how good their computerization program was. *I* panted with relief, because I wasn't shown up as something less than qualified.

But what interested me most of all was that the computer and I had agreed on the one key finding that served to channel all research in a new direction—yet the scientist who was responsible for that finding remains unknown to the general public. A dozen men in the field have received Nobel prizes for exploring the new road he had pointed out, but not he himself. Some men's names have become almost household words in consequence, but not his.

So let me tell you what it was that that computer and I agreed upon, especially since it will tie in with the previous two chapters. To do that, let's begin by going back a century.

In 1869, a Swiss biochemist, Johann Friedrich Miescher, only twenty-five years old at the time, found that cell nuclei seemed rather resistant to the action of pepsin, an enzyme that acts to break up proteins. From the nuclei, he extracted sizable quantities of something that, whatever it was, was not protein. Considering the source, he called it "nucleir."

Miescher analyzed nuclein and found that it contained both nitrogen and phosphorus. At once, Ernst Felix Hoppe-Seyler, the German biochemist under whom Miescher was working, clamped down on the work and wouldn't let it be published for two years. This was not because he had some foreboding as to the great importance of the discovery; it was because until then only one other compound ever isolated from living tissue had proved to have both nitrogen and phosphorus atoms in its molecule, and that was lecithin—which Hoppe-Seyler himself had discovered.

Hoppe-Seyler, being human as well as a biochemist, didn't like to have the uniqueness of his discovery lightly smashed, and it was only till he himself had completely confirmed Miescher's work that he let the news out of the laboratory.

Eventually nuclein was found to show a pronounced acid reaction, so the name was changed to "nucleic acid."

In 1879 another of Hoppe-Seyler's students, Albrecht Kossel, began to break up the nucleic acid structure and to identify some of the smaller fragments he obtained. He found a number of compounds with molecules composed of rings of both carbon and nitrogen atoms. These had the chemical names of "purines" and "pyrimidines." There were also present in the mixture of fragments sugar molecules that he could not quite identify.

Kossel's work eventually led to the demonstration that the nucleic acid molecule was made up of a string of smaller units called "nucleotides." Each nucleotide consisted of a purine (or a pyrimidine), a sugar, and a phosphorus-oxygen combination called a phosphate.

In a particular nucleic acid molecule there were nucleotides of four different kinds, the important difference lying in the detailed structure of the purine or pyrimidine component. The sugar and the phosphate were the same in all the nucleotides. We needn't bother with the exact chemical names of the different nucleotides. We can just call them 1, 2, 3, and 4.

The man who actually identified the nucleotides as the basic unit of the nucleic-acid structure was a Russian-American chemist named Phoebus Aaron Theodore Levene, who had studied under Kossel. In 1909 he identified the sugar in the nucleic acid as "ribose," a five-carbon-atom sugar that had been studied in the laboratory as a synthetic but had never been found in living tissue.

Then, in 1929, he found that some nucleic acids contained a sugar that was not quite ribose. The new sugar had one oxygen atom less in its molecule than ribose did, so it was called "deoxyribose." Prior to Levene's discovery, deoxyribose had never been known, either in the laboratory or in nature.

Any particular sample of nucleic acid had among its constituent units either ribose or deoxyribose—never both. Chemists therefore began to speak of two kinds of nucleic acid: "ribonucleic acid" and "deoxyribonucleic acid," usually abbreviated as RNA and DNA respectively. Each variety was built up out of nucleotides containing the particular sugar unit characteristic of itself, plus any one of four different types of purines or pyrimidines. Three of these different types were found in each of the two varieties of nucleic acid. The fourth was different in the two but only slightly. We might say that RNA was built up of 1, 2, 3, and 4a, while DNA was built up of 1, 2, 3, and 4b.

Next question: What were the nucleic acids doing in the body; what was their function?

Whatever it was, it had something to do with protein. Kossel had discovered that nucleic acids were associated with protein, and the combination was called "nucleoprotein."

That astonished nobody. In the first third of the nineteenth century, the general classes of compounds contained in living tissue were worked out, and one of those classes was found to be the most complicated by far, and the most fragile. That class seemed made up of just the kind of substances you would expect to be involved in something as versatile and delicate as life.

In 1839 the Dutch chemist Gerardus Johannes Mulder first applied the word "protein" to this complicated group of compounds. The name comes from a Greek word meaning "of first importance." Mulder had used the name to stress the importance of a particular formula he had worked out for certain protein fragments. The formula proved completely unimportant, but in every succeeding decade for a hundred years the aptness of the name became steadily more apparent.

By the time nucleic acids were discovered, no biochemist alive doubted that proteins were "of first importance" and were indeed the key molecules of life. In the twentieth century, new discoveries seemed to make protein's position in this respect more and more secure. Enzymes, which tightly controlled the chemical reactions within the body, proved to be proteins. Hormones, vitamins, antibiotics, trace minerals (poisons, too, for that matter) all seemed to work, one way or another, through their effect on enzymes.

Proteins were *it*.

The various protein molecules were built up of chains of smaller units called "amino acids." There were some twenty varieties of amino acids, each of which was found in almost every protein.

Some protein molecules were made up of nothing more than a chain of amino acids; these were called "simple proteins" in a system of classification worked out, to begin with, by Hoppe-Seyler. Those protein molecules that contained, as more or less minor parts of their molecules, atom groupings that were *not* amino acids, were called "conjugated proteins."

The conjugated proteins were classified further according to the nature of the non-amino-acid portions of the molecule. Where fatty molecules were associated with the protein, the result was a "lipoprotein" or a "lecithoprotein." Carbohydrate attachments gave rise to the classes of "glycoproteins" and "mucoproteins." Where added groups lent color to the protein, the result was "chromoproteins." There were also "phosphoproteins," "metalloproteins," and so on.

One thing biochemists were certain of was that in the case of all the conjugated proteins, it was the protein portion that was the critical part. The non-amino-acid portion, called a "prosthetic group," might have a function, even a crucial function, but somehow it was never considered as more than the tool of the protein portion of the molecule.

The well-known protein hemoglobin, for instance, which carries oxygen from lungs to tissue cells, has as its prosthetic group something called "heme." It is the heme which actually picks up the oxygen and transports it. Nevertheless heme by itself cannot do the job, and abnormal hemoglobins that function badly (as in sickle-cell anemia) don't have anything wrong with the heme, but generally have minor deviations in the amino-acid chains of the protein portion of the molecule.

It is as though you were picturing a man using a brush to paint a picture, or an ax to chop down a tree, or a gun to shoot a duck. The tool used may be essential to the function in question, but there can be no doubt that it is the man who counts every time; that the man can do things without tools (and many a simple protein can do important work), but tools can do nothing without the man.

It was customary to think of prosthetic groups as comparatively small and stable molecules fit to perform some simple function, while the protein was a large and delicate molecule very versatile in its functioning. Because that was the way it clearly was in the case of many conjugated proteins, it was too easily assumed that it had to be that way in the case of nucleoproteins too. Nucleic acid was considered a small and stable molecule that performed its task under the guidance, so to speak, of the protein.

Even as late as 1939, when I was studying organic chemistry at Columbia, I was taught that the nucleic acid molecule was a "tetranucleotide"; that is, a molecule made up of a string of four nucleotides, one of each kind: 1-2-3-4.

A tetranucleotide is middling large for an organic molecule, but it is only about one-fiftieth as large as an average protein molecule. Nucleic acid therefore was easily and casually dismissed as just a protein auxiliary, a kind of Cinderella compound sitting in the ashes while big sister, Protein, went sweeping off to the ball.

Of course no one knew exactly what it was that nucleic acid did, but whatever it was, biochemists were certain, it had to be something routine. They persisted in thinking this even though nucleic acids were found in some pretty important places. It turned out that the chromosomes were made up of nucleoproteins, for instance, and the chromosomes were strings of "genes" that controlled the inheritance of physical characteristics—a pretty basic job.

That didn't shake anyone. Those little tetranucleotides undoubtedly had some cute little genetic function, but whatever that might be, it clearly had to be the protein of the chromosomes that controlled the physical characteristics of the body. Only the protein molecule could be complicated enough to do so.

But then it turned out that the nucleic acid molecule might not be as small as it appeared. In isolating the nucleic acid from cells and tearing it loose from whatever it was hanging onto, it was broken into small fragments. Gentler treatment was devised, which resulted in larger fragments being obtained, and still larger. It began to appear that nucleic acid molecules might be rather on the large side indeed.

That didn't shake anyone, either. If the molecule was large, it just meant that the tetranucleotides repeated themselves: 1-2-3-4-1-2-3-4-1-2 . . . and so on forever, with easy breaking points every four nucleotides, rather like a perforated chain of stamps. And if that were so, the nucleic acids still couldn't be complicated enough to be very important in the living scheme of things.

All this insistence on concentrating on protein and ignoring nucleic acid could only be achieved by more or less ignoring a major and very peculiar finding reported in 1896 by Kossel.

He was studying sperm cells, which are rich in nucleic acid. It isn't hard to see why they must be rich in nucleic acid. Since sperm cells carry substances controlling the inheritance of physical characteristics (else how is it that youngsters so frequently resemble their fathers in this or that aspect of their appearance?), they must contain at least one half set of the paternal chromosomes. (On fertilizing the egg cell, the sperm half set combines with the egg half set and the young organism inherits a full set, half from one parent, half from the other.)

A sperm cell is so tiny, however, that it just barely has room for that half set; consequently it must be nearly pure chromosomal material—which is nucleoprotein—and it should be rich in nucleic acid.

Kossel used salmon sperm (easy to get in quantity) and other fish sperm and discovered that the protein contained in it was quite atypical. The molecules were relatively small and relatively simple. Salmon sperm was extreme in this respect, its chief protein, salmine, being made up of small molecules containing a single amino acid, called arginine, almost to the exclusion of the others. Only 10–20 per cent of the amino acids in salmine were anything other than arginine.

A small protein molecule made up almost entirely of a single amino acid could have none of the vastly intricate complexity of the usual protein molecule, of considerably larger size, made up of up to twenty varieties of amino acids. Could the protein molecules of salmon sperm possibly carry the information required to lead the developing egg in the direction of a large and perfect adult salmon?

Yet, on the other hand, the nucleic acid in salmon sperm seemed to be no different from the nucleic acid in other cells.

We might reason as follows: The sperm cell has to swim like mad to get to an egg cell before some other sperm cell makes it. It cannot afford to carry any useless ballast. It must carry only that which is barely essential for inheritance plus just enough fuel for the race and just enough of whatever molecular machinery is required to effect entrance into the egg cell.

Even the chromosomes the sperm carries have to be cut to the bone. If anything can be eliminated without bad effect, let it be eliminated. Time enough to restore it when the sperm is safely inside the egg with a large supply of raw material to draw upon.

So if most of the protein is eliminated from the sperm contents while nucleic acid remains untouched, it might be deduced that the nucleic acid is essential to the transmission of genetic information and protein is not.

Unfortunately, in order to draw that conclusion biochemists had to abandon a preconception too strong to abandon. Biochemists *knew* that protein was important and nucleic acids weren't, so if they thought about Kossel's findings at all, they decided that the proteins of the sperm, no matter how simple they seemed, somehow managed (once they were safely in the egg cell) to guide the buildup of more complex proteins that *did* suffice to carry genetic information.

As for the nucleic acids, they were too small to carry the information, and that was that. If the sperm cells insisted on hanging on to a full complement of nucleic acids, that was puzzling—but it simply had to be non-crucial.

The break-through came with studies of the pneumococcus, the small germ that causes pneumonia.

There are two strains of these pneumococci, different in appearance through the presence or absence of a carbohydrate capsule. The strain in which the capsule was present looked smooth-surfaced; the one that lacked the capsule was rough-surfaced. They were differentiated as the "S strain" and the "R strain" (for smooth and rough respectively).

The two strains were the same species of bacterium, but the R strain lacked the necessary piece of genetic information required to manufacture the carbohydrate that formed the capsule.

An English bacteriologist, Fred Griffith, had discovered as far back as 1928 that if a sample of S strain that had been boiled till it was quite dead was added to a living colony of R strain, then living S-strain pneumococci eventually began to appear.

What happened? Surely the dead S strain had not come back to life. A logical explanation short of that would be that when the S strain was killed by boiling, the chemical that carried the necessary genetic information for manufacturing the carbohydrate was *not* destroyed, or, at the very least, not entirely destroyed. When the dead S strain was added to the living R strain, the non-destroyed information chemical was somehow incorporated into the structure of at least some of the living R-strain pneumococci, which then began to develop carbohydrate capsules and became S strain.

In 1931 it was found that intact dead bacteria were not needed for the conversion. A quantity of dead S bacteria soaked in some solvent and filtered off would leave behind an "extract" containing some of the material in the cells. This extract (containing not a single scrap of intact cell) would nevertheless serve to transform R strain to S strain.

The question was, What was the nature of the information molecule in the extract that was acting as a "transforming principle"? Surely some kind of protein—but it would have to be an unusual one that was capable of surviving boiling water temperature, which no complex proteins could.

In 1944 an American biochemist, Oswald Theodore Avery, with two coworkers, Colin Munro Macleod and Maclyn McCarty, purified that extract of transforming principle and finally identified its chemical nature.

It was *not* a protein. It was *pure nucleic acid*—DNA, to be more precise.

That simply transformed everything. It could now be seen that it was the DNA component of chromosomes that was important and the protein component that was merely the auxiliary force, and Kossel's findings concerning sperm protein suddenly made brilliant sense. Nucleic acid was now a Cinderella compound that had reached the ball with a coach and horses, coachmen, and a beautiful gown. Prince Biochemistry fell in love with her at once.

Once biochemists finally looked at DNA instead of dismissing it, advances came thick and fast. The true complexity of its structure was worked out in 1953, and the method by which it stored information that guided the formation of specific enzymes was worked out in the 1960s.

How does this apply to viruses, which we left in the previous chapter at the moment of crystallization by Stanley?

In 1937, two years after Stanley's demonstration, two British biochemists, Frederick Charles Bawden and Norman W. Pirie, had found that tobacco mosaic virus (the very one that had been the first to be crystallized) was not entirely protein. Some 6 per cent of it was nucleic acid of the RNA variety.

At the time, nothing was thought of it, since this was

before the Avery break-through. As time passed, other viruses were found to possess nucleic acid components, either RNA or DNA or, sometimes, both. In fact, every undoubted virus has been found to contain nucleic acid.

Once Avery published his paper, that viral nucleic acid was looked on with new eyes too, and fortunately biochemistry in the postwar days had a whole battery of new instrumental techniques at hand. Electron microscopes brought viruses into the field of vision, and when X rays were bounced off them something could be learned about the nature of their molecular structure.

It began to appear that the virus molecule was made up of a container and something contained in that container. The container was composed of protein, and inside it was the contained: a coil of nucleic acid. The protein began to appear rather like a mere capsule, which might contain here and there an enzyme molecule that might help dissolve a cell wall or membrane so that the virus could get inside.

In 1952 two American biochemists, Alfred D. Hershey and M. Chase, tried a crucial experiment with bacteriophage, a rather large and complicated virus that had bacterial cells as its chosen prey.

To begin with, bacteria were grown in media that contained both radioactive sulfur atoms and radioactive phosphorus atoms. Both types of atoms were incorporated into the structure of the bacterial cells; their presence was easily detected by the radiations they emitted.

Bacteriophages were then allowed to infest these "tagged" bacteria, and they, too, incorporated radioactive atoms into their structure. Both sulfur and phosphorus were incorporated into the virus protein. Since nucleic acid contained phosphorus but no sulfur, only radioactive phosphorus was incorporated into the virus nucleic acid.

Finally the tagged bacteriophages were allowed to infest normal untagged bacteria. After enough time had been allowed for the virus to get into the bacterial cells, those cells were carefully rinsed so that anything clinging to the outside of the cells would be washed off. It turned out that only radioactive phosphorus was present inside the cell. There was *no radioactive sulfur* to be detected inside.

That meant that the protein capsule of the virus, which included radioactive sulfur atoms in its structure, could not be inside the cell. It might help provide entry for the virus through enzyme action, but after that was done, *only the nucleic acid part of the virus entered the cell.*

Within the cell the virus nucleic acid brought about the production of more nucleic acid molecules like itself, imposing its own directions on the cell and making use of the cell's own enzymatic machinery for its purposes. Not only did it make more nucleic acid molecules like itself, but it also supervised the production of its own specific protein molecules to make new capsules for itself, at the expense of the cell's own needs. Eventually the bacterial cell was destroyed, and where one bacteriophage had entered, some two hundred were in existence, each ready to invade a new cell.

It must be the nucleic acid, then, that is the truly living part of the virus—and therefore of all creatures, including ourselves.

Furthermore, while ordinary micro-organisms were free-living cells, that could, in some cases, invade and parasitize large organisms made up of numerous cells, viruses were something still more basic. They might be compared to free-living chromosomes capable of invading and parasitizing cells containing numerous chromosomes.

Avery was sixty-seven years old at the time his revolutionary paper was published, and was near the end of his distinguished career in medical research—but not so near that there was no time to appreciate him. He did not die till 1955, eleven years later, and by that time the nucleic-acid triumph was clear and unmistakable, and Avery's finding was clearly the beginning of that triumph.

Yet Avery never got a Nobel prize, and by the clear estimate of both myself and the computer, that was a miscarriage of scientific justice.

E

ABOUT THE THYROID GLAND

twelve

DOCTOR, DOCTOR, CUT MY THROAT

Two months ago, I was persuaded to visit a doctor for a routine medical examination. This was something I resisted, because I generally enjoy perfect health and I don't want any doctor telling me anything different. Eventually, though, pouting and sulking, I let myself be examined.

The doctor said, "You are in perfect health, Isaac."

"I told you so," I said heatedly, "before you started."

"Except," he said, "for a thyroid tumor."

Sure enough, there was a clear bulge in the smooth and youthful lines of my throat when I tilted my head backward. The lump was easily felt, too. Since I had never seen or felt it before, I naturally accused my doctor of putting it there. He smiled indulgently and asked me how I expected him to make a living otherwise.

Let us not go into what took place over the next month or so. Completely overlooking my protests and my sudden interest in the possibility of faith healing, my doctor callously laid his insidious plans for surgery, and on February 12, 1972, I found myself inducted into a hospital room. I watched, with increasing apprehension, as preparations were made for an operation on my throat on the morning of the fifteenth.

Carefully my surgeon (a cheerful rascal with sparkling eyes and a lighthearted chuckle) described the incision he would make from ear to ear, and the slow, four-hour inspection he expected to make of every item in my throat.

I brooded quite a bit, you can imagine.

The night before, they forced me to take a sleeping pill (the first one I had ever taken), and the next morning, they came in and jabbed me thrice with, I presume, three different tranquilizers and/or sedatives. This was designed (it was explained to me) to keep me from climbing the walls as they tried to wheel me down to the carving room.

Alas, they did not count on my peculiar emotional make-up. Inside me there are only two emotions: anxiety and hilarity. When anything is done to remove the anxiety, whether that be a piece of good news, some convivial company, or half a finger of light wine . . . I get hilarious.

So now, very early on the morning of the fifteenth, when I was given an injection of the first tranquilizers I had ever taken, away went my worries, and I was left feeling hilarious.

They put me on the meat cart and, as they wheeled me down the corridors, I waved my arms and sang at the top of my resonant voice. I kept it up all the way to the torture chamber. I distinctly heard one nurse saying to another, "Did you ever come across *this* reaction to medication before?"

They got me to the chopping block at last, tipped the cart, and rolled me down under that big light. And there came my surgeon, with his green mask on and his eyes sparkling jovially.

As soon as I saw him, I reached up, grabbed him, and intoned:

> "Doctor, doctor, with green coat,
> Doctor, doctor, cut my throat.
> And when you've cut it, doctor, then,
> Won't you sew it up again?"

By that time they had managed to jab me with the anesthesia and I lost touch with everything. But, my surgeon told me afterward, he stood there laughing, and wondering if he could get his hand steady enough to make that first incision.*

Well, the operation is over; half my thyroid is gone; and I'm recovering. So let's get *something* out of it. Let me tell you about hormones.

It took a while for mankind to appreciate his nervous system. There are about one hundred thousand miles of nerve fibers in the adult human body, and these focus upon

---

* I've often said that I'd do anything for a laugh, but having a surgeon with his scalpel at my throat and setting his hand to shaking with laughter goes, I think, about five miles beyond the bounds of reason.

the brain and spinal cord, which consist of three pounds of the most complex organization of matter known to man. Yet Aristotle could think of no function for the brain other than to serve as a cooling organ for the blood that passed through it.

In 1766 the Swiss physiologist Albrecht von Haller published his researches. These showed that the stimulation of a nerve leading to a muscle was more effective in producing a muscle contraction than direct stimulation of the muscle would be. He also showed that all nerves led eventually to the brain or spinal cord. He was the founder of neurology, and throughout the nineteenth century, physiologists were increasingly interested in working out the intricacies of the nervous system.

For instance when you eat, the gastric juices of your stomach start to flow while the food is still in your mouth. The glands in the stomach lining know that food is on the way before anything reaches them.

Presumably, this advance "knowledge" on the part of the stomach glands comes through nerve action. The food in the mouth stimulates certain nerves, which carry the message to the brain, which, in turn, sends out a new message along nerves leading to the stomach lining, saying, "Secrete!"

A "presumable" solution, however, cuts no ice in science, as long as the phenomenon can be tested by experiment. In 1889 the Russian physiologist Ivan Petrovich Pavlov therefore set about testing the presumable.

He severed a dog's gullet and led the upper end through an opening in the neck. The dog could then be fed, but the food would drop out through the open gullet and never reach the stomach.* Nevertheless the gastric secretion flowed at the proper moment. Pavlov then cut appropriate nerves to the stomach, or from the mouth and throat, and though the dog then ate as heartily as before, the gastric juices did not flow.

For these and other researches into the physiology of

---

* I recognize the necessity of animal experiments with my mind but not with my heart. When I was doing active, full-time work at a medical school, I did no animal experiments myself, and I always walked out when animals were brought in by anyone else. . . . Yet there are many times when there is simply no substitute for work on an intact organism.

digestion and for establishing the importance of the autonomic nervous system, Pavlov received the Nobel Prize for Medicine and Physiology in 1904.

The nature of the nerve connection between mouth and stomach raised the question of the nature of the nerve connection between stomach and small intestine—the next step along the pathway of the alimentary canal.

When food leaves the stomach and enters the small intestine, a large digestive gland called the pancreas is suddenly galvanized into activity and pours its digestive secretion into the duodenum, the first section of the small intestine. The result is that the stomach contents, as they are squirted into the duodenum, are promptly bathed by a digestive secretion that is well designed to continue the process of digestion from the point where the stomach's work left off.

Here is an example of excellent organization. If the pancreas secreted its juices continuously, that would represent a great waste, for most of the time, they would be expended to no purpose. On the other hand, if the pancreas secreted its juices intermittently (as it does), but did so at either regular or random intervals, the secretions would not be likely to synchronize with food entry into the duodenum, and not only would the secretions then be wasted, but food would remain imperfectly digested.

The fact that food entry and pancreas secretion *are* perfectly synchronized seems to indicate the presence of nerve action. If there were any doubt, Pavlov's experiments on mouth and stomach would surely prove it, by analogy.

However, proofs by analogy are shaky. Direct testing is much preferred. In 1902, then, two English physiologists, William Maddock Bayliss and Ernest Henry Starling, decided to spend some time on the unrewarding task of taking Pavlov's findings one short step farther. (You get the Nobel prize for the first step, a footnote in the history books for the second.)

Bayliss and Starling cut the nerves to the pancreas of a laboratory animal and, presumably, fell off their respective chairs when the pancreas kept on working in perfect synchronization even though it lacked the nerves that would bring it messages.

How could that be?

The stomach contents are unique in the body in that

they are strongly acid. The gastric juice contains not only the enzyme pepsin, which digests protein, but also a surprising quantity of hydrochloric acid, which keeps the gastric juices at the strong acidity required for the most efficient working of the pepsin and does a little protein digestion on its own.* The discovery of this production of hydrochloric acid (a strong mineral acid that would, on the face of it, seem incompatible with life) came in 1824 and was a profound shock to biologists.

The quick discharge of pancreatic juice not only carries on digestive breakdown of the food in the stomach contents but helps to neutralize the acidity, for the pancreatic juice is mildly alkaline. (Failure to take care of the acidity properly is surely a contributing factor to duodenal ulcer.)

With all this in mind, Bayliss and Starling set about trying to find the factor that produced pancreatic synchronization. If it was not a question of nerve action, was it something in the stomach contents itself? If it was, what could it be but that distinctive characteristic, the acidity of those contents? To begin with, why not separate the acidity from all the rest, and test it alone?

They therefore introduced a small quantity of hydrochloric acid into the small intestine at a time when the animal was fasting and its stomach was empty. Promptly the pancreas, without nerve attachments, did its job with great vigor, and the empty duodenum was aslosh with pancreatic juice.

If, then, it was the acidification of the duodenal lining that triggered the pancreas, Bayliss and Starling decided to carry things one step farther. They obtained a section of the duodenum from a newly killed animal and soaked it in hydrochloric acid. Something in that duodenum was now converted (perhaps) into the triggering factor (whatever it was).

If the message was not carried by nerves, it might well be carried by the blood, which was the one moving tissue of the body, and connecting every organ in the body with every other—specifically, the duodenum with the pancreas.

---

* It is a perennial puzzle that digestive enzymes don't digest the linings of the alimentary canal. For that matter, how is it that hydrochloric acid doesn't wreak havoc on the stomach lining? Whatever the protective device is, it isn't perfect, and when it fails, a gastric ulcer can result.

In that case, suppose a small quantity of the acid in which the duodenal lining had been soaked were injected into the blood stream of a living animal. If the acid now had the triggering factor in it, then . . . what would happen?

A fasting animal was chosen, one with nothing in the duodenum, neither gastric content nor artificially inserted hydrochloric acid. Nevertheless, because of the injection of whatever-it-was into the blood stream, the pancreas sprang into action.

The conclusion seemed unavoidable. The intestinal lining reacted to acidity by producing a chemical that was secreted into the blood stream. The blood stream carried the chemical throughout the body to every organ, including the pancreas. When the chemical reached the pancreas, it somehow stimulated that organ into secreting its juice.

Bayliss and Starling named the substance produced by the intestinal lining "secretin," for obvious reasons. Assuming that there might be other examples of such substances in the body, Bayliss in the course of a lecture in 1905 suggested a general name. He called these chemical messengers hormones, from a Greek word meaning "I arouse," since hormones roused some dormant organ or organs to activity.

Bayliss and Starling never got a Nobel prize for their discovery of hormones, though in my opinion their work was of more fundamental importance than that of Pavlov. Perhaps Pavlov thought this too, for after the discovery of hormones, he left the field of orthodox digestive physiology and began to study the various ways salivation in dogs could be stimulated. In doing so, he worked out the details of the conditioned response in the 1920s, and for this he more clearly deserves the Nobel prize than for the research for which he actually received it.

Although hormones were discovered after nerve action, it is the hormone that is the older and more basic messenger. Very simple animals and all plants lack a nervous system and yet manage to get along on the basis of chemical messages alone.

In fact we might suppose that nerves developed in the more complex animals because the necessity of swift muscular motion (plants and very simple animals have no muscles, either) placed a premium upon swift sensations and swift reactions.

The shift from hormones to nerves is somehow analogous (it seems to me) to the shift from mechanical interaction to electronic interaction in man's technology. Control through electron flow is much quicker and more delicate than control through intermeshing gears. The brain would, by this analogy, resemble the central control room, where distant objects are adjusted delicately by observing the reading of pivoting needles and flashing lights and then closing appropriate contacts.

In fact, one would ask why hormones continued to function in organisms in which the nerve network and the brain were highly developed. Why do we bother with the horse-and-buggy system of carrying chemicals by the blood stream to every part of the body in the hope that some one part will make use of it, when we have available the jet-plane system of nerves carrying their messages quickly and *specifically* to the places where needed?

One answer is that evolution is a conservative process, one that tends to hold on to everything possible, modifying and adjusting rather than abandoning.

Then, too, hormones have their advantages. For one thing, they can control portions of the physiology without bothering the nervous system, which is loaded down as it is and would welcome any respite. For another, hormones manage to keep a permanent adjustment of some factors in a simple and automatic way that requires little investment of effort on the part of the body generally.

For instance, secretin is produced by the action of acidity on the duodenal lining. The secretin, once produced, stimulates the pancreas into discharging pancreatic juice into the duodenum. The mildly alkaline pancreatic juice quickly diminishes the acidity of the stomach contents that have entered the duodenum. And the decline of acidity cuts down the production of secretin, which in turn cuts down pancreatic activity.

In short, the formation of the secretin stimulates an action that brings about a halt in the formation of secretion. It is a self-limiting process. There is "feedback." The result is that the flow of pancreatic juice is not merely initiated by hormone activity, but the rate of that flow is carefully adjusted from moment to moment by hormone activity and the feed-back it produces.

As the twentieth century wore on, other hormones were discovered, some of which were produced by small organs that had that production as their only function. One of these—and the one that has a morbid interest for me right now—is a yellowish-red mass of glandular tissue about two inches high, a bit more than two inches wide, and weighing an ounce or a little less. It exists in two lobes, one on either side of the windpipe, with a narrow connecting band running in front of the windpipe just on the bottom boundary of the Adam's apple.

The Adam's apple is more properly called the thyroid (from a Greek word meaning shieldlike) cartilage. This is in reference to the large, oblong shields carried by Homeric and pre-Homeric warriors. These had a notch on top where the head might cautiously emerge to survey the situation. There is just such a notch on top of the Adam's apple, hence the name.

The glandular tissue in the neighborhood of the Adam's apple borrows that name and is called the thyroid gland.

Before the end of the nineteenth century the function of the thyroid gland was not known. It was somewhat more prominent in women than in men, and one opinion maintained that the thyroid was nothing more than padding designed to fill out the neck (of women particularly) and make it plumply attractive. There were regions in Europe where the thyroid (again particularly in women) was enlarged beyond the normal size, and this, which meant a somewhat swollen neck, was accepted as an enhancement of beauty, rather than otherwise.

This enlargement, called a goiter (from an old French word for throat) was sometimes associated with one of two opposing sets of symptoms. Some goiterous individuals were dull, listless, and apathetic, while others were nervous, tense, and unstable. (Through hindsight, we know that the thyroid controls the metabolic rate of the body, the general speed of the body's motor, so to speak. An enlarged thyroid all parts of which are functioning, races the motor; while an enlarged thyroid where few parts are functioning, throttles it down to a murmur.)

In 1896 a German chemist, Eugen Baumann, located iodine in the thyroid gland. This was surprising, for iodine had not been known to be a component of living tissue before. What's more, no other element has ever been found to be so lopsidedly present in an organism, either before or since. The concentration of iodine in the thyroid is sixty thousand times as great as in the rest of the body.

In 1905 an American physicist, David Marine, just out of medical school, brooded over this fact. Iodine was not a common element and was obtained chiefly from sea organisms, which concentrated it out of its very dilute presence in ocean water. Salt spray from the ocean might scatter thin quantities of iodine over the land, but there were places on land where the iodine content of the soil was very low, and, behold, those were the places where goiter was particularly common.

Perhaps the absence of iodine resulted in less-than-normal functioning of the thyroid, which tried to correct the situation (uselessly) by enlarging itself. Marine experimented on animals, depriving them of iodine and producing both goiter and the dull listlessness characteristic (we now know) of an underfunctioning thyroid. He cured the condition by adding small quantities of iodine to their food.

By 1916 he felt confident enough to experiment on young people and was able to show that traces of iodine in the food cut down the incidence of goiter in humans. He then launched a campaign to add small quantities of iodine compounds to the water supply of Cleveland, a process that virtually eliminated goiter. The campaign, meeting the usual resistance from those who preferred goiter to change, took ten years.

In general, the thyroid hormone is produced in proportion to need. If the rate of metabolism needs to be high, thyroid hormone is consumed rapidly and the blood level falls. This fall and the consequent less-than-normal level of the hormone in the blood stimulates heightened activity on the part of the thyroid and keeps the level normal despite the greater use. If the rate of metabolism needs to be low, thyroid hormone is but slowly consumed and the blood level rises. This, we might suppose, would inhibit thyroid activity and slow it down.

We might suppose that the high or low level of thyroid hormone in the blood would affect the thyroid gland directly, but not so. Since the thyroid gland produces the hormone, the blood concentration in its own vicinity would always be higher than in the remainder of the body and would respond less rapidly to changes in metabolic rate. The thyroid gland, if it relied on itself and its immediate surroundings, would receive but a blurred and distorted picture of what was going on. (It would be something like an executive judging the worth of his ideas by the opinions of his yes-men.)

A better solution is to set a separate gland to work, one in a different part of the body. In this case, it is the pituitary gland, situated at the base of the brain.

The pituitary produces a number of hormones, one of which is called the thyroid-stimulating hormone, a phrase often abbreviated as TSH.

TSH, though poured into the blood stream generally, as all hormones are, affects only the thyroid. TSH stimulates it and causes it to increase its production of thyroid hormone. When the blood level of thyroid hormone falls too low, this stimulates the production of TSH by the pituitary, which is far enough from the thyroid so that the blood passing through it accurately reflects the thyroid-hormone level in the body generally.

The increase of TSH stimulates the activity of the thyroid gland. The level of thyroid hormone in the blood then rises, and this depresses pituitary activity. As TSH goes down, so does thyroid activity, and as the thyroid hormone goes down, up goes TSH, and therefore up goes thyroid activity.

The result of the thyroid and the pituitary working together is that the thyroid hormone is kept at a markedly steady level in the blood stream despite the rise and fall of the body's need for the hormone at different times and under different conditions of activity.

Let's see, now, how all this affects me.

The fact that half my thyroid is gone is not in itself a terribly serious thing. The remaining half of my thyroid, forced to work twice as hard as usual by the unrelenting demands of my pituitary, would hypertrophy (that is, grow larger) and easily produce all the thyroid hormone I would need.

This, however, is viewed without enthusiasm by my doctors. One half of my thyroid has already displayed undisciplined growth and has had to be taken out. Given that, the rest of my thyroid can't be trusted to know how to hypertrophy with discretion. It must be dealt with in a spirit of keen suspicion.

The result is that I am going to be taking thyroid pills for the rest of my life. The thyroid hormone is a modified amino acid that is not subject to digestion but is absorbed directly. This means that I don't have to inject the stuff as I would if it were insulin I needed. Instead I just swallow it. In addition, since thyroid pills are prepared from the thyroid glands of slaughtered livestock and there is no other use for those glands, the pills are relatively cheap and readily available.

With a constant supply of thyroid hormone entering my body from the outside, my pituitary gland (unable to differentiate the thyroid hormone in a pill from the thyroid hormone in my very own thyroid gland) lowers its production of TSH and keeps it lowered.

With TSH chronically lowered, what is left of my thyroid gland remains understimulated and, far from growing, shrinks. As a result, the chance of my developing a tumor on the left to match the one I once had on my right is significantly decreased.

So there you are, and there I am, and I don't like it, but the universe doesn't care whether I like it or not, and I can only be thankful it was no worse. And now, barring further incidents of a distressing nature, it may well be that I will continue writing these essays for some time to come.

I hope.

F

ABOUT SOCIETY

thirteen

LOST IN NON-TRANSLATION

At the Noreascon (the 29th World Science Fiction Convention), which was held in Boston on the Labor Day weekend of 1971, I sat on the dais, of course, since, as the Bob Hope of science fiction, it is my perennial duty to hand out the Hugos. On my left was my daughter, Robyn, sixteen, blond, blue-eyed, shapely, and beautiful. (No, that last adjective is not a father's proud partiality. Ask anyone.)

My old friend Clifford D. Simak was guest of honor, and he began his talk by introducing, with thoroughly justified pride, his two children, who were in the audience. A look of alarm instantly crossed Robyn's face.

"Daddy," she whispered urgently, knowing full well my capacity for inflicting embarrassment, "are you planning to introduce *me*?"

"Would that bother you, Robyn?" I asked.

"Yes, it would."

"Then I won't, I said, and patted her hand reassuringly.

She thought a while. Then she said, "Of course, Daddy, if you have the urge to refer, in a casual sort of way, to your beautiful daughter, that would be all right."

So you can bet I did just that, while she allowed her eyes to drop in a charmingly modest way.

But I couldn't help but think of the blond, blue-eyed stereotype or Nordic beauty that has filled Western literature ever since the blond, blue-eyed Germanic tribes took over the western portions of the Roman Empire, fifteen centuries ago, and set themselves up as an aristocracy.

. . . And of the manner in which that has been used to subvert one of the clearest and most important lessons in the Bible—a subversion that contributes its little bit to the serious crisis that today faces the world, and the United States in particular.

In line with my penchant for beginning at the beginning, come back with me to the sixth century B.C. A party of Jews have returned from Babylonian Exile to rebuild the Temple at Jerusalem, which Nebuchadrezzar had destroyed seventy years before.

During the Exile, under the guidance of the prophet Ezekiel the Jews had firmly held to their national identity by modifying, complicating, and idealizing their worship of Yahweh into a form that was directly ancestral to the Judaism of today. (In fact Ezekiel is sometimes called "the father of Judaism.")

This meant that when the exiles returned to Jerusalem, they faced a religious problem. There were people who, all through the period of the Exile, had been living in what had once been Judah, and who worshipped Yahweh in what they considered the correct, time-honored ritual. Because their chief city (with Jerusalem destroyed) was Samaria, the returning Jews called them Samaritans.

The Samaritans rejected the newfangled modifications of the returning Jews, and the Jews abhorred the old-fashioned beliefs of the Samaritans. Between them arose an undying hostility, the kind that is exacerbated because the differences in belief are comparatively small.

In addition, there were, of course, also living in the land, those who worshipped other gods altogether—Ammonites, Edomites, Philistines, and so on.

The pressures on the returning band of Jews were not primarily military, for the entire area was under the more or less beneficent rule of the Persian Empire, but it was social, and perhaps even stronger for that. To maintain a strict ritual in the face of overwhelming numbers of nonbelievers is difficult, and the tendency to relax that ritual was almost irresistible. Then, too, young male returnees were attracted to the women at hand and there were intermarriages. Naturally, to humor the wife, ritual was further relaxed.

But then, possibly as late as about 400 B.C., a full century after the Second Temple had been built, Ezra arrived in Jerusalem. He was a scholar of the Mosaic law, which had been edited and put into final form in the course of the Exile. He was horrified at the backsliding and put through a tub-thumping revival. He called the people together, led them in chanting the law and expounding upon it, raised their religious fervor, and called for confession of sins and renewal of faith.

One thing he demanded most rigorously was the abandonment of all non-Jewish wives and their children. Only so could the holiness of strict Judaism be maintained, in his view. To quote the Bible (and I will use the recent New English Bible for the purpose):

"Ezra the priest stood up and said, 'You have committed an offence in marrying foreign wives and have added to Israel's guilt. Make your confession now to the Lord the God of your fathers and do his will, and separate yourselves from the foreign population and from your foreign wives.' Then all the assembled people shouted in reply, 'Yes; we must do what you say. . . .'" (Ezra 10:10–12)

From that time on, the Jews as a whole began to practice an exclusivism, a voluntary separation from others, a multiplication of peculiar customs that further emphasized their separateness; and all of this helped them maintain their identity through all the miseries and catastrophes that were to come, through all the crises, and through exiles and persecutions that fragmented them over the face of the Earth.

The exclusivism, to be sure, also served to make them socially indigestible and imparted to them a high social visibility that helped give rise to conditions that made exiles and persecutions more likely.

Not everyone among the Jews adhered to this policy of exclusivism. There were some who believed that all men were equal in the sight of God and that no one should be excluded from the community on the basis of group identity alone.

And one who believed this (but who is forever nameless) attempted to present this case in the form of a short piece of historical fiction. In this fourth-century-B.C. tale the heroine was Ruth, a Moabite woman. (The tale was presented as having taken place in the time of the judges, so the traditional view was that it was written by the prophet Samuel in the eleventh century B.C. No modern student of the Bible believes this.)

Why a Moabite woman, by the way?

It seems that the Jews, returning from Exile, had traditions concerning their initial arrival at the borders of Canaan under first Moses, then Joshua, nearly a thousand

years before. At that time, the small nation of Moab, which
lay east of the lower course of the Jordan and of the Dead
Sea, understandably alarmed at the incursion of tough desert raiders, took steps to oppose them. Not only did they
prevent the Israelites from passing through their territory,
but, tradition had it, they called in a seer, Balaam, and
asked him to use his magical abilities to bring misfortune
and destruction upon the invaders.

That failed, and Balaam, on departing, was supposed to
have advised the king of Moab to let the Moabite girls lure
the desert raiders into liaisons, which might subvert their
stern dedication to their task. The Bible records the following:

"When the Israelites were in Shittim, the people began to
have intercourse with Moabite women, who invited them
to the sacrifices offered to their gods; and they ate the sac-
rificial food and prostrated themselves before the gods of
Moab. The Israelites joined in the worship of the Baal of
Peor, and the Lord was angry with them." (Numbers
25:1–3)

As a result of this, "Moabite women" became the quin-
tessence of the type of outside influence that by sexual attraction tried to subvert pious Jews. Indeed Moab and the
neighboring kingdom to the north, Ammon, were singled
out in the Mosaic code:

"No Ammonite or Moabite, even down to the tenth generation, shall become a member of the assembly of the
Lord . . . because they did not meet you with food and
water on your way out of Egypt, and because they hired
Balaam . . . to revile you. . . . You shall never seek their
welfare or their good all your life long." (Deuteronomy
23:3–4, 6)

And yet there were times in later history when there was
friendship between Moab and at least some men of Israel,
possibly because they were brought together by some common enemy.

For instance, shortly before 1000 B.C. Israel was ruled
by Saul. He had held off the Philistines, conquered the
Amalekites, and brought Israel to its greatest pitch of
power to that point. Moab naturally feared his expansionist
policies and so befriended anyone rebelling against Saul.
Such a rebel was the Judean warrior David of Bethlehem.
When David was pressed hard by Saul and had retired to a

fortified stronghold, he used Moab as a refuge for his family.

"David . . . said to the king of Moab, 'Let my father and mother come and take shelter with you until I know what God will do for me.' So he left them at the court of the king of Moab, and they stayed there as long as David was in his stronghold." (1 Samuel 22:3–4)

As it happened, David eventually won out, became king first of Judah, then of all Israel, and established an empire that took in the entire east coast of the Mediterranean, from Egypt to the Euphrates, with the Phoenician cities independent but in alliance with him. Later, Jews always looked back to the time of David and of his son Solomon as a golden age, and David's position in Jewish legend and thought was unassailable. David founded a dynasty that ruled over Judah for four centuries, and the Jews never stopped believing that some descendant of David would yet return to rule over them again in some idealized future time.

Yet, on the basis of the verses describing David's use of Moab as a refuge for his family, there may have arisen a tale to the effect that there was a Moabite strain in David's ancestry. Apparently, the author of the Book of Ruth determined to make use of this tale to point up the doctrine of non-exclusivism by using the supremely hated Moabite woman as his heroine.

The Book of Ruth tells of a Judean family of Bethlehem—a man, his wife, and two sons—who are driven by famine to Moab. There the two sons marry Moabite girls, but after a space of time all three men die, leaving the three women—Naomi, the mother-in-law, and Ruth and Orpah, the two daughters-in-law—as survivors.

Those were times when women were chattels and when unmarried women, without a man to own them and care for them, could subsist only on charity. (Hence the frequent biblical injunction to care for widows and orphans.)

Naomi determined to return to Bethlehem, where kinsmen might possibly care for her, but urged Ruth and Orpah to remain in Moab. She does not say, but we might plausibly suppose she is thinking, that Moabite girls would have a rough time of it in Moab-hating Judah.

Orpah remains in Moab, but Ruth refuses to leave Naomi, saying "Do not urge me to go back and desert you. . . .

Where you go, I will go, and where you stay, I will stay.
Your people shall be my people, and your God my God.
Where you die I will die, and there I will be buried. I
swear a solemn oath before the Lord your God: nothing
but death shall divide us." (Ruth 1:16–17)

Once in Bethlehem, the two were faced with the direst
poverty and Ruth volunteered to support herself and her
mother-in-law by gleaning in the fields. It was harvesttime
and it was customary to allow any stalks of grain that fell
to the ground in the process of gathering to remain there to
be collected by the poor. This gleaning was a kind of welfare program for those in need. It was, however, back-
breaking work, and any young woman, particularly a Moabite, who engaged in it, underwent certain obvious risks at
the hands of the lusty young reapers. Ruth's offer was simply heroic.

As it happened, Ruth gleaned in the lands of a rich Judean farmer named Boaz, who coming to oversee the work,
noticed her working tirelessly. He asked after her, and his
reapers answered, "She is a Moabite girl . . . who had
just come back with Naomi from the Moabite country."
(Ruth 2:6)

Boaz speaks kindly to her and Ruth says, "Why are you
so kind as to take notice of me when I am only a for-
eigner?" (Ruth 2:10) Boaz explains that he has heard how
she has forsaken her own land for love of Naomi and how
hard she must work to take care of her.

As it turned out, Boaz was a relative of Naomi's dead
husband, which must be one reason why he was touched by
Ruth's love and fidelity. Naomi, on hearing the story, had
an idea. In those days, if a widow was left childless, she
had the right to expect her dead husband's brother to
marry her and offer her his protection. If the dead husband
had no brother, some other relative would fulfill the task.

Naomi was past the age of childbearing, so she could not
qualify for marriage, which in those days centered about
children; but what about Ruth? To be sure, Ruth was a
Moabite woman and it might well be that no Judean would
marry her, but Boaz had proven kind. Naomi therefore in-
structed Ruth how to approach Boaz at night and, without
crudely seductive intent, appeal for his protection.

Boaz, touched by Ruth's modesty and helplessness,
promised to do his duty, but pointed out that there was a

kinsman closer than he and that, by right, this other kinsman had to have his chance first.

The very next day, Boaz approached the other kinsman and suggested that he buy some property in Naomi's charge and, along with it, take over another responsibility. Boaz said, "On the day when you acquire the field from Naomi, you also acquire Ruth the Moabitess, the dead man's wife. . . ." (Ruth 4:5)

Perhaps Boaz carefully stressed the adjectival phrase "the Moabitess," for the other kinsman drew back at once. Boaz therefore married Ruth, who in time bore him a son. The proud and happy Naomi held the child in her bosom and her women friends said to her, "The child will give you new life and cherish you in your old age; for your daughter-in-law who loves you, who has proved better to you than seven sons, has borne him." (Ruth 4:15)

This verdict of Judean women on Ruth, a woman of the hated land of Moab, in a society that valued sons infinitely more than daughters, a verdict that she "has proved better to you than seven sons" is the author's moral—that there are nobility and virtue in all groups and that none must be excluded from consideration in advance simply because of their group identification.

And then, to clinch the argument for any Judean so nationalistic as to be impervious to mere idealism, the story concludes: "Her neighbors gave him a name: 'Naomi has a son,' they said; 'we will call him Obed.' He was the father of Jesse, the father of David." (Ruth 4:17)

Where would Israel have been, then, if there had been an Ezra present then to forbid the marriage of Boaz with a "foreign wife"?

Where does that leave us? That the Book of Ruth is a pleasant story, no one will deny. It is almost always referred to as a "delightful idyl" or words to that effect. That Ruth is a most successful characterization of a sweet and virtuous woman is beyond dispute.

In fact everyone is so in love with the story and with Ruth that the whole point is lost. It is, by right, a tale of tolerance for the despised, of love for the hated, of the reward that comes of brotherhood. By mixing the genes of mankind, by forming the hybrid, great men will come.

The Jews included the Book of Ruth in the canon partly because it is so wonderfully told a tale but mostly (I suspect) because it gives the lineage of the great David, a lineage that is *not* given beyond David's father, Jesse, in the soberly historic books of the Bible that anteceded Ruth. But the Jews remained, by and large, exclusivistic and did not learn the lesson of universalism preached by the Book of Ruth.

Nor have people taken its lesson to heart since. Why should they, since every effort is made to wipe out that lesson? The story of Ruth has been retold any number of times, from children's tales to serious novels. Even movies have been made of it. Ruth herself must have been pictured in hundreds of illustrations. And in every illustration I have ever seen, she is presented as blond, blue-eyed, shapely, and beautiful—the perfect Nordic stereotype I referred to at the beginning of the article.

For goodness' sake, why shouldn't Boaz have fallen in love with her? What great credit was there in marrying her? If a girl like that had fallen at your feet and asked you humbly to do your duty by her and kindly marry her, you would probably have done it like a shot.

Of course she was a Moabite woman, but so what? What does the word "Moabite" mean to you? Does it arouse any violent reaction? Are there many Moabites among your acquaintances? Have your children been chased by a bunch of lousy Moabites lately? Have they been reducing property values in your neighborhood? When was the last time you heard someone say, "Got to get those rotten Moabites out of here. They just fill up the welfare rolls."

In fact, judging by the way Ruth is drawn, Moabites are English aristocrats and their presence would raise property values.

The trouble is that the one word that is *not translated* in the Book of Ruth is the key word "Moabite," and as long as it is not translated, the point is lost; it is lost in nontranslation.

The word Moabite really means "someone of a group that receives from us and deserves from us nothing but hatred and contempt." How should this word be translated into a single word that means the same thing to, say, many modern Greeks? . . . Why, "Turk." And to many modern Turks? . . . Why, "Greek." And to many modern white Americans? . . . Why, "Black."

To get the proper flavor of the Book of Ruth, suppose

we think of Ruth not as a Moabite woman but as a Black woman.

Reread the story of Ruth and translate Moabite to Black every time you see it. Naomi (imagine) is coming back to the United States with her two Black daughters-in-law. No wonder she urges them not to come with her. It *is* a marvel that Ruth so loved her mother-in-law that she was willing to face a society that hated her unreasoningly and to take the risk of gleaning in the face of leering reapers who could not possibly suppose they need treat her with any consideration whatever.

And when Boaz asked who she was, don't read the answer as "She is a Moabite girl," but as "She is a Black girl." More likely, in fact, the reapers might have said to Boaz something that was the equivalent of (if you'll excuse the language), "She is a nigger girl."

Think of it that way and you find the whole point is found in translation and only in translation. Boaz' action in being willing to marry Ruth because she was virtuous (and not because she was a Nordic beauty) takes on a kind of nobility. The neighbors' decision that she was better to Naomi than seven sons becomes something that could have been forced out of them only by overwhelming evidence to that effect. And the final stroke that out of this miscegenation was born none other than the great David is rather breath-taking.

We get something similar in the New Testament. On one occasion a student of the law asks Jesus what must be done to gain eternal life, and answers his own question by saying, "Love the Lord your God with all your heart, with all your soul, with all your strength, and with all your mind; and your neighbor as yourself." (Luke 10:27)

These admonitions are taken from the Old Testament, of course. That last bit about your neighbor comes from a verse that says, "You shall not seek revenge, or cherish anger towards your kinsfolk; you shall love your neighbour as a man like yourself." (Leviticus 19:18)

(The New English Bible translations sounds better to me here than the King James's: "Thou shalt love thy neighbour as thyself." Where is the saint who can truly feel another's pain or ecstasy precisely as he feels his own? We must not ask too much. But if we simply grant that some-

one else is "a man like yourself," then he can be treated
with decency at least. It is when we refuse to grant even
this and talk of another as our inferior that contempt and
cruelty come to seem natural, and even laudable.)

Jesus approves the lawyer's saying, and the lawyer
promptly asks, "And who is my neighbour?" (Luke 10:29)
After all, the verse in Leviticus first speaks of refraining
from revenge and anger toward *kinsfolk;* might not, then,
the concept of "neighbour" be restricted to kinsfolk, to
one's own kind, only?

In response, Jesus replies with perhaps the greatest of the
parables—of a traveler who fell in with robbers, who was
mugged and robbed and left half dead by the road. Jesus
goes on, "It so happened that a priest was going down by
the same road; but when he saw him, he went past on the
other side. So too a Levite came to the place, and when he
saw him went past on the other side. But a Samaritan who
was making the journey came upon him, and when he saw
him was moved to pity. He went up and bandaged his
wounds, bathing them with oil and wine. Then he lifted
him on to his own beast, brought him to an inn, and
looked after him there." (Luke 10:31–34)

Then Jesus asks who the traveler's neighbor was, and the
lawyer is forced to say, "The one who showed him kind-
ness." (Luke 10:37)

This is known as the Parable of the Good Samaritan,
even though nowhere in the parable is the rescuer called a
good Samaritan, merely a Samaritan.

The force of the parable is entirely vitiated by the common phrase "good" Samaritan, for that has cast a false light
on who the Samaritans were. In a free-association test, say
"Samaritan" and probably every person being tested will
answer, "Good." It has become so imprinted in all our
brains that Samaritans are good that we take it for granted
that a Samaritan would act like that and wonder why Jesus
is making a point of it.

We forget who the Samaritans were, in the time of Jesus!

To the Jews, they were *not* good. They were hated, despised, contemptible heretics with whom no good Jew
would have anything to do. Again, the whole point is lost
through non-translation.

Suppose, instead, that it is a white traveler in Mississippi
who has been mugged and left half dead. And suppose it

was a minister and a deacon who passed by and refused to "become involved." And suppose it was a Black sharecropper who stopped and took care of the man.

Now ask yourself: Who was the neighbor whom you must love as though he were a man like yourself if you are to be saved?

The Parable of the Good Samaritan clearly teaches that there is nothing parochial in the concept "neighbor," that you cannot confine your decency to your own group and your own kind. All mankind, right down to those you most despise, are your neighbors.

Well, then, we have in the Bible two examples—in the Book of Ruth and in the Parable of the Good Samaritan— of teachings that are lost in non-translation, yet are terribly applicable to us today.

The whole world over, there are confrontations between sections of mankind defined by race, nationality, economic philosophy, religion, or language as belonging to different groups, so that one is not "neighbor" to the other.

These more or less arbitrary differences among peoples who are members of a single biological species are terribly dangerous and nowhere more so than here in the United States, where the most perilous confrontation (I need not tell you) is between White and Black.

Next to the population problem generally, mankind faces no danger greater than this confrontation, particularly in the United States.

It seems to me that more and more, each year, both Whites and Blacks are turning, in anger and hatred, to violence. I see no reasonable end to the steady escalation but an actual civil war.

In such a civil war, the Whites, with a preponderance of numbers and an even greater preponderance of organized power would, in all likelihood, "win." They would do so, however, at an enormous material cost and, I suspect, at a fatal spiritual one.

And why? Is it so hard to recognize that we are all neighbors, after all? Can we, on both sides—on *both* sides—find no way of accepting the biblical lesson?

Or if quoting the Bible sounds too mealymouthed and if repeating the words of Jesus seems too pietistic, let's put it another way, a practical way:

Is the privilege of feeling hatred so luxurious a sensation that it is worth the material and spiritual hell of a White-Black civil war?

If the answer is really "Yes," then one can only despair.

fourteen

THE ANCIENT AND THE ULTIMATE

About three weeks ago (as I write this) I attended a seminar in upstate New York, one that dealt with communications and society. The role assigned was a small one, but I spent four full days there, so I had a chance to hear all the goings on.*

The very first night I was there I heard a particularly good lecture by an extraordinarily intelligent and charming gentleman who was involved in the field of TV cassettes. He made out an attractive and, to my way of thinking, irrefutable case in favor of the cassettes as representing the communications wave of the future—or, anyway, one of the waves.

He pointed out that for the commercial programs intended to support the fearfully expensive TV stations and the frightfully avid advertisers, audiences in the tens of millions were an absolute necessity.

As we all know, the only things that have a chance of pleasing twenty-five to fifty million different people are those that carefully avoid giving any occasion for offense. Anything that will add spice or flavor will offend someone and lose.

So it's the unflavored pap that survives, not because it pleases, but because it gives no occasion for displeasing. (Well, some people, you and I, for instance, are displeased, but when advertising magnates add up the total number of you and me and others like us, the final sum sends them into fits of scornful laughter.)

Cassettes, however, that please specialized tastes are selling content only, and don't have to mask it with a spurious

* Lest you think I was violating my principles by taking a vacation, I might as well tell you that I brought my hand typewriter with me, and used it, too.

and costly polish or the presence of a high-priced entertainment star. Present a cassette on chess strategy with chessmen symbols moving on a chessboard, and nothing else is needed to sell x number of cassettes to x number of chess enthusiasts. If enough is charged per cassette to cover the expense of making the tape (plus an honest profit) and if the expected number of sales are made, then all is well. There may be unexpected flops, but there may be unexpected best sellers too.

In short, the television-cassette business will rather resemble the book-publishing business.

The speaker made this point perfectly clear, and when he said, "The manuscript of the future will not be a badly typed sheaf of papers but a neatly photographed sequence of images," I could not help but fidget.

Maybe the fidgeting made me conspicuous as I sat there in the front row, for the speaker then added, "And men like Isaac Asimov will find themselves outmoded and replaced."

Naturally I jumped—and everybody laughed cheerfully at the thought of my being outmoded and replaced.

Two days later, the speaker scheduled for that evening made a trans-Atlantic call to say he was unavoidably detained in London, so the charming lady who was running the seminar came to me and asked me sweetly if I would fill in.

Naturally I said I hadn't prepared anything, and naturally she said that it was well known that I needed no preparation to give a terrific talk, and naturally I melted at the first sign of flattery, and naturally I got up that evening, and naturally I gave a terrific talk.* It was all very natural.

I can't possibly tell you exactly what I said, because, like all my talks, it was off the cuff, but, as I recall, the essence was something like this:

The speaker of two days before having spoken of TV cassettes and having given a fascinating and quite brilliant picture of a future in which cassettes and satellites dominated the communications picture, I was now going to make use of my science-fiction expertise to look still further ahead

* Well, everybody said so.

and see how cassettes could be further improved and refined, and made still more sophisticated.

In the first place, the cassettes, as demonstrated by the speaker, needed a rather bulky and expensive piece of apparatus to decode the tape, to place images on a television screen, and to put the accompanying sound on a speaker.

Obviously we would expect this auxiliary equipment to be made smaller, lighter, and more mobile. Ultimately we would expect it to disappear altogether and become part of the cassette itself.

Secondly, energy is required to convert the information contained in the cassette into image and sound, and this places a strain on the environment. (All use of energy does that, and while we can't avoid using energy, there is no value in using more than we must.)

Consequently we can expect the amount of energy required to translate the cassette to decrease. Ultimately we would expect it to reach a value of zero and disappear.

Therefore we can imagine a cassette that is completely mobile and self-contained. Though it requires energy in its formation, it requires no energy and no special equipment for its use thereafter. It needn't be plugged into the wall; it needs no battery replacements; it can be carried with you wherever you feel most comfortable about viewing it: in bed, in the bathroom, in a tree, in the attic.

A cassette as ordinarily viewed makes sounds, of course, and casts light. Naturally it should make itself plain to you in both image and sound, but for it to obtrude on the attention of others, who may not be interested, is a flaw. Ideally, the self-contained mobile cassette should be seen and heard only by you.

No matter how sophisticated the cassettes now on the market, or those visualized for the immediate future, they do require controls. There is an on-off knob or switch, and others to regulate color, volume, brightness, contrast, and all that sort of thing. In my vision, I want to make such controls operated, as far as possible, by the will.

I foresee a cassette in which the tape stops as soon as you remove your eye. It remains stopped till you bring your eye back, at which point it begins to move again immediately. I foresee a cassette that plays its tape quickly or slowly, forward or backward, by skips, or with repetitions, entirely at will.

You'll have to admit that such a cassette would be a perfect futuristic dream: self-contained, mobile, non-energy-consuming, perfectly private, and largely under the control of the will.

Ah, but dreams are cheap, so let's get practical. Can such a cassette possibly exist? To this, my answer is, Yes, of course.

The next question is: How many years will we have to wait for such a deliriously perfect cassette?

I have that answer too, and quite a definite one. We will have it in minus five thousand years—because what I have been describing (as perhaps you have guessed) is the book!

Am I cheating? Does it seem to you, O Gentle Reader, that the book is *not* the ultimately refined cassette, for it presents words only, and no image, that words without images are somehow one-dimensional and divorced from reality, that we cannot expect to get information by words alone concerning a universe that exists in images?

Well, let's consider that. Is the image more important than the word?

Certainly if we consider man's purely physical activities, the sense of sight is by far the most important way in which he gathers information concerning the universe. Given my choice of running across rough country with my eyes blindfolded and my hearing sharp, or with my eyes open and my hearing out of action, I would certainly use my eyes. In fact, with my eyes closed I would move at all only with the greatest caution.

But at some early stage in man's development he invented speech. He learned how to modulate his expired breath and how to use different modulations of sound to serve as agreed-upon symbols of material objects and actions and—far more important—of abstractions.

Eventually he learned to encode modulated sounds into markings that could be seen by the eye and translated into the corresponding sound in the brain. A book, I need not tell you, is a device that contains what we might call "stored speech."

It is speech that represents the most fundamental distinction between man and all other animals (except possibly the dolphin, which may conceivably have speech but has never worked out a system for storing it).

Not only do speech and the potential capacity to store speech differentiate man from all other species of life who have lived now or in the past, but it is something all men have in common. All known groups of human beings, however "primitive" they may be, can and do speak, and can and do have a language. Some "primitive" peoples have very complex and sophisticated languages, I understand.

What's more, all human beings who are even nearly normal in mentality learn to speak at an early age.

With speech the universal attribute of mankind, it becomes true that more information reaches us—as *social* animals—through speech than through images.

The comparison isn't even close. Speech and its stored forms (the written or printed word) are so overwhelmingly a source of the information we get, that without them we are helpless.

To see what I mean, let's consider a television program, since that ordinarily involves both speech and image, and let's ask ourselves what happens if we do without the one or the other.

Suppose you darken the picture and allow the sound to remain. Won't you still get a pretty good notion of what's going on? There may be spots rich in action and poor in sound and may leave you frustrated by dark silence, but if it were anticipated that you would not see the image, a few lines could be added and you would miss nothing.

Indeed radio got by on sound alone. It used speech and "sound effects." This meant that there were occasional moments when the dialogue was artificial to make up for the lack of image: "There comes Harry now. Oh, he doesn't see the banana. Oh, he's stepping on the banana. There he goes." By and large, though, you could get along. I doubt that anyone listening to radio seriously missed the absence of image.

Back to the TV tube, however. Now turn off the sound and allow the vision to remain untouched—in perfect focus and full color. What do you get out of it? Very little. Not all the play of emotion on the face, not all the impassioned gestures, not all the tricks of the camera as it focuses here and there are going to give you more than the haziest notion of what is going on.

Corresponding to radio, which is only speech and miscellaneous sound, there were the silent movies, which were only images. In the absence of sound and speech, the actors in the silent films had to "emote." Oh, the flashing eyes; oh, the hands at the throat, in the air, raised to heaven; oh, the fingers pointing trustingly to heaven, firmly to the floor, angrily to the door; oh, the camera moving in to show the banana skin on the floor, the ace in the sleeve, the fly on the nose. And with every extreme of inventiveness of visualization in its most exaggerated form, what did we have every fifteen seconds? An utter halt to the action, while words flashed on the screen.

This is not to say that one cannot communicate after a fashion by vision alone—by the use of pictorial images. A clever pantomimist like Marcel Marceau or Charlie Chaplin or Red Skelton can do wonders—but the very reason we watch them and applaud is that they communicate so much with so poor a medium as pictorialization.

As a matter of fact, we amuse ourselves by playing charades and trying to have someone guess some simple phrase we "act out." It wouldn't be a successful game if it didn't require much ingenuity, and, even so, practitioners of the game work up sets of signals and devices that (whether they know it or not) take advantage of the mechanics of speech.

They divide words into syllables, they indicate whether a word is short or long, they use synonyms and "sounds like." In all this, they are using visual images to *speak*. Without using any trick that involves any of the properties of speech, but simply by gesture and action alone, can you get across as simple a sentence as, "Yesterday the sunset was beautiful in rose and green"?

Of course a movie camera can photograph a beautiful sunset and you can point to that. This involves a great investment of technology, however, and I'm not sure that it will tell you that the sunset was like that *yesterday* (unless the film plays tricks with calendars—which represent a form of speech).

Or consider this: Shakespeare's plays were written to be acted. The image was of the essence. To get the full flavor, you must see the actors and what they are doing. How much do you miss if you go to *Hamlet* and close your eyes and merely listen? How much do you miss if you plug your ears and merely look?

Having made clear my belief that a book, which consists of words but no images, loses very little by its lack of images and has therefore every right to be considered an extremely sophisticated example of a television cassette, let me change my ground and use an even better argument.

Far from lacking the image, a book *does* have images, and what's more, far better images, because personal, than any that can possibly be presented to you on television.

When you are reading an interesting book, are there no images in your mind? Do you not see all that is going on, in your mind's eye?

Those images are *yours*. They belong to you and to you alone, and they are infinitely better for you than those wished on you by others.

I saw Gene Kelly in *The Three Musketeers* once (the only version I ever saw that was reasonably faithful to the book). The sword fight between D'Artagnan, Athos, Porthos, and Aramis on one side and the five men of the Cardinal's Guard on the other, which occurs near the beginning of the picture, was absolutely beautiful. It was a dance of course, and I reveled in it. . . . But Gene Kelly, however talented a dancer he might be, does not happen to fit the picture of D'Artagnan that I have in my mind's eye, and I was unhappy all through the picture because it did violence to "my" *The Three Musketeers*.

This is not to say that sometimes an actor might not just happen to match your own vision. Sherlock Holmes in my mind just happens to be Basil Rathbone. In *your* mind, however, Sherlock Holmes might *not* be Basil Rathbone; he might be Dustin Hoffman, for all I know. Why should all our millions of Sherlock Holmeses have to be fitted into a single Basil Rathbone?

You see, then, why a television program, however excellent, can never give as much pleasure, be as absorbing, fill so important a niche in the life of the imagination, as a book can. To the television program we need only bring an empty mind and sit torpidly while the display of sound and image fills us, requiring nothing of our imagination. If others are watching, they are filled to the brim in precisely the same way, all of them, and with precisely the same sounding images.

The book, on the other hand, demands co-operation from the reader. It insists he take part in the process.

In doing so, it offers an interrelationship that is made to order by the reader himself for the reader himself—one that most neatly fits his own peculiarities and idiosyncrasies.

When you read a book, you create your own images, you create the sound of various voices, you create gestures, expressions, emotions. You create *everything* but the bare words themselves. And if you take the slightest pleasure in creation, the book has given you something the television program can't.

Furthermore, if ten thousand people read the same book at the same time, each nevertheless creates his own images, his own sound of the voice, his own gestures, expressions, emotions. It will be not one book but ten thousand books. It will not be the product of the author alone, but the product of the interaction of the author and each of the readers separately.

What, then, can replace the book?

I admit that the book may undergo changes in nonessentials. It was once handwritten; it is now printed. The technology of publishing the printed book has advanced in a hundred ways, and in the future books may be turned out electronically from a television set in your house.

In the end, though, you will be alone with the printed word, and what can replace it?

Is all this wishful thinking? Is it just that I make my living out of books, so I don't want to accept the fact that books may be replaced? Am I just inventing ingenious arguments to console myself?

Not at all. I am certain that books will not be replaced in the future, because they have not been replaced in the past.

To be sure, many more people watch television than read books, but that is not new. Books were *always* a minority activity. Few people read books before television, and before radio, and before anything you care to name.

As I said, books are demanding, and require creative activity on the part of the reader. Not everyone, in fact darned few, are ready to give what is demanded, so they don't read, and they *won't* read. They are not lost just because the book fails them somehow; they are lost by nature.

In fact let me make the point that reading itself is difficult, inordinately difficult. It is not like talking, which every even halfway normal child learns without any program of conscious teaching. Imitation beginning at the age of one will do the trick.

Reading, on the other hand, must be carefully taught and, usually, without much luck.

The trouble is that we mislead ourselves by our own definition of literacy. We can teach almost anyone (if we try hard enough and long enough) to read traffic signs and to make out instructions and warnings on posters, and to puzzle out newspaper headlines. Provided the printed message is short and reasonably simple and the motivation to read it is great, almost everyone can read.

And if this is called literacy, then almost every American is literate. But if you then begin to wonder why so few Americans read books (the average American out of school, I understand, does not even read one complete book a year), you are being misled by your own use of the term literate.

Few people who are literate in the sense of being able to read a sign that says NO SMOKING ever become so familiar with the printed word and so at ease with the process of quickly decoding by eye the small and complicated shapes that stand for modulated sounds that they are willing to tackle any extended reading task—as for instance making their way through one thousand consecutive words.

Nor do I think it's entirely a matter of the failure of our educational system (though heaven knows it's a failure). No one expects that if one teaches every child how to play baseball, they will all be talented baseball players, or that every child taught how to play the piano will be a talented pianist. We accept in almost every field of endeavor the notion of a talent that can be encouraged and developed but cannot be created from nothing.

Well, in my view, reading is a talent too. It is a very difficult activity. Let me tell you how I discovered that.

When I was a teen-ager, I sometimes read comic magazines, and my favorite character, if you're interested, was Scrooge McDuck. In those days, comic magazines cost ten cents, but of course I read them for nothing off my father's newsstand. I used to wonder, though, how anyone would be so foolish as to pay ten cents, when by simply glancing through the magazine for two minutes at the newsstand, he could read the whole thing.

Then one day on the subway to Columbia University, I found myself hanging from a strap in a crowded car with nothing handy to read. Fortunately the teen-age girl seated in front of me was reading a comic magazine. Something is better than nothing, so I arranged myself so I could look down on the pages and read along with her. (Fortunately I can read upside down as easily as right side up.)

Then, after a few seconds, I thought, Why doesn't she turn the page?

She did, eventually. It took minutes for her to finish each double-page spread, and as I watched her eyes going from one panel to the next and her lips carefully mumbling the words, I had a flash of insight.

What she was doing was what I would be doing if I were faced with English words written phonetically in the Hebrew, Greek, or Cyrillic alphabet. Knowing the respective alphabets dimly, I would have to first recognize each letter, then sound it, then put them together, then recognize the word. Then I would have to pass on to the next word and do the same. Then, when I had done several words this way, I would have to go back and try to get them in combination.

You can bet that under those circumstances, I would do very little reading. The *only* reason I read is that when I look at a line of print I see it all as words, and at once.

And the difference between the reader and the non-reader grows steadily wider with the years. The more a reader reads, the more information he picks up, the larger his vocabulary grows, the more familiar various literary allusions become. It becomes steadily easier and more fun for him to read, while for the non-reader it becomes steadily harder and less worth while.

The result of this is that there are and *always have been* (whatever the state of supposed literacy in a particular society) both readers and non-readers, with the former making up a tiny minority, of, I guess, less than 1 per cent.

I have estimated that four hundred thousand Americans have read some of my books (out of a population of two hundred million), and I am considered, and consider myself, a successful writer. If a particular book should sell two million copies in all its American editions, it would be a remarkable best seller—and all that would mean would be that 1 per cent of the American population had managed to nerve themselves to buy it. Of that total, moreover, I'm willing to bet that at least half would manage to do no more than stumble through some of it in order to find the dirty parts.

Those people, those non-readers, those passive receptacles for entertainment, are terribly fickle. They will switch from one thing to another in the eternal search for some device that will give them as much as possible and ask of them as little as possible.

From minstrels to theatrical performances, from the theater to the movies, from the silents to the talkies, from black-and-white to color, from the record player to the radio and back, from the movies to television to color television to cassettes.

What does it matter?

But through it all, the faithful less-than-1-per-cent minority stick to the books. Only the printed word can demand as much from them, only the printed word can force creativity out of them, only the printed word can tailor itself to their needs and desires, only the printed word can give them what nothing else can.

The book may be ancient but it is also the ultimate, and readers will never be seduced away from it. They will remain a minority, but they will *remain*.

So despite what my friend said in his speech on cassettes, writers of books will never be outmoded and replaced. Writing books may be no way to get rich (oh, well, what's money!), but as a profession, it will always be there.

fifteen

BY THE NUMBERS

Hypocrisy is a universal phenomenon. It ends with death, but not before. When the hypocrisy is conscious, it is of course disgusting, but few of us are conscious hypocrites. It is so easy to argue ourselves into views that pander to our own self-interests and prejudices and *sincerely* find nobility in them.

I do it myself, I'm certain, but by the very nature of things, it is difficult to see self-examples clearly. Let me give you instead an example involving a good friend of mine.

He was talking about professors. He could have been one, he said, if he had followed the proper path after college graduation. Now, he said, he was glad he hadn't, for he wouldn't want to be associated with so uniformly cowardly a profession. He wouldn't want to bear a title borne by those who so weakly and supinely gave in to the vicious demands of rascally students.

His eyes glinted feverishly at this point and he lifted his arms so that they cradled an imaginary machine gun. He said, from between gritted teeth, "What I would have given those bastards would have been a rat-tat-tat-tat—" And he sprayed the entire room with imaginary bullets, killing (in imagination) every person in it.

I was rather taken aback. My friend was, under ordinary conditions, one of the most kindly and reasonable persons I know—and I made excuses (hypocritically doing for a friend what I would not have done for an enemy). He had a few drinks, and I knew that he had had a lonely, miserable, and scapegoated youth. No doubt at the other end of that machine gun were the shades of those young men who had hounded him for sport so many years ago.

So I made no comment and changed the subject, bringing up a political campaign then in progress. It quickly turned out, again to my discomfiture, that my friend, who usually saw eye to eye with me, had deserted our standard and was voting for the other fellow. I could not help expressing dismay, and my friend at once began to explain at great length his reasons for deserting.

I shook my head, eager to cut him short. "It's no use," I said. "You won't convince me. I hate your man too much ever to vote for him."

Whereupon my friend threw himself back in his chair with a simper of self-conscious virtue* and said, "I'm afraid I'm not a very good hater."

And the vision of the imaginary machine gun with which he had imaginarily killed hundreds of students not three minutes before rose in front of my eyes. I sighed and changed the subject again. What was the use of protesting? It was clear he honestly thought he was not a good hater.

But my friend reminded me of men generally. What of the similar hypocrisy of all those who nowadays are against technology?

Heaven only knows how many people are now occupied in denouncing our technological society and all the evils it has brought upon us. They do so with a self-conscious virtue that tends to mask the fact that they are all as eager a group of beneficiaries of that society as anyone else. They may denounce the other guy's electric razor, so to speak, but do so while strumming on an electric guitar.

There must be some idealists who "return to the soil" and remain there for longer than the month or two required to develop calluses. I may conceive of them using sticks and rocks as tools, scorning the fancy metal devices manufactured by modern blast furnaces and factories. But *even so,* they are free to do this only because they take advantage of the fact that our technological society can feed (however imperfectly) billions of human beings and still leave land for simple-lifers to grub in.

Our technological society was not forced on mankind. It grew out of the demand of human beings for plenty of food, for warmth in winter, coolness in summer, less work

---

* If self-conscious virtue could be sold at a dollar a pound, we'd all be rich. Me too, for I am loaded down with as many tons of self-conscious virtue as anyone. Just the same, events since that election have abundantly justified me.

and more play and amusement. Unfortunately, people want all of this plus all the children they feel like having, and the result is that technology* in its command performance has brought us to a situation of considerable danger.

Very well; we must pull through safely—but how? To me, the only possible answer is through the continued and *wiser* use of technology. I don't say that this will surely work. I *do* say, though, that nothing else will.

For one thing, it seems to me that we must continue, extend, and intensify the computerization of society.

Is that thought offensive? Why?

Is it that computers are soulless? Is it that they don't treat human beings as human beings, but merely as punch-cards (or as the electronic equivalent)?

Well, then, let's get it straight. Computers don't treat anyone as anything. They are mathematical tools designed to store and manipulate data. It is the human beings who program and control computers who are responsible, and if they sometimes hide behind the computer to mask their own incapacity, that is really a human fault rather than a computer fault, isn't it?

Of course, one might argue that if the computer weren't there to hide behind, the human beings in charge would be flushed out and be forced to treat us all more decently.

Don't you believe it! The history of administrative ineptitude, of bureaucratic savagery, of all the injustices and tyranny of petty officialdom, long antedates the computer. And that's what you'd be dealing with if you abolished the computer.

Of course, if you dealt with a human being, you could reason and persuade—which means that a person with intelligence and articulacy would have an advantage over

---

* Mind you, I say "technology" and not "science." Science is a systematic method for studying and working out those generalizations that seem to describe the behavior of the universe. It could exist as a purely intellectual game that would never affect the practical life of human beings either for good or evil, and that was very nearly the case in ancient Greece, for instance. Technology is the application of scientific findings to the tools of everyday life, and that application can be wise or unwise, useful or harmful. Very often, those who govern technological decisions are not scientists and know little about science but are perfectly willing to pander to human greed for the immediate short-term benefit and the immediate dollar.

others with just as good a case who happen to be unsophisticated, inarticulate, and scared. Or you might be able to bend an official decision by slipping someone a few dollars, by doing a favor, or by calling upon an influential friend. In which case, those with money or importance have the advantage over those without.

But that's wrong, isn't it? It is to soulless impartiality that we all give lip service. The laws, we proclaim, must be enforced without favor. The law, we maintain, is no respecter of persons. If we really believe that, then we should welcome computerization, which would apply the rules of society without the capacity for being blarneyed or bribed out of it. To be sure, cases may be different from person to person, but the more elaborately a computer is programmed, the more the difference in cases can be taken into account.

Or is it that we don't really want to be treated impartially? Very likely; and that's why I suspect hypocrisy has a lot to do with the outcry against computerization.

Do we lose our individuality in a computerized society? Do we become numbers instead of people?

Alas, we can't be people without having handles. We are all coded and *must* be. If you must deal with someone who resolutely refuses to give you a name, you will refer to him by some description, such as "The guy with the red hair and bad breath." Eventually, you will reduce that to "Old Bad-breath."

With time and generations, that could become "Obreth" or something and may even come to be considered an aristocratic name.

In other words, we *are* coded. We can't be a "person" to more than the bare handful of people who deal with us every day. To everyone else, we are known only as a code. The problem, then, is not whether we are to be coded; the problem is whether we are to be coded *efficiently*.

It amounts to a difference between a number and a name. Most people seem to think that a number is much more villainous than a name. A name is somehow personal and endearing, while a number is impersonal and wicked.

I recognize the feeling. I happen to love my own name, and I invariably make a big fuss if it is misspelled or mispronounced (both of which are easy to do). But I find excuses for myself. In the first place, my name is intensely personal. I am the only Isaac Asimov in the world, as far as I know; certainly the only one in the United States. Furthermore, if anyone knows my name without knowing me, it is entirely because of what I myself, personally, have done with my life.

And yet it has its drawbacks. My name is difficult to spell and difficult to pronounce and I spend what seems several hours a year negotiating with telephone operators and attempting to persuade them, in vain, to pronounce my name just approximately correctly.

Ought I to have some simpler and more pronounceable name? . . . But then I would be lost in a nominal ocean. There must be many people who prefer names to numbers and have names like Fred Smith, Bob Jones, and Pat McCarthy. Each of these is shared by myriads, and of what real value is a sound combination endlessly duplicated? Imagine the history of mistakes such duplication has led to, from the billing of someone for an article he didn't buy to the execution of someone for a crime he didn't commit.

Numbers are names also—but *efficient* names. If they are properly distributed, there need be no duplications *ever*. Every single numbername can be unique through all of earthly space and time. And they would all be equally amenable to spelling and pronunciation.

Naturally we should distinguish between a man's official code designation and his personal one. Even today, a man may have the name of Montmorency Quintus Blodgett, and no document involving him may be legal without every letter of that name carefully formed in his own handwriting—yet his friends may call him Spike. To have an official number does not mean that you must be *called* by that number.

Just have that number on record. Have it unique. Have it convenient. And have it easily stored and manipulated by computer. You will be infinitely more a person, because there is something that is uniquely and ineradicably you forever reachable, than by having a meaningless name dubiously known to a few dozen people.

The day of the number is upon us already, in fact, although in a very primitive fashion. It is here because we insist on it. We insist on overloading the post office to a further extent each year, so we need ZIP codes to expedite delivery. As true hypocrites, we complain bitterly about those ZIP codes and would complain just as bitterly if we abandoned them and delayed our mail, as we would then necessarily have to do.

In the same way, the upward spiraling number of long-distance calls we all make and the reluctance of people to be telephone operators rather than telephone users (or to pay telephone bills that will enable the phone companies to lure operators to the switchboards) makes area codes necessary.

And as for social-security numbers, try running the tax system without them.

Of course you are about to say, Who needs the tax system? and oh boy, do those words fall upon sympathetic ears! My tax payments each year are higher by an order of magnitude than I ever dreamed (when I got my doctorate) I would ever make as total income—and I pay none of it joyously.

Nevertheless those taxes are there, despite the objections of every one of us, because of the absolute demand—of every one of us. We insist that the government maintain various expensive services and that means enormous and complicated taxes. To demand the service and complain of the payment is hypocrisy if the contradiction is understood and idiocy if it is not.

The greatest and most expensive of our demands is that the government maintain an enormous military establishment of the most advanced and expensive type in order to protect us in our position as richest and most powerful nation against the envious hordes without.

What? *You* don't demand it? *You* don't either? I guess that is because you and I are anti-militaristic and believe in peace and love. The fact is, however, that the American people, by a large majority, would rather pay for arms than for anything else. If you doubt it, study the record of Congressional votes and remember that there are few senators and representatives who would dream of offending their constituents and risking the loss of their precious jobs.

Yes, you're for cutting government spending. And I'm for cutting government spending. The only catch is that you and I and all the rest of us are for cutting it only in those areas that don't hurt us either emotionally or economically. . . . Which is natural for hypocrites.

And if we all yell for reduction but all keep our heads firmly in the trough, there will be no reduction as long as our technological civilization remains stable.

Now, then, if we insist on huge and expensive government activities, and if we therefore expect the government to collect about a quarter of a trillion dollars a year from generally reluctant taxpayers who, by and large, find nothing unpatriotic in cheating, you place the government in a difficult spot.

It is because of that difficult spot that the Internal Revenue Service has the most unpopular job in the country (and I tell you frankly that I myself hate them from top to bottom—being, unlike my friend, a fairly good hater). Yet that hateful job is essential, and it couldn't be done at all without social-security numbers and computers.

Since the job must be done, let's make it less hateful. To me it seems that the way out is to develop a national computer bank, government-run (inevitably) that will record in its vitals every bit of ascertainable information about every individual in the United States (or in the world, if we are ever intelligent enough to work out a world government).

I don't look forward to this with sad resignation or with fearful apprehension, but with longing.

I want to see every man receive a long and complicated code of identification, with symbols representing age, income, education, housing, occupation, family size, hobbies, political views, sexual tastes, *everything* that can be conceivably coded. I would like to have all these symbols periodically brought up to date so that every birth, every death, every change of address, every new job, every new degree earned, every arrest, every sickness, is constantly recorded. Naturally any attempt to evade or falsify such symbols would clearly be an anti-social act and would be treated and punished as such.

Wouldn't such coding be an invasion of privacy? Yes, of course, but why bring that up? We lost *that* fight long ago. Once we agreed to an income tax at all, we gave the government the right to know what our income was. Once we insisted on having the income tax made equitable by permitting deductions for business expenses and losses, for contributions, depreciation, and who knows what else, we made it necessary for the government to deal with it all, to pry into every check we make out, to poke into every meal in every restaurant, to leaf through our every record.

I don't like it. I hate and resent being treated as though I were guilty until I prove myself innocent. I hate dealing in an unequal fight with an agency that is at once prosecutor and judge.

And yet it is necessary. I myself have never been caught, so far, in anything but overpayments, and have therefore received only refunds, but I understand this is not typical. The IRS, by turning everyone upside down and shaking hard, collects millions of dollars that rightfully belong to the government.

Well, what if we were all thoroughly encoded and that all this encoding were manipulated and handled by computers? Our privacy would be no more destroyed than it is now, but the effects of that destruction might be less noticeable and irritating. The IRS would not need to fumble over our records. They would *have* our records.

I, for one, would love to be in a situation where I couldn't possibly cheat, as long as no one else could possibly cheat, either. For most of us, it would mean a saving in taxes.

In fact, I would like to see a cashless society. I would like to see everyone work through a computerized credit-card arrangement. I would like to see every transaction of whatever nature and size, from the purchase of General Motors to the purchase of a newspaper, involve that credit card, so that money is always transferred electronically from one account to another.

Everyone would know what his assets are at any time. Furthermore the government could take its cut out of every transaction and adjust matters, plus or minus, at the end of each year. You could not cheat, you would not be concerned.

Will all this personal snooping enable the government to control and repress us more ruthlessly? Is it compatible with democracy?

The truth is that no government is ever at a loss for methods of controlling its population. No computer is needed, no codes, no dossiers. The history of mankind is a history of tyranny and of government by repression, and

some of the most repressive and efficiently despotic govern-
ments have had very little in the way of technology at their
service.

Did the Spanish Inquisition use computers to track down
heretics? Did the Puritans of New England? The Calvinists
of Geneva?

The difficulty, in fact, is finding a government that is not
repressive. Even the most liberal and gentle government, in
which civil liberties are ordinarily scrupulously respected,
quickly turns repressive when an emergency arises and it
feels threatened. It does this without any difficulty at all,
breaking through any legal barriers as though they weren't
there.

In World War II, for instance, the United States Government—which I love and respect—placed thousands of
Americans of Japanese descent into concentration camps
without any trace of legal right. It could not even be considered a necessary war measure, since the same was not
done (or even dreamed of) with respect to Americans of
German or Italian descent, although we were at war with
Germany and Italy as well as with Japan. Yet the action
met with little resistance from the population generally,
and was actually popular, entirely because of our suspicion
of people with funny-looking eyes and because of our fear
of Japan in the immediate aftermath of Pearl Harbor.

That's the key word: fear. Every repression is aroused
by fear. If by no general fear, then by the fear of a tyrant
for his own safety.

In the absence of detailed knowledge about its population, a government can only feel safe if it represses *everybody*. In the absence of knowledge, a government *must* play
it safe, *must* react to rumors and suppositions, and *must*
strike hard at everybody, lest it be struck. The worst tyrannies are the tyrannies of fearful men.

If a government knows its population thoroughly, it need
not fear uselessly; it will know *whom* to fear. There will be
repression, certainly, since the government never existed
that did not repress those it considered dangerous, but the
repression will not need to be as general, as enduring, or as
forceful. In other words, there will be less fear at the top
and *therefore* more freedom below.

Might not a government repress just for the hell of it, if
it has the kind of opportunity computerization gives it? Not

unless it is psychotic. Repression makes enemies and conspirators, and however efficiently a computer may help you fight them, why create them if you don't have to?

Then, too, a thorough knowledge of the characteristics of its population can make more efficient those government services we now demand. We cannot expect the government to act intelligently if it does not, at any time, know what it is doing; or what, in detail, is being demanded of it. We must buy service with money in the first place, as all taxpayers know; but we must then buy useful and efficient service by paying out, in return, information about ourselves.

Nor is this something new. The decennial census has grown steadily more complex with the years, to the benefit of the businessman and the administrator, who find in it the information that can help guide their responses. Well, I only suggest this be carried to its ultimate conclusion.*

Will such an ultimate computerization, such a total conversion into a society following a by-the-numbers organization, wipe out initiative and creativity and individualism?

Such as in what society that we have ever had?

Show me the society at any time in the world's history in which there was no war, no famine, no pestilence, no injustice. We have had societies in which there was initiative and creativity and individualism, yes, but in only a small upper layer of aristocrats and sophisticates.

The philosophers of Athens had time to think and speculate, because Athenian society was rich in slaves that had no free time at all. The Roman senators lived lives of luxury by plundering all the Mediterranean world. The royal courts of every nation, our own southern gentry, our own northern industrialists lived easy on the backs of peasants, and slaves, and laborers.

Do you want those societies? If so, where will you yourself fit in, given such a society? Do you see yourself as an Athenian slave, or as an Athenian philosopher; as an Italian peasant, or as a Roman senator; a southern sharecropper, or a southern plantation owner? Would you like to be

---

* Actually, now that I think of it, I used this notion in my story, "All the Troubles of the World," first published in 1958 and included in my collection *Nine Tomorrows* (Doubleday, 1959).

transported into such a society and run your fair share of risk as to the position you will occupy in it, remembering that for everyone in comfort there were a hundred or a thousand scrabbling in the dark?

Hypocrite! You don't want the simple society at all. You just want to be comfortable, and the hell with everyone else.

Fortunately we can't have simple societies anyway. The only thing we can legitimately aspire to is exactly the complex society we now have—but *one that works*. The only alternative, the *only* alternative, is utter destruction.

And that means complete computerization, because the society has grown too complex to be made to work in any other way.

If we program our computers properly, we will be able to apply minimum taxes, we will be able to hold corruption to a minimum, we will be able to minimize social injustice. After all, any society in which the people are plundered, in which the few enrich themselves, in which large segments of the population are poor, hungry, alienated, and angry, contributes to its own instability.

Individuals may be short-sighted enough to prefer their own immediate benefit and the hell with all others, including their children, but computers are not that soulless. They would be geared to the working of a society and not to the comfort of individuals, and, unlike the uncontrolled human being, would not sell our society's birthright for an individual's mess of pottage.

Again, individuals may be emotional enough to want war to enforce their views, even though a war almost invariably ends with both sides generally losing (though particular individuals may profit) and no war can conceivably be as useful as a sensible compromise. But a computer, properly programmed, can't possibly be so soulless as to recommend war as an optimum solution.

And if the various nations all computerized themselves in a properly programmed fashion, I suspect that all the national computers would, so to speak, agree on solutions. They would all recommend compatible programs, since it is clear that in this day, and even more so in future days, no one portion of the Earth can profit from evil to another.

The world is small. We rise together, all of us; or we sink together.*

So that's what I want, a world without war and without injustice, made possible by the computer.

And because I try *not* to be a hypocrite, I will admit frankly that I want such a world for purely selfish reasons: It will make me feel good.

* Actually, I first made this point in a story entitled "The Evitable Conflict," first published in 1950 and included in my collection *I, Robot* (Doubleday, 1950).

G

AND (YOU GUESSED IT!)
ABOUT ME

sixteen

THE CRUISE AND I

In the introduction to chapter 2, I casually mentioned having stood on the deck of a liner off Florida. It occurs to me that I ought not let it go at that. Especially since I am notoriously a non-traveler and my faithful Gentle Readers may wish to know how I came to make the trip and how I survived it.

The truth is that only twice in my life, prior to the cruise of the good ship *Statendam*, have I crossed the ocean, and neither time was it voluntary.

At the age of three I was taken from Europe to America. I *had* to go; my parents insisted. I presume we traveled steerage. Fortunately I remember nothing about it.

While I was serving with the Army, proudly bearing the exalted rank of buck private, I made my second sea voyage, this time from San Francisco to Hawaii. Again, I had to go; a sergeant seemed to expect it of me. I traveled on what seemed to be a converted garbage scow, in which first class was steerage. Unfortunately I remember this voyage.

With that kind of record, I reacted with stubborn silence when, in late spring 1972 I was approached by Richard C. Hoagland, who was aflame with the desire to lead a party of idealists southward to see the launch of Apollo 17.

It was, he explained, the last manned expedition to the Moon in the Apollo series, probably the last of any kind for decades to come. It was, he explained further, the only night launch in the series and would be a spectacular sight, especially since we would be watching it from the sea, with the sky clear from horizon to horizon.

I pointed out an insuperable objection: "But it's almost a thousand miles away," I said, "and I get separation anxiety as soon as I am out of sight of my study."

"Fine," he said, "I'll put down your name. No longer will people be able to sneer contemptuously when they say that Isaac Asimov, the greatest science-fiction writer alive, has never seen a rocket launching."

"Is that what people do?" I asked.

"Sneer contemptuously?"

"No, say I am the greatest science-fiction writer alive."

"I have it in writing and notarized," he said.

So I went. After all, I have my position to think of.

I boarded the S.S. *Statendam* shortly after 2 P.M. on Monday, December 4, 1972. I was all set to give speeches, to participate in discussions, to lead seminars, and to cower in my bunk—not necessarily in that order.

On board I found four other science-fiction writers: There was Robert A. Heinlein, with whom I had shared nearly four years of precarious desk duty during the arduous days of World War II. There was Theodore Sturgeon, looking like Don Quixote in buckskin. There was Frederik Pohl, who, at various times in the thirty-four years since we first met, has been my agent, my editor, my collaborator, and, always, my friend. And there was Ben Bova, who last year stepped into the difficult-to-fill shoes of John W. Campbell as editor of *Analog*.

By a curious coincidence, Hoagland possessed written evidence to prove that each one of them was the best science-fiction writer alive.

Bob Heinlein, who had been in Annapolis in his time, introduced me to the mysteries of seagoing cryptography. The front of the ship was the prow. You went forward to go toward it and aft to go away from it. When you stood facing forward, your left was port and your right was starboard. I asked Bob why this was, and he said it was part of the Mosaic code as handed down from Sinai.

The floors, he said, were decks, and the windows were portholes. We were on the port side when he said this, and I nodded with ready intelligence. "I see," I said. "The windows on the other side are starboardholes, right?"

He hit me with a marlinespike.

At five to four I made my way out to a place on the side of the ship where I could hang on to a railing and witness whatever was going to happen at four o'clock, when the ship was scheduled to leave. A sleety drizzle filled the air, it being a typical fine December day in New York. It slowly froze me to the deck, for the ship did not leave till six o'clock, and we all waved good-by then to the New York skyline as it bleared through the smog.

I met Norman Mailer during the wait. He was on board to represent the non-science-fiction literary response to the space effort (assuming that anything that is non-science-fiction can be considered literary).

The first and only previous time I had ever met him was in an elevator in the midtown building in which (unknown to me) he maintained an office. We were the only ones in the elevator. I studied his shock of iron-gray hair and said to him, "Has anyone ever told you you look like Norman Mailer?"

"A few people," he said, and got off.

This time I introduced myself and he told me he read *Asimov's Guide to Science* every morning while meditating. I congratulated him on his taste in reading matter.

On board also was a white-haired, fragile lady named Katherine Anne Porter. I had no sooner had her pointed out to me when an extraordinarily clever witticism occurred to me. It was clear that her mere presence made of us a sort of "ship of fools."

I sought out Fred Pohl. "Do you know Katherine Anne Porter is on board?" I said, neatly setting him up for the kill.

"Yes," he said. "It makes us rather a ship of fools, right?"

I thought it a foolish remark.

My first meal on board introduced me to the rigors of life on shipboard. I had already discovered the elevators, the boutique, the library, the fifteen bars and lounges, and now I was handed a dinner menu modeled on feasts given by the more decadent Roman emperors. Having ascertained that the meals were included in the price of the cruise, I ordered one of everything.

The waiters were all Indonesians, more or less fresh from the old country, so they were still underdeveloped enough to be quiet, industrious, efficient, and pleasant. It was disconcerting, but we all forced ourselves to be tolerant of their strange, foreign ways.

Somewhere in the course of the meal a sudden spasm of dizziness struck me. It was for all the world as though the entire room had swayed. I autodiagnosed a small stroke and was grateful that the ship's doctor (a handsome, somber man in an admiral's uniform) was at my very table.

"Sir," I said anxiously, "the room seemed to sway just now, and I suspect I suffered—"

"Yes, the sea is a little rough," he said.

I decided not to mention my stroke. He was a busy man.

Marvin Minsky, who works on robots at M.I.T., called across from the next table to ask me how far I thought the ship was swaying. I made a quick, shrewd estimate of the angle and said I didn't know.

Whereupon he pointed to a pencil he had attached to a fork so that it dangled over the table and said, "Hardly at all. Maybe two degrees. That should make everybody feel better."

I don't think it did. (Later in the cruise, Marvin, who has a magnificently bald head, put on a Charles II wig and, in the guise of a fan, came to me with bated breath and humbly asked for my autograph. He said it was his ambition to grow up to be like me. I gave him my autograph in the kindest and most condescending way and patted his head.)

It was not until the second day that I decided that I was *not* going to be seasick. Once I had reached that decision, I went off to serve as angel of mercy to those of my colleagues who were not as talented as I.

To my indignation, there were surprisingly few who suffered. Late in the cruise I discovered that Carl Sagan (the well-known astronomer from Cornell) did not take kindly to the swaying of the ship. At once I told him, in full and moving detail, of the exact manner in which the various ship's motions failed to affect me, attributing my immunity to nausea to superior genes and a ready intelligence.

Carl showed no signs of gratitude.

I was less adaptable to the chief indoor sport of seagoing mankind, which consisted of the continuous and steady consumption of a variety of spirituous liquors. The shipping line co-operated with this fully; an indefinite supply of strong drink was made available to all.

This made life hard for me, since the continuous and steady consumption of as much as one small jigger of wine reduces me to a state of swinish intoxication. I was forced to such subterfuges as asking for a glass of ice water and then sneaking an olive into it.

At 10:30 the second morning, we had a boat drill. We had to put on warm clothing and a kind of life preserver. Then we went out on the upper promenade deck (if that's what it was called) and clustered about the lifeboats assigned to us.

I didn't like the symbolism of the whole thing, and someone who noted the concern on my finely chiseled features said, "Women and children first, Asimov."

"Women, children, and *geniuses*," I replied haughtily.

"*Young* geniuses," said a twenty-two-year-old whippersnapper behind me.

Actually the ship became home very quickly and I lost all terror of the sea. In fact, it was on land that the worst dangers were to be found.

On Saturday, the ninth, we reached St. Thomas, in the Virgin Islands, and were driven around in an open bus in a kind of midsummer heat that was most unusual for December. I mentioned the matter to the driver, but it only seemed to confuse him. "What heat wave?" he asked.

Since he insisted on driving on the left-hand side of the road, it was obviously useless to expect intelligent conversation from him. (Everyone else drove on the left-hand side too. Ridiculous!)

We stopped off at what had once been the governor's mansion, and I got into a conversation with a gentleman who explained that the island's water source was rainfall. This was wonderful, except in droughts. The previous summer, he said, had been extraordinarily dry. From his house on the hill he could see innumerable squalls out on the Atlantic. Every single one of them, he said, had missed the island, despite his own best efforts to lure them into the right direction by the use of body English.

Now, of course (he concluded), it was the dry season. I looked up at the gathering clouds and said, "Are you sure?"

"Oh, there might be a light tropical storm," he admitted casually, "but it will only last five minutes."

On the way back to the ship there was a light tropical storm. It lasted five hours, and some three inches of rain fell.

The next day, we were in Puerto Rico, and the plan was to get a look at Arecibo (two and a half hours away by dubious bus), where we would see the world's largest radio telescope.

Having spent all night wringing myself out, I looked up at the sky and said, "I don't think I'll go. It looks like rain."

"You're judging by New York skies," someone said. "Here in sunny Puerto Rico, the Sun shines 360 days a year." He showed me a propaganda leaflet put out by the chamber of commerce, and that indeed was what it said.

Sure enough, even as I read it, the Sun popped smilingly out from behind the clouds, so I got on the bus. The Sun at once popped smilingly into the clouds and it rained heavily all the way to Arecibo. Too late, I realized the propaganda leaflet had failed to say how *long* the Sun shone on each of the 360 days.

The bus ride began in what seemed to be one of the slum areas of the island. We had not quite emerged from that slum area two and a half hours later, when we reached our destination. The last five or six miles was up a precipitous mountainside along a road that made a right-angle curve every five feet. The driver blew his horn melodiously at every curve, taking his hand off the wheel each time.

I was quite sure I would never experience a rottener ride, and I didn't—until an hour and a half later, when we went down that same road. There was more seasickness on the bus than on the ship, and there was a rush for Dramamine pills. I used my own methods and clung tightly to the nearest girl.

The huge radio telescope was a magnificently impressive sight though, and was easily almost worth the trip. They had a kind of ski lift that would raise any maniac to the huge devices far above the big bowl itself. There was also a catwalk that stretched out for hundreds of feet, high up over blank emptiness. We were told it had a rudimentary railing that would serve to delay our fall a moment or two, and a flooring of slats with enough space in between to drop us half through.

Some of the party decided to break the rules and make use of these devices. I did not crowd forward, however, since I don't like to be pushy, and in the end I never got to go. I was philosophical about it.

* * *

On the second morning of the cruise, right after the boat drill, we all got down to the serious business of the cruise. Ken Franklin, of the American Museum of Natural History, started us off with a rousing keynote speech, and I settled back to a week or more of pure enjoyment, pure relaxation, pure somnolence—but I began to worry.

It seems there were reporters on board; narrow-eyed, cynical, and sophisticated men; who found fault with the food, the accommodations, the arrangements, the personnel. The only thing they didn't find fault with, as near as I could see, was the liquor—and they might have, in between drinks, if there had been any in-between-drinks for them.

Alas, I thought. They will write narrow-eyed, cynical, and sophisticated articles making fun of the cruise* and it will be up to me to do what I can to make things better.

So, to begin with, I persuaded the men in charge to allow Hugh Downs to moderate the discussions. He had come aboard to do some announcing in the last stages of the launch countdown and I thought there was no point in wasting his professional expertise. It was an inspiration. He kept the sessions moving in perfect shape. It was a pity he left us at St. Thomas.

On Wednesday, the sixth, Ben Bova started the day with a pleasant talk on space exploration. He did so without benefit of a public-address system. The efforts of twelve high-powered scientists to deal with a recalcitrant microphone came to naught. I did not involve myself, of course, since my own level of engineering competence is limited. I can with considerable skill push a switch down if it happens to be up, or up if it happens to be down; but beyond that, I am shaky.

Ben had completed his speech when the ship's engineer was located in some obscure corner of the vessel and brought in. He looked at the switch on the microphone, noted it was down, and pushed it up. Instantly the miracle of electronic amplification of sound was upon us and I was sorry I had not volunteered to help; switch-pushing is my engineering specialty.

---

* They did, as a matter of fact. They let it be known that they themselves were far too superior in every respect to enjoy themselves and they all reached the very tiptop heights of wit by mentioning the presence of Miss Porter and implying that we were a ship of fools. Thank the good Lord for reportorial wit, say I.

Actually the public-address system gave us trouble all through. So did the slide projectors. So did the overhead lights. So did the screen-lowering device. Technology defeated us at every turn, and we were all thankful that we weren't in charge of the countdown then proceeding on the Florida shore.

On the next to the last night of the cruise, for instance, Ken Franklin set up eight slide projectors and a recorded commentary on the flat part of the ship in the rear (the fantail, I think). By clever manipulation of the various projectors, he planned to have the next-best thing to an actual planetarium show.

Unfortunately there seemed no way of arranging wires to run the projectors without also blowing a fuse. Ken had to improvise a speech and carried it off magnificently without any visual aids other than the stars in the sky. The sky was partly cloudy, however, and the cloud-removal device did not work either.

My own first speech, on Wednesday, dealt with the possibility of colonizing the asteroids, and I sawed the air pretty effectively. Norman Mailer, who followed me, referred to me as a "distinguished writer" and spoke of my "brilliant speech." I tried to look modest and nearly succeeded.

Mailer then went on to give a most unusual speech of his own, intending to serve as a "devil's advocate." He deplored the fact that we were left with only two diseases, the common cold and the ubiquitous "virus," and bemoaned the loss of the diseases of yesteryear: diphtheria, scarlet fever, typhoid, and all the rest of the jolly bunch. He also speculated on the existence of ghostly spirits in a "thanatosphere" around the Earth (a suggestion I had last seen mentioned in Dickens' *A Christmas Carol*), and plumped strenuously for experimentation on the Moon in the fields of levitation, ESP, and magic generally.

The rest of us managed to be unconvinced.

Mailer left at St. Thomas, and Carl Sagan joined us there. On the next Monday and Tuesday, the eleventh and twelfth, Carl delivered three speeches that were absolutely magnificent, particularly a two-hour presentation of the new views of Mars resulting from the latest photographs taken by a rocket sent into an orbit about the planet.

At one point I raised my hand. "Carl," I said, "didn't

you predict all this out of purely theoretical considerations a couple of years before the Mars probe was sent out, and didn't the photographs prove you exactly right?"

"Yes, Isaac," he said, "but I thought I would leave that unmentioned as a matter of modesty." And he beamed at the audience.*

But, of course, everything, everything—Sagan's speech on Mars, Mailer's role as devil's advocate, Fred Pohl's charming speech in which he defined progress as that which opened more options to mankind—served only as background for the real purpose of the cruise, the viewing of the launching of Apollo 17.

Increasing excitement pervaded the ship all that first Wednesday, December sixth. The ship had anchored off Florida during the day, and the giant rocket stood out against the flat Florida coast like a misplaced Washington's Monument.

The day darkened; night came; clouds banked on the eastern horizon; and there was a continuous display of far-away lightning-without-thunder ducking in and out of the distant thunderheads. The countdown proceeded toward the 9:53 zero minute, and I worried. There had never been any hitch, any hold, any delay in an Apollo launch, but, on the other hand, it was an undeniable fact that I had never watched one, either.

I was not quite myself, then, when Hugh Downs interviewed me for the benefit of the ship's passengers in those last minutes before the launch. By the time I broke away, almost every spot on every railing was occupied. I found a place at last, on the upper promenade deck, that had been left unoccupied because brilliant lights over the ping-pong table reduced everything else to a blur. Nor was there silence, for with the launch ten minutes away, several members of the crew were engaged in a heart-stopping, nerve-wrenching game of ping-pong.

Richard Hoagland passed me. "Dick," I cried, "get me a good spot, will you, old boy, and don't put me under the painful necessity of tearing your heart out."

He dragged me through numberless corridors up to the bridge and to a hidden spot he had saved.

---

* The reporters left with Mailer, so Mailer's speech got a big play afterward and Sagan's went unmentioned. Next to reportorial wit, I suppose, there is nothing better than repertorial judgment.

"What if something goes wrong?" I asked.

"How can anything go wrong?" asked Dick. "There's less than a minute to the launching."

"T minus thirty seconds and holding," said the radio.

I knew it! I knew it!

And I knew what would be the worst of what was to come, too: The radio would now indulge in its own particular cancer, the inability to tolerate a soothing silence.

For two and a half hours, the cultured and pleasant voice of the radio announcer maintained a steady commentary about nothing at all. Sentence followed sentence, paragraph followed paragraph, with a smoothly unwinding and unvarying content of zero; a soft and irritating repetition of nothing, goose egg, naught, nil, cipher; round and round in infinite variation on a non-theme.

Mailer had said sardonically that NASA had succeeded in making mankind's greatest adventure dull. Difficult? Not at all. In a world that has forgotten the virtue of silence, anything can be forced into dullness.

Not that the cultured voice dripped on forever. At periodic intervals, the forces of radio paid homage to their economic gods by running off a few singing commercials and ebullient sales messages at an enhanced sound level.

It was not till 12:20 A.M., with Dick Hoagland on the bridge telling the Captain that he would have to keep the ship at the cape for another day because he had written and notarized proof that the Captain was the best mariner in the world, that all the holds were over and the countdown began to proceed toward zero.

By then it was past midnight, and only I, on the entire ship, seemed aware that we had slipped into Pearl Harbor Day. But zero was reached, and a cloud of vapor enveloped the rocket. I held my breath and waited for it to rise, in sick suspense.

It did rise, at last, and the vast red flower at its tail bloomed. What was surely the most concentrated manmade light on an enormous scale that the world had ever seen, illuminated the nightbound shores of Florida.

As I said briefly in my introduction to chapter 2, the night vanished from horizon to horizon. We, and the ship, and all the world we could see, were suddenly under the dim copper dome of a sky from which the stars had washed out, while below us the black sea turned an orange-gray.

In the deepest silence, the artificial sun that had so changed our immediate world rose higher and higher, and then—forty seconds after ignition—the violent shaking of the air all about the rocket engines made its way across the seven miles of sea that separated us and the shore, and reached us. With the rocket high in the air, we were shaken with a rumbling thunder so that our private and temporary day was accompanied by a private and temporary earthquake.

Sound and light ebbed majestically as the rocket continued to rise until it was a ruddy blotch in the high sky. The night was falling once more; the stars were coming out, and the sea darkened. In the sky there was a flash as the second stage came loose, and then the rocket was a star among stars; moving, and moving, and moving, and growing dimmer . . .

And in all this, it was useless to try to speak, for there was nothing to say. The words and phrases had not been invented that would serve as an accompaniment to that magnificent leap to the Moon, and I did not try to invent any.

Had I had the time and the folly, and had I not been utterly crushed under sights and sounds so much greater than anything I had ever experienced, I might have tried to apostrophize the world about me and say: Oh, wonder of wonders! Oh, soaring spirit of man, that conquers space, and reaches indomitably toward the stars . . .

But I couldn't, and I didn't, and it was some young man behind me who contributed the spoken accompaniment to the rise of the spaceship.

With all the magnificent resources of the English language at his command, he chose the phrase that perhaps most intimately expressed his inner workings.

"Oh, shit," he said, as his head tilted slowly upward. And then, with his tenor voice rising over all the silent heads on board, he added, "Oh, *shi-i-i-i-it!*"

Well, to each his own. I said nothing.

seventeen

ACADEME AND I

Would you believe that I have reached the point where I am the subject of advanced-degree work?

Well, I am. People get their master's degrees by preparing bibliographies of my stories, books, and articles. They earn it, too, because trying to prepare a complete Asimov bibliography is almost impossible. I wouldn't care to tackle it myself.

One gentleman, Lloyd Neil Goble, has earned his Master of Science degree by analyzing, very carefully, the techniques I use in science writing; as in these chapters, for instance. His dissertation has been published by Mirage Press and is entitled *Asimov Analyzed*.

I have read *Asimov Analyzed* with a mixture of gratification and fear.

The gratification is easy to explain. It's true that there are some people who gather from my writings that I am just a little bit on the immodest side, but never in my most outrageous sweeps of self-love would I dare be as pro-Asimov as Mr. Goble allows himself to be.

The fear arises from the fact that Mr. Goble mistakes me: He carefully works out the average lengths of sentences, and my systems for using parentheses, and seems to think it is all part of a carefully constructed plot on my part to devise a style particularly suited for science writing.

No such thing! The fact of the matter, of course, is that I haven't worked out anything and haven't the faintest idea as to what I'm doing. I just bang the typewriter, that's all. Consequently I turn the pages of Mr. Goble's dissertation *very* carefully and try not to read it in detail, because if I find out too much about all my devices, I will get self-conscious and lose that fine, easy style that arises only out of my innocent naïveté.

But, to top it all off, here's something else:

It so happens that the college crowd has discovered science fiction. . . . I don't mean the students; I mean the faculty. Colleges are giving *courses* in science fiction. And at the University of Dayton a course is being given entitled The Science Fiction of Isaac Asimov.

When I found that out, I went and lay down for a while. I am a rational person, after all, and there are some things I consider hallucinations.

Of course I was in a peculiar position with regard to the academic world even before the sudden mushrooming popularity of science fiction in the college classroom. You see, I have long had one foot in each world.

I don't for one moment intend to imply that I am the only college professor who writes science fiction, or that I am the only science-fiction writer with a professorial appointment. I do suspect, though, that no writing professor writes as much science fiction as I do or (dare I say it?) as good science fiction as I do. And I don't think that any science-fiction writer has quite as notable a professorial position in a science department as I do.

It has its disadvantages. I am sometimes interviewed by gentlemen or ladies of the media, and this combination of careers seems to fascinate them. They find the juxtaposition anything from eccentric to outrageous, and they ask me questions about it; the same questions, over and over.

Let me, then, take this opportunity of answering some of the questions I am overfrequently asked. Perhaps if I do so, that will encourage the invention of new questions.

1. *Dr. Asimov, isn't it odd that a biochemist should write science fiction? What made you abandon your lectures and your test tubes and turn to writing sensational stories?*

Believe it or not, I am asked this question often, and the mere fact that it is asked shows that the questioner doesn't know much about my writing, or he would know that I never turned from biochemistry to science fiction. The science fiction came first—by years!

I have, after all, been a writer since well before I was a teen-ager, and I sold my first science-fiction story in 1938, when I was eighteen years old and a senior at Columbia University.

In fact I was a major science-fiction writer by mid-1942, by which time I had written forty-two stories and published thirty-one,* including "Nightfall," the first three positronic-robot stories, and the first two Foundation novelettes. And I was still just a graduate student with a freshly minted master's degree.

By the time seven more years had passed and I had joined the faculty of the medical school, I had written all the Foundation stories and all but one of the stories that were to appear in *I, Robot*.

So I am not, *not*, NOT a biochemist who turned to science fiction. I am a science-fiction writer who eventually became a professor, and that's an entirely different thing.

2. *I see. Well, then, in that case, Professor Asimov, what made you decide to become a biochemistry professor? If you had established yourself as a science-fiction writer, why did you turn away from it?*

Because I never intended to be a science-fiction writer for a *living*. I might as well have intended to be a ragpicker for a living. Let me explain:

My ambition, as a child, was to be a medical doctor. At least my parents told me that that was my ambition and I believed it. It was the normal ambition for Jewish parents of the ghetto to have for their sons. It was the surest way of getting those sons out of the ghetto.

So when I entered Columbia University, in 1935, it was with the purpose of applying to medical school at the conclusion of my college years. I wasn't overcome with joy at the thought, because being involved with pain, disease, and death did not appeal to me. On the other hand, I didn't know any other alternative to inheriting my father's candy store with its sixteen-hour workday and its seven-day week.

Fortunately I didn't get into medical school. I was unenthusiastic enough to apply for entrance to only five schools all together and none of them would have me. By that time, though, I had discovered another alternative. I was majoring in chemistry, something I had started with routine premedical notions, and discovered that I loved the

---

* Eleven of my early stories were never sold, never published, and no longer exist. I'm sorry, but that's the way it is. And no, I can't reconstruct them. If you want to know the full story of my early writing life, you will find it, along with twenty-seven of my early stories, hitherto uncollected in any of my books, in *The Early Asimov* (Doubleday, 1972).

science for itself. Consequently when I didn't score with the medical schools, I applied, in 1939, for permission to continue on at Columbia so that I might do graduate work in chemistry with the objective of a Ph.D.

My notion was that once I got my Ph.D., I could use it to get a position on some good college faculty. There I would teach chemistry and do research.

Actually World War II delayed me, but I finally got my Ph.D. in 1948 and joined the faculty at Boston University School of Medicine in 1949. . . . My plan had worked.

All through my life, then, it was the one doctorate or the other—the medical for my parents, the philosophical for myself—that was my goal and my hoped-for device for earning a living.

Science-fiction writing had nothing to do with that—nothing at all. When I first began to write, it was merely through an uncontrollable impulse. I had no vision of money, not even a vision of readers; just a desire to spin stories for my own happiness.

When I finally did sell my first story, in 1938, I was, as aforesaid, an eighteen-year-old college senior. I was still in my premedical stage, still looking forward uneasily to the possibility of starting medical school within the year—and wondering where I would get the money for it. For that matter, it was hard enough to get money for college tuition itself, and those were the days when Columbia charged only four hundred dollars a year.

Consequently when the first few science-fiction checks came in, I saw in them only one thing: a contribution toward my tuition. That's what they were, and that's all they could be.

Was I stupid not to see that they might someday be more? Well, consider . . .

When I started writing science fiction, the *top* word rate was one cent. I was much more likely to get half a cent per word. The number of science-fiction magazines was exactly three, and only one of them was prosperous. Science fiction was all I wrote or, it seemed to me, could write. I didn't even *want* to write anything but science fiction.

With a market that limited and that poor, could any sane person expect to make a living as a writer? With the years, to be sure, a few more magazines were started and rates went up a little, but, even so, the prospects remained dim.

In fact let me be precise: During my first eleven years as a science-fiction writer, my total earnings, my *total* earnings, through my labors at my typewriter, amounted to less than eight thousand dollars. And I was doing well. I was selling everything I wrote, after the first four years.

With that kind of record, is it any surprise that my science-fiction writing never for a moment deflected me from the serious task of preparing myself for what seemed to be my real career? Naturally, then, when, in June 1949, I had a chance at joining a faculty for the princely payment of five thousand dollars each and every year, I jumped at it.

3. *I understand, Professor. But tell me, did this double career of yours ever bring about a conflict? Did your academic colleagues ever look down at you for your disreputable avocation?*

I guess there was some amusement at it in Columbia. A good portion of the student body had read science fiction sometime or other in their early life. Back in the forties, however, science fiction was looked upon as essentially children's literature. The pattern generally was that you read science fiction in high school and abandoned it in college. They smiled at me not so much for reading science fiction, but merely for *still* reading it.

The fact that I *wrote* science fiction was easier to accept and understand than the fact that I read it. After all, I was paid for writing it, and I was using the money to help me get my education. There was nothing wrong with that.

Through all my schooling there was only one time when I got nervous about my science fiction.

In 1947 I had my forthcoming Ph.D. dissertation much on my mind, and it was one of the few periods when I was doing little writing. So the pressure was building up to do some writing of some kind.

I was conducting experiments that involved a substance called catechol. This existed in fluffy, white, extremely soluble crystals. As soon as they hit the water surface they were gone, dissolved. I thought idly that perhaps they dissolved a fraction of a millimeter above the water surface, and it occurred to me to write a story about a substance that dissolved *before* water was added.

Because my dissertation was so much on my mind, I

couldn't resist writing it in the form of a mock dissertation, complete with turgid sentences, tables, graphs, and fake references. I called it "The Endochronic Properties of Resublimated Thiotimoline" and sold it to John Campbell, editor of *Astounding Science Fiction*.

Then I got nervous. My position at Columbia was rocky anyway, because I was considered eccentric even aside from the science-fiction bit. My scholarship was all right, but I was loud, boisterous, and irreverent (behaving in the hallowed halls of Columbia, a quarter of a century ago, much as I behave in the hallowed halls of Doubleday these days). I knew that some of the faculty thought I lacked the proper gravity to make a good scientist, and it occurred to me that the thiotimoline article, which clearly made fun of science and scientists, would be the last straw. . . . And the article would be published just about the time I was getting ready for my oral examination for the doctorate.

So I called Mr. Campbell and told him I wanted the article run under a pseudonym. He agreed.

But he forgot. It came out under my own name about three months before my orals. Yes, sir; yes, ma'am; the entire faculty read it.

When I stood before the examining committee, I was put through the usual hell, and then when they had me beaten down into a quivering mass of panic, one of them said, "And now, Mr. Asimov, could you tell us something about the thermodynamic properties of thiotimoline?" and I had to be led out of the room in hysterics.

They passed me, obviously, or I wouldn't be the Good Doctor now.

4. *I wasn't really asking whether you had trouble when you were a student, Good Doctor; I meant, did you have trouble with your fellow faculty members when you were yourself on the faculty?*

I certainly didn't expect to. Several of the members were science-fiction fans, notably the one who recommended me for the job, and knew my writing well.

In fact I had only one bad moment, to begin with. My first book had been sold just a couple of weeks before I accepted the faculty position and went to Boston. That book, *Pebble in the Sky,* was to be published by Doubleday, on January 19, 1950, and I knew they were going to

publicize my relationship to the school. I found this out
when I read the material on samples of the cover jacket
Doubleday sent me. On the back cover (along with a very
good likeness of myself that breaks my heart when I look at
it now) was an account of the thiotimoline question at my
oral examination, and a final sentence which read:

"Dr. Asimov lives in Boston, where he is engaged in cancer research at Boston University School of Medicine."

I thought about that for quite a while, then decided to
bite the bullet. I asked to see the Dean and put it to him
frankly. I was a science-fiction writer, I said, and had been
for years. My first book was coming out under my own
name, and my association with the medical school would
be mentioned. Did he want my resignation?

The Dean considered thoughtfully and said, "Is it a good
book?"

Cautiously I said, "The publishers think so."

And he said, "In that case the medical school will be
glad to be identified with it."

And that took care of that.

5. *But if you were a science-fiction writer, Professor, didn't
that cast doubt on the validity of your scientific work? I
mean, if you published a scientific paper, might that not be
dismissed by someone as "just more science fiction"?*

That would be a very obvious half-witticism, but it has
never happened, that I know of.

To be sure, my career as an active researcher was short
and the number of papers I put out was not large, but they
were all perfectly good and sober papers and I don't know
that anyone ever dismissed them because of my other profession.

Naturally I don't know what happened behind my back,
but stories would reach me indirectly . . .

A fellow member of the department, who got his appointment only a month after I did, and who was *not* a
science-fiction reader, told me years later that when he discovered I was a science-fiction writer, he was sure that
would ruin my scientific career. He told me he was curious
enough to sound out the feelings of others and that nobody
minded.

Well, almost nobody. I was doubtful sometimes about
the socially conservative individual with whom I did my

early research. I don't know that he objected to my science fiction particularly, as much as to my personality in general.

He hinted to me, for instance, that in the heat of the Boston summer I should nevertheless, in accord with my social status as a faculty member, wear a jacket and tie. I smiled genially and turned a deaf ear, of course. I also ignored all hints that my relations with students were too informal. (If he had looked more carefully, he would have noted that my relations with *everybody* were too informal.)

Anyway, I heard one story about him that I cannot vouch for personally but that my informant swore to me was true. My research colleague went to Washington once to push for an increase in grant funds, and of those functionaries he consulted, one looked over the report, pointed to my name on the list of those engaged in the project, and said, "Isn't that the science-fiction writer?"

My research colleague, in an immediate sweat at the possibility of losing the grant, began to assure the other that I never allowed my science fiction to mix with my real science.

But the functionary shook that off and proceeded to ask many more questions about me. It turned out that he was a science-fiction fan and was far more interested in me than in the project. My colleague got all the money he asked for that time, but I think he was annoyed about it all, anyway.

But it didn't matter. I only worked with him for a few years and then got out from under.

6. *To change the subject, Professor Asimov: you write a good deal, don't you?*

I publish seven or eight books a year on the average— say, half a million words a year.

7. *But how can you do that and still keep up a full teaching load?*

I can't, and I don't.

A funny thing happened after I took my job at the medical school. Once I finally had the scientific career I had striven toward for so many years, my writing activiti which until then had only been a helpful adjunct, sudd took on a life of their own.

My first book was followed by another, then

Royalties began to arrive regularly. Anthologies began to multiply, and book clubs and paperbacks and foreign interest. My writing income began to bound upward.

Then something else happened. Working with two other members of the department, I helped write a textbook on biochemistry for medical students and discovered I liked to write non-fiction. Then I found out there was a larger market for non-fiction than for fiction and that the word rates were considerably better. Then I found out I could write non-fiction on all sorts of subjects.

So I wrote more and more, both non-fiction and fiction, and enjoyed myself hugely. After I had been on the job for several years, I discovered two more things: one, I made more money writing than professoring, and the disparity increased each year; two, I *liked* writing better than professoring, and that disparity, too, increased each year.

I kept having the impulse to quit my job and just devote myself to my writing, but how could I? I had spent too much of my life educating myself for this job to throw it away. So I dithered.

The dithering came to an end in 1957, by which time I had a new department head and the school had a new dean. The old ones had been tolerant of my eccentricities, even fond of them perhaps, but the new ones were not. In fact, they viewed my activities with keen disapproval.

What bothered them most was the status of my research. As long as I had written only science fiction, my research was not affected. My science fiction was written on my own time. No matter how hot the story, or how pressing the deadline, it was written evenings and weekends only.

Non-fiction was different. I considered my books on science for the public to be a scholarly activity, and I worked on them during school hours. I continued to carry a full teaching load, of course, but I gave up my research.

I was called on the carpet for this by the new administration, but I held my ground stubbornly and even a little fiercely. I said that I was paid primarily to be a teacher, that I fulfilled all my teaching duties, and that it was generally recognized that I was one of the best teachers in the

m r my research, I said, I didn't think I would ever be a merely adequate researcher, and that while my scientific work would be respectable enough, it would never shed luster on the school. My writing, on the other hand (I said), was first-class, and it would bring a great deal of fame to the school. On that basis (I continued) not only would I not abandon my writing in favor of research as a matter of personal preference, but also out of a concern for the welfare of the school.

I did not manage to put that across. I was told, quite coldly, that the school could not afford to pay someone sixty-five hundred dollars a year (that was my salary by then) in order to have him write science books.

So I said contemptuously, "Then keep the darned money, and I won't teach for you."

"Good," I was told, "your appointment will be ended as of June 1958."

"No it won't," I said. "Just the salary. The title I keep, for I've got tenure."

Well, what followed was a Homeric struggle that lasted for two years. Never mind the details, but I still have the title. Since June 1958, however, I don't teach and I don't collect a salary. I give one lecture a year and I fulfill some honorary duties (such as sitting on committees), but I am now a full-time writer and will continue to be one. And I am still Associate Professor of Biochemistry.

The school is now very happy with the situation. As I predicted, my writing has indeed brought them favorable publicity. And I am happy with the situation too, because I value my academic connection. It is pleasant to be able to walk into a large university and feel you belong, and are there by right.

As a matter of fact, the administrator with whom I had the trouble has long since retired and, since that time, a succession of presidents, directors, and deans have all been extremely kind to me. I would like to emphasize that, except for that one argument in 1957 and 1958, I have always been treated with surpassing generosity by everyone at the school from top to bottom.

I must also emphasize, once again, that even during that argument it was *not* my science-fiction writing that was in question. The quarrel was entirely over my abandonment of research, and I had abandoned that in favor of my *non-fiction*.

8. In view of the fact that you no longer teach, Dr. Asimov, do you still view yourself as a scientist?

Certainly. Why shouldn't I? I've had professional training in chemistry. I've lectured for years, at a professional level, in biochemistry. I've written textbooks in these subjects. None of that has been wiped out.

I consider one of the most important duties of any scientist the teaching of science to students and to the general public. Although I don't often lecture to formal classes, my books on science reach more people and teach more people than I could possibly manage by voice alone.

It is true I no longer teach class, but that is not at all the same as saying that I no longer teach. I teach science now more than I ever did in school, and so I consider myself not only a scientist, but a *practicing* scientist.

Naturally I also consider myself a writer.

9. In view of the wide variety of writings you turn out, what kind of writer do you consider yourself?

Sometimes I wonder. In the past two years I have published an annotation of Byron, a two-volume work on Shakespeare, a satire on sex books, and a joke book* in addition to my books on science and on history.

So I let others decide. To others I seem to be identified always as a science-fiction writer. It was how I began, how I made my first and perhaps still my greatest impact.

Nor have I really retired as a science-fiction writer. It is no longer my major field of endeavor, but I have never stopped writing it. My most recent novel is *The Gods Themselves* (Doubleday, 1972).

So there you are . . .

I'm a science-fiction writer.

* These are, respectively, for those of you who are curious: *Asimov's Annotated Don Juan* (Doubleday, 1972); *Asimov's Guide to Shakespeare* (Doubleday, 1970); *The Sensuous Dirty Old Man* (Walker, 1971, under the transparent pseudonym of Dr. A.); and *Treasury of Humor* (Houghton Mifflin, 1971).